The
Widow's
Irish Secret

BOOKS BY SUSANNE O'LEARY

Susanne O'Leary

The
Widow's
Irish Secret

bookouture

Published by Bookouture in 2025

An imprint of Storyfire Ltd.
Carmelite House
50 Victoria Embankment
London EC4Y 0DZ

www.bookouture.com

The authorised representative in the EEA is Hachette Ireland
8 Castlecourt Centre
Dublin 15 D15 XTP3
Ireland
(email: info@hbgi.ie)

ISBN: 978-1-83618-616-8
eBook ISBN: 978-1-83618-617-5

This book is a work of fiction. Names, characters, businesses, organizations,
places and events other than those clearly in the public domain, are either the
product of the author's imagination or are used fictitiously. Any resemblance to
actual persons, living or dead, events or locales is entirely coincidental.

For Isobel

1

Tricia was sitting at her desk in the living room of her small flat in Dublin, looking out through the open window, lost in thought. It was a beautiful day in early spring and the gentle breeze brought with it the sound of birdsong and faint traffic noises from the main road nearby.

Tricia had only been here for two years; but it had been a difficult time, after the loss of her husband. She had thought she'd pick up her life again. But Dublin didn't appeal to her after years of living on a farm in the wilds of Donegal. City life was not for her, she had come to realise. And it had been hard sorting out the belongings Sean had left behind in their Dublin flat. She knew she needed to finally say goodbye to their life together. They were just things, but they all had memories attached to them. The guitar he used to play, sitting at the window looking lovingly at her while he softly sang some romantic song. The rucksack he used for hikes up the Dublin mountains which he found rather tame compared to the high peaks of Donegal; the leather boots, the hipflask and the binoculars for birdwatching all had to go. Only the little crystal vase that he had liked to put red roses into every evening when they were in town, and the silver bowl he had given her on their twentieth wedding anniversary were things she would keep and treasure. But what remained, including his suits and leather jacket, would be given to charity.

Tricia had felt a mixture of sadness and relief as the last items were disposed of. She could now concentrate on her own life and what to do in order to get as far away from her recent past as possible.

Lately, her Kerry roots had begun to beckon. Even though Donegal was beautiful in a wild way, it didn't have the soft air or the gentleness of Kerry and its people. She was beginning to pine for the views of the Atlantic she'd grown up with, the beautiful beaches and the colourful houses of Dingle town on the edge of the ocean. She longed to live again, to laugh, to dance and do fun things with friends, to be happy and carefree. *I'm only in my early sixties*, she thought. *Still young enough to have a life worth living.* She thought of her daughters. Lily, Rose and Violet had all settled there, the two eldest now mothers with children of their own. Tricia had been too busy with the probate and everything to do with the will to visit her grandchildren, which made her sad. She sighed, thinking of the predicament she was in that she had kept from her daughters. She wanted to keep it secret from them for as long as she could. It would be too painful to talk about it just yet and she didn't know how they'd react. She had done something that could cause a lot of trouble and might even bring shame on the family. Now rumours were flying around, all started by someone who wanted to put pressure on her.

She had left it all behind in Donegal, hoping that somehow it could all be resolved in time and forgotten about. Now that she was able to live a little again, the time had come when she could finally be a real hands-on grandmother. Kerry felt like the place where she could escape it all and begin afresh. She longed to go back to the place where she had first fallen in love.

Tricia ran her fingers through her hair knowing she needed a cut and colour before she went anywhere. Her blonde curls had become dull with strands of grey running through them, which was a bit ageing. The latest trend of showing off the grey didn't appeal to her. She hadn't had the time or energy to do anything about her appearance during the past difficult years. But now she felt ready to face the challenge of going out into the world again and meeting new people.

Tricia made a mental note to make an appointment with her hairdresser. Then she turned her thoughts to the plan she and Sean had had a few years ago, to rent a cottage in Dingle for the summer. The one they had found had been tiny but the rent had been cheap. Located near the road to Ventry, where her eldest daughter, Lily, and her family lived, it would have been ideal for Tricia and Sean. Rose, her second daughter, lived nearby as well with her husband and little girl, Sophie. *The children are growing up so fast. I want them to get to know me and Sean properly before it's too late*, Tricia had thought then. But she had dropped the idea when Sean fell ill. She had been so taken up with his illness, nursing him while he slowly faded away during the heartbreaking year before his passing. And then the deep sorrow when he was gone and the winding up of his estate that had taken so long. But now here she was, finally able to look forward and live again. Maybe that little cottage was still available?

Right now seemed to Tricia the best time to start her new life, to connect with her daughters and their children, and to get far away from all the trouble in Donegal. A whole summer near the beach, long lazy days playing with those little children, spoiling them with ice cream and trips to town and the Aqua Dome, picnics on the beach, teaching them to swim and all the things she had done when her own daughters were small. Fish and chips on the pier, walks in the gardens of Magnolia Manor, where she had spent so many happy years with Fred, her first husband and the father of her girls. It all seemed like an idyll that was hard to resist. It was as if all Tricia needed to do was to find that cottage, make the downpayment and get ready to go. But she knew it would not be that easy. There was one obstacle to all that perceived happiness. Sylvia, her former mother-in-law. She would have taken over as the most important person to the children, the grandmother and great-grandmother, the matriarch of the family. It would be hard to compete with her.

The front door opening and then slamming shut pulled Tricia out of her reverie. She turned to find Violet, her youngest daughter, running into the room.

'Mum,' Vi exclaimed. 'I have some amazing news.'

Tricia got up from the desk. 'What has happened now?' she asked. Vi had a habit of bursting in with 'amazing news' at regular intervals, be it a part in a movie or TV series; she had a flair for the dramatic. 'Did you get another part in something amazing?'

'Yes, in a way.' Vi wrapped her arms around her mother in a tight hug. 'I'm getting married! Jack proposed last night. Got down on his knee in the middle of a restaurant and held out a box with a ring. How cheesy is that? And just look at this rock.' Vi held up her left hand with a beautiful square-cut emerald surrounded by tiny diamonds. '"It's to match your eyes," he said.' Vi drew breath and looked at her mother, her green eyes shining. 'We want to have the wedding at Magnolia Manor the end of August, before Jack goes to Cornwall to film. Isn't it incredible?'

'Yes. Quite... wonderful.' Tricia sat down on the sofa feeling as if she had been hit by a tornado. But that was Vi, always dramatic, never calm and composed like her sisters. 'Congratulations, darling. Where is Jack?' she asked, suddenly feeling overwhelmed that a film star like Jack Montgomery was going to be her son-in-law.

'He's on his way. I wanted to tell you first before he comes.'

Vi joined her mother on the sofa. 'Please say you're happy for me. I mean, we've been together for two years, so you should have known it was on the cards.'

'I didn't think it would happen so soon,' Tricia confessed. 'I knew you were dating, of course, everyone did. And that you bought the gatehouse together as well. But...' She ran her hand down Vi's silky red hair that hung to the middle of her back. 'I thought maybe you'd wait a bit. We've only started to get to know each other, you and I, after all that's been going on with me.' Vi had arrived in Dublin only a few days ago to see a play and to meet Jack at the airport as he arrived from England. They were planning to drive to Kerry later that week.

Vi nodded. 'I know, Mum. You've been through a tough time. But we'll be together while we plan the wedding. After all, the mother of the bride is a very important person.'

'What about the grandmother of the bride?' Tricia asked with a wry smile. 'I'm sure she'll have opinions and ideas about the wedding.'

'Oh, I can handle Granny,' Vi said. 'I know she'll want to take over if she gets a chance. But we won't let her, will we?'

'We can try,' Tricia mumbled. But she knew Sylvia would be a tough nut to crack. In her mid-eighties, she was still as strong and feisty as she had always been. Age certainly hadn't withered Sylvia, or made her mellow in any way. Tricia had always admired Sylvia for her strength during the many tragedies that had hit her through her life and felt a huge respect for her mother-in-law. They had been united during many difficult years. Fred had died in a freak accident at sea with his own father. So Tricia and Sylvia had mourned their husbands together. Sylvia had been a tower of strength and helped Tricia both financially and morally while she was bringing up three daughters single-handed. But there had always been a feeling of rivalry under the surface, a feeling of not quite living up to Sylvia's high standards. 'Never explain, never complain' had always been Sylvia's motto. Tricia had never been able to follow that example.

'Does Sylvia know about your engagement?' Tricia asked.

Vi squirmed. 'Eh, yes. Sorry, Mum.'

'I see,' Tricia said, trying to hide the slight resentment she felt that Sylvia had been told about the engagement before they'd told her.

'But she doesn't know about our wedding plans,' Vi continued. 'I wanted to talk to you about it first and then tell Granny when we had decided everything. That way she'd find it hard to put her oar in and...'

'She'll do that anyway.' Tricia sighed and got up. 'I was actually planning to look at cottages for rent near Magnolia right now. I thought I'd spend the summer there. Now with your wedding coming up, I will definitely spend as much time there as I can.' Tricia felt calmer now that she had the perfect excuse to move down to Kerry for a few months. It would be natural for her to help plan her daughter's wedding. Nobody would question why she'd run away.

'Oh, that's terrific,' Vi exclaimed, bouncing up from the sofa. 'Let's look at them together.'

Tricia tried to find the website but couldn't remember which one it had been. 'I thought I'd rent something near Ventry.'

'But they're all so tiny,' Vi argued, staring at the screen when a list of cottages came up. 'Maybe you can stay with us at the gatehouse? But we're doing it up at the moment, so it could be a bit noisy.'

'What are you doing with the gatehouse?' Tricia asked. 'Wasn't it restored with all mod cons recently?'

'Yes, four years ago,' Vi replied. 'But we're changing the heating system to electric and putting solar panels on the roof. We want to do as much for the environment as we can. And we're turning the small bedroom into Jack's office. He's getting more into writing screenplays and directing than acting, you see.'

'So he'll be spending more time at home?' Tricia asked.

'That's right. Once he's finished with the film in Cornwall. Our plan is to open a production company, to work locally as much as possible.'

'I'm sure Jack is pleased about that,' Tricia remarked.

'Of course. That's why we decided to get married now. I'll be home a lot and we can plan everything together. And now that you're coming, it'll be even better.' Vi looked at the screen again. 'But there is nothing there that would suit you. Too far away if we're to plan a wedding at Magnolia Manor together. Maybe...' She paused. 'You know what? I have an idea that could work a lot better. Look up houses for sale instead, and you'll see what I mean.'

'Okay. Not that I had planned to buy anything at the moment.' Tricia put in the appropriate words into Google and clicked on the first link that came up. She scrolled down for a moment and then stared at the picture of a little house with a slate roof that looked eerily familiar. 'Is that... Oh yes, it is. The gardener's cottage.'

'That's right, Mum,' Vi said, looking excited. 'It's just come up for sale. Granny didn't want it to be sitting there a total wreck, so she was hoping someone would buy it and do it up.'

'Oh,' Tricia said. 'I had no idea.' She knew the house well as it could be seen from the manor house that had been in the family for generations. The manor had been her home when she married Fred, and the girls had all spent their early childhood there. Until the tragedy happened and Tricia's life changed forever. 'That cottage is near the big house,' Tricia said, looking at the photos.

'On land that belongs to the Fleury estate,' Vi filled in. 'Down the lane from the manor house, just off the path to the pier where...' She stopped, looking suddenly appalled. 'Oh. I'm sorry, Mum. Didn't mean to...'

'The pier where Fred used to moor his boat,' Tricia mumbled. 'The boat that killed him and Liam.' She put her hand to her mouth, feeling tears stinging her eyes, all the memories of that horrible day coming to the surface.

Vi touched her mother's shoulder. 'Mum, I'm really sorry. How thoughtless of me. I can see you're upset.'

Tricia looked at her daughter and touched Vi's cheek. 'Not your fault. You don't remember what happened. You were just a toddler. You wouldn't have any idea of how it felt and how I still feel, even after more than thirty years. That's why I haven't spent much time at Magnolia. It is still so hard.'

'Maybe a cottage for rent at Ventry isn't so bad after all,' Vi suggested.

Tricia didn't reply while she stared at the image of the cottage. 'No, that's too far away from you. You were right about that. And maybe I should go back and face the fear. Lay the ghosts, so to speak. That little house is so pretty,' she continued, looking at the slate roof, the whitewashed walls with rambling roses and the tiny front garden that could be made as lovely as it had once been. 'Fred wanted to do it up, you see. And we had planned to start just after we were married. But then I got pregnant with Lily and...' She kept staring at the photo. 'Maybe I could do what we had planned after all. It could be healing rather than upsetting to live there.'

'Mum, you don't have to,' Vi protested, putting a hand on Tricia's shoulder. 'We'll think of something else. In any case, that house is for sale and not for rent and it needs a lot of work to make it comfortable.'

But Tricia wasn't listening. 'This place is going for a song, so I think I might be able to afford it,' she said as if to herself. She made a quick calculation in her head, wondering if she had enough to buy it. The farm was up for sale and once it was sold and all taxes paid, there wouldn't be a lot left. She was handy with a hammer and good at fixing things so she could do a lot herself. She had a little nest egg that she hadn't planned to touch, but maybe... 'The shed at the back looks like it could be made into something,' she continued. 'Maybe it could join the house and make it bigger...' She was lost in thought, weighing up the possibilities. She had been in the cottage a few times many years ago when Fred was considering doing it up for them to live in during the first year of their marriage. She could see from the photos that it still had the same kitchen with a wood-burning range and those old solid oak cupboards. The living–dining room had a big fireplace and lovely views of the little bay. It should be restored carefully without ruining the period feel or the charm. Tricia suddenly felt excited at the prospect. Maybe this was a chance not to be missed? Something to occupy her mind, a new project and then the wedding... *I could buy the cottage, do it up and then sell it*, she thought. It could solve all of her problems. She looked at the screen again, at the dear little cottage that seemed to speak to her and urge her to come and do it up and make it liveable again. *It must have a history; old houses always do*, Tricia thought, her heart beating faster.

'Please, Mum,' Vi pleaded. 'Forget I said anything. You don't have to go back to all that pain.'

'I'm not so sure,' Tricia argued. 'Maybe going back is a way to go forward?' She nodded, as a steely determination seemed to come from nowhere. That little house carried with it too many memories, but it was the perfect hideaway. Remote and beautiful but very rundown. Nobody would think of looking for her there.

'Yes. I can do this,' she murmured. 'I can face the past. If Sylvia could, why shouldn't I?' She suddenly felt a dart of excitement mixed with fear, knowing she had come to a turning point in her life. If she didn't take the right path now, she might regret it for a very long time.

2

It didn't take long to finalise the deal. The next morning, Tricia rang the estate agent handling the sale of the cottage and put in an offer a little above the asking price, just to make sure it would be accepted. Tricia wasn't worried about the money, not right now anyway. It would clear out all her savings, but she needed to take the plunge. She told the nice woman at the agency that her name was Patricia Ryan, hoping it was a common enough name. 'That's not my full name, but it's what I will be known as for the moment,' she said. 'I want to keep a low profile until the sale goes through. I hope you understand.' *Not only that*, she thought. *I don't want anyone from Sean's family to find me...*

'Of course,' the woman said. 'We don't actually reveal the name of the buyer anyway. A lot of famous people have been buying property around here. They often want to be incognito until everything is finalised.'

'That's great. Not that I'm famous in any way,' Tricia said with a laugh. 'Oh, and I want to get access as soon as possible,' she added. 'My daughter is getting married and the wedding is in the area, so it'd be great if I can be there in good time.'

'That shouldn't be a problem,' the woman said, 'as you're a

cash buyer. But don't you want to view the property first? And perhaps have a survey organised? It's an old house and there could be problems...'

'I know it very well,' Tricia replied. 'I've seen it many times and I know what it will take to do it up.'

'A lot of hard work and more than a little bit of money,' the woman said with a chuckle. 'But worth it in the end. It's in a lovely location. So if you're sure, we'll contact the seller and then, if they agree, we'll start the conveyancing with the solicitors.'

'Excellent,' Tricia said, her spirits rising. 'I'll talk to my solicitor and organise the downpayment as soon as I hear back from you.' She hung up, crossing her fingers and saying a silent prayer that her offer would be accepted and she could start planning her move.

While she waited, she called the hairdresser's and asked for an appointment for a cut and colour as soon as possible. As luck would have it, they had a cancellation and Tricia could come in that very afternoon. Happy to have something to distract her, Tricia went along to the little salon around the corner that didn't charge too much and came out two hours later, her hair cut in a short, layered bob and the roots touched up to give her back the gleaming blonde head of hair she had always been so proud of. It made her look a lot brighter and years younger. *Whatever happens next*, she thought, as she looked in the mirror noticing how her blue eyes sparkled, *I feel better and more confident than I have for a very long time.*

And then it all happened very fast. Everything fell into place as soon as Sylvia had accepted the offer a few days later. Tricia announced the purchase that very evening at dinner with Jack and Vi at a little restaurant near the flat. Tricia often had dinner there as it was cosy and intimate and never too crowded. 'Sylvia has accepted my offer and I've paid the downpayment and signed the contract. So it's all going ahead,' she said. 'Isn't it exciting?'

Looking worried, Vi stared at her mother. 'Mum, are you sure? It's a huge undertaking and then you'll have to face a lot of painful memories. The wedding will be stressful for you anyway and then this, on top of it.'

'I like a challenge,' Tricia said with a grin. 'And you know how I love to paint and decorate. I can do a lot myself and I'm sure Dominic can find me workmen who don't charge too much to do what I can't.' She turned to Jack. 'You're very quiet. Do you think I'm mad as well?'

Jack looked up from the menu. 'Not at all, Tricia. I know that cottage from my walks around the grounds of Magnolia Manor. It's very nice and still in fairly good nick. Needs an upgrade and all that but it could be made into something fabulous. I'd say go for it, Tricia. Love your hair, by the way.'

'Thanks, Jack. I'm glad someone is on my side.' Tricia smiled at him, thinking how lucky Vi was to have found such a nice man. In many ways he was just like Fred. They shared an interest in the arts, and his strong jaw and beautiful eyes were very similar, too, even though Fred had had green eyes like Vi. Tricia often wondered if that was what had made Vi fall in love with Jack. A kind of innate knowledge of her father despite not really remembering him. It was eerie and wonderful at the same time.

'I'm on your side too,' Vi protested. 'I just don't want you to take on too much.'

'It'll be good for me,' Tricia said. 'I feel a whole new chapter of my life is just beginning.' Then she turned to the waiter who had just arrived to take their order. 'I'll have the lamb cutlets, please.'

Vi and Jack said they'd have the same. 'And a bottle of that nice Merlot,' Tricia ordered. 'But first, could you bring us a bottle of your best champagne? We have a lot to celebrate tonight.'

'Of course, Mrs Fleury,' the waiter said and left to place the order.

'Mrs Fleury?' Vi asked. 'Are you changing your name back?'

'That's right,' Tricia replied. 'I feel my life in Donegal is over since Sean passed away. I want to leave it all behind. I was so proud to be Tricia Fleury when I married your father all those years ago. I was only in my early twenties then. And now I want to be a Fleury girl again.'

'That will make Granny very happy,' Vi said as the champagne arrived in a bucket full of ice at their table.

'I'm not doing it for Granny, but for me,' Tricia argued, glad that they weren't questioning her. She didn't want to reveal the real reason her new name was so important.

'Good for you,' Jack said. 'I adore Sylvia but she can be a little overbearing if you let her.'

'And we're not going to,' Tricia said with feeling. Then, when the champagne had been opened, she raised her glass. 'Here's to you two, Jack and Vi. May you have a wonderful life together, wherever you are in the world. I couldn't be happier for you and I will make sure the wedding is just the way you want.'

Jack clinked glasses with Tricia. 'And here's to my very smart and brave future mother-in-law.'

Vi held her glass up. 'To my darling mummy,' she said, her eyes gleaming with tears of happiness. 'Welcome back to Kerry and – us.'

Those words echoed through Tricia's mind all through the journey from Dublin to Dingle a few weeks later. It was a long drive that took over four hours but Tricia enjoyed it enormously. The traffic was light as she had decided to drive down on a

Sunday, even though she wouldn't get possession of the cottage until the following Wednesday.

She would stay with Vi at the gatehouse as Jack was off to Cornwall. This way she would have time to take a look at the cottage – at least from the outside – and then see Sylvia and break the news that she was the new owner. It would be too late for Sylvia to back out of the deal, but then why would she? The cottage had been for sale for the past year, after all, and Sylvia should be happy that it was being sold for a very good price. The manor had been converted into apartments for seniors, so she knew Sylvia must have been selling the property to fund further expansion. She'd be happy it was finally sold. Except she might not be happy about who had bought it.

When Fred and Tricia had got engaged and he took her to Magnolia Manor to introduce her to his parents, Sylvia had looked as if she didn't quite approve of her son's choice of future wife. Tricia, whose parents had modest means, was not quite the wife Sylvia would have liked to see Fred marry. Or so Tricia had always thought. She had had to work part time to pay for her tuition as her parents couldn't afford college fees. The fact that Tricia had a degree in accountancy with top marks didn't seem to impress Sylvia. But then not many girls would have been good enough for Sylvia, Nora, the housekeeper at Magnolia Manor, had once declared. Nora had been a huge help to Tricia in the early days and they still kept in touch. She wondered what they would think of the legal tangle she had left behind in Donegal.

Tricia turned her mind away from the problem and tried to enjoy the beautiful vistas she was driving through. She was relieved that she hadn't had any further calls from Sean's family. The rolling green hills, the farms with their old houses and barns, the little villages with cottages and taller houses, façades adorned with carved stone in intricate patterns. She stopped for lunch in Adare, a lovely village with chocolate-box cottages, their thatched roofs lending a charming old-world image to the main street.

Then Tricia continued her journey through Newcastle West, tempted to stop and visit the old castle but drove on, feeling she needed to get to Dingle as soon as she could. She had decided while she was having lunch that she had to tell Sylvia as soon as she arrived that she was the buyer of the cottage. It would be better to take the bull by the horns straight away. Not that Sylvia was anything like a bull, but she might not like having been kept in the dark. They had to get on if Vi's wedding was to be as lovely as she hoped. It wouldn't be fair, Tricia thought, to have two women at daggers drawn while they were planning the most important day in her youngest daughter's life. That thought both calmed and terrified her. But better to get it over with.

'Let the battle commence,' Tricia said to herself, smiling as she felt that even if there would be arguments, and problems, life was suddenly worth living again.

3

Vi stood in the doorway of the gatehouse when Tricia arrived. She ran down the steps, her red hair flying, and hugged her mother as soon as Tricia had got out of the car. 'Welcome home, Mum. I'm so happy you're here at last.'

'Me too, darling,' Tricia said, breathing in the floral scent in Vi's hair. Then she stepped back and looked at her daughter. 'You look so good. Happy and healthy and rested.'

'It's this place,' Vi said. 'The air, the peace, the garden, well, you know. The Magnolia magic as we call it.'

'I hope it'll have the same effect on me,' Tricia remarked.

'I'm sure it will.'

Tricia looked up at the house, the façade of which had been recently painted a sunny yellow. The old sash windows had been replaced and the window sills were picked out in white. There was a small patio at the side where she could see garden furniture and flowers in large pots. It was a lovely little house but she remembered how it had been a near wreck before it was rescued by Lily when she came to live here permanently. 'This is a very pretty house now.'

'We love it,' Vi said. 'Jack says it's the best place he's ever lived in. Hey, are you hungry? I could make you an omelette or something.'

Tricia patted Vi's cheek. 'Thanks, pet, but I had lunch in Adare at that place we always used to stop at. And we can go out to eat tonight if you like.'

'Oh, but Granny has invited us both for dinner tonight,' Vi announced. 'To welcome you, she said.'

'That was kind of her,' Tricia said, knowing kindness had nothing to do with it. 'We'd better draw up some plans for the wedding beforehand, though. Just in case.'

'I know. Jack and I made a list. We can go through it together when you've settled in.'

'Settled in?' Tricia said. 'I feel settled already. But do you know what I'd like? A swim. That would help me relax.' She squinted up at the sky where the sun peeked through the clouds. 'It's not too cold today.'

'When did that ever stop you?' Vi asked, smiling. 'You love a swim even on a freezing cold day.'

'Best way to unwind.' Tricia pulled one of her bags from the boot of the car. 'I think my togs are in here. I'll just put this in my room and then get changed. Can't wait to have a swim.'

'You're going down to the pier?' Vi asked, looking worried.

'Yes. I always used to swim from there.' Then Tricia noticed the look in Vi's eyes. 'Oh, I know. The pier where the boat was tied up at high tide. Hard to face but it's something I have to get through. And I've been there a lot of times through the years afterwards. Don't worry, sweetheart, I'm moving forward, not back to sad times.'

'I hope so.' Vi peered into the boot. 'Do you want me to help you with the other bags?'

'No. Leave them until I move into the cottage.'

'You can stay with us as long as you need,' Vi offered. 'If you find the cottage too... rustic.'

Tricia laughed. 'Rustic? I know what you're hinting at. But

I'll be fine. It's summertime and I won't need much except the basics. I can't wait to move in, no matter how primitive it is.'

'That's great.' Vi smiled at Tricia. 'You're so brave, Mum. But I have a feeling you can't wait to start your new life down here. Even if it's going to be a challenge with the new house and then the wedding and... Granny.'

'Bring it on,' Tricia said with more bravado than she really felt.

Tricia wasted no time finding her swimsuit and a towel. She told Vi she would be back soon and got ready for her swim. Throwing on a bathrobe she found on the back of the bathroom door, she left the house and walked down the path that led to the wooden pier. The walk felt like a trip down memory lane for Tricia. Even though the path was overgrown with weeds and the trees had grown much taller than she remembered, the memories kept tumbling into her mind. She and Fred had often walked down this path hand in hand, chatting and laughing, taking a break from minding their little girls and running the estate. Then they had raced each other onto the planks of the pier and jumped into the often freezing cold water. They had swum out into the bay and climbed onto the raft that used to be anchored there from early spring. She smiled at the memories, thinking how lucky she had been to have experienced such a love story even though it hadn't lasted more than ten years.

Losing Fred had been the worst trauma in her life. With Sean it had been different. He was older than her by nearly ten years and his illness had lasted over a year. She had been prepared for his death and had come to accept it, even if she missed him terribly when he was gone. She had been more accepting the second time and, in a way, relieved as nursing him had worn her out. Coming back to Magnolia Manor, where she had spent the happiest years of her life, now felt like a balm to her soul and she was able to enjoy the memories rather than push them away. Being here made her feel young again in a very odd way.

As she walked on, she looked up at the canopies of oaks and ash, delighting in the birdsong and the warmth of the dappled sunlight. The breeze from the north-west was a little chilly but it felt so fresh with that salty tang she remembered so well. Fred had loved coming down here for a swim and she could nearly feel him walking with her. He had always enjoyed these little escapes from his busy time running the estate. In those days, Tricia had been braver than Fred, however, and always swam from late April into mid-October. She loved the pier as the worn wooden planks had been soft under her bare feet and she didn't get sand everywhere like on the beach.

Now, here she was at the pier, stepping onto the wood, worn to a silky softness by time and weather. It was nearly high tide and the waves lapped against the rocks at the base of the pier. Tricia kicked off her sandals and walked barefoot to the end, throwing off her bathrobe, preparing to dive into the dark water. She turned as she heard a soft rustle nearby and saw an egret flapping its wings and then rising out of the rushes and flying off across the water, its white wings gleaming in the sunlight. It was a beautiful sight and Tricia felt a dart of sheer joy as she watched the bird in graceful flight disappear over the hills across the bay. Then she dove into the water, gasping as she came up for air. The water was cold but she soon got used to it and began to swim with strong, even strokes towards the raft that she saw to her delight was still there. She arrived breathless and heaved herself up to sit and rest for a while before the swim back.

She hadn't been swimming much lately and her heart was pounding in her chest which annoyed her. *Well, you're over sixty now, girl*, she told herself, *no longer young and fit like in the old days. But I'll work on it and get as fit as I can be at my age.* She looked across the bay and thought of Fred, feeling that familiar sense of loss that still came back from time to time, like a sudden stab in her heart. It was as if he had stolen her youth when he died and left her sad and grumpy and middle-aged. It was such a different sense of loss to that which she felt about Sean. Fred had died so young. *Oh stop it,* she ordered herself. *Self-pity is not the way to go. Fred would not be impressed.*

A sudden glint blinded her momentarily and Tricia blinked and looked to the shore, her hand over her eyes to see better. Something had reflected the sunlight for a second and then it disappeared. Was someone watching her? Or maybe it was just a window opening in the manor house, the top of which she could see over the tree tops. She shrugged and prepared to heave herself into the water to swim back, which she did with slow, even strokes, not wanting to exhaust herself. She had to be all bright-eyed and bushy-tailed for Sylvia's dinner tonight, which might be a bit of an ordeal if they started to discuss the wedding plans. But she couldn't quite get the flash of light out of her mind, despite the distraction of the cold water.

She reached the pier and climbed up the rather rickety ladder and put on the bathrobe and sandals. As she walked back across the planks, she spotted something in the rushes that she hadn't noticed earlier. It was a rubber dinghy, also called a rib, pulled up onto the shore and half hidden by the clump of reeds. It had a brand new outboard motor and there was a wetsuit on one of the seats and an oxygen tank underneath it. Mystified, Tricia stared at it wondering who owned it and what they were doing there. Someone seemed to be either diving or snorkelling from there. Could it be Henri, Arnaud's son who now ran the Magnolia business with Rose? Arnaud was Sylvia's French fiancé and was also on the board of Magnolia Manor.

Tricia shot a final glance at the rib as she walked back up the path, telling herself there was a perfectly good explanation.

But deep down she had an eerie feeling there was something strange going on. She had hoped to escape from all the troubles and suspicions in the north, but maybe they had already caught up with her...

4

Back at the gatehouse, Tricia spent the next few hours settling in and getting ready for dinner with Sylvia. Vi had said there was no need to dress up, but Tricia knew she had to at least dress in what Sylvia called 'casual chic' which was the most difficult dress code to pull off. But if she didn't look at least well groomed, she would feel less confident and be at a disadvantage as the wedding plans were discussed. She unpacked her suitcase and found her beige linen trousers and a bright blue cotton sweater she had bought in the Ralph Lauren outlet shop in Kildare Village on the way down to Kerry. Simple and perfect – just the thing to wear under Sylvia's critical gaze. Tricia quickly showered and washed and blow-dried her hair, mentally blessing her hairdresser for giving her a cut that was so easy to manage.

Vi was in the living room putting together the list with her and Jack's wedding plans. She looked up as Tricia entered, smiling approvingly. 'You look great, Mum. The swim was obviously what you needed.'

'That and a little spit and polish,' Tricia replied, looking at herself in the mirror over the mantelpiece. She did look a lot better already, even if there were still shadows under her eyes and lines around her mouth. The light makeup she had applied had brightened her complexion and her hair bouncing around her face was an added bonus. 'Let's have a look at the list,' she said, turning away from the mirror. 'We'll want to be prepared to stay strong and ready to resist any arguments.'

'You're right. Granny means well, even if she'll want everything her way.' Vi handed Tricia her list. 'As you see, we want a small cosy affair with the wedding ceremony in the little church up the hill and the reception in the orangery. It'll be so gorgeous there within the old walls and the garden to wander around in should it get too hot. I think Lily will love the idea to have the reception there. It's going to be a barbecue but we'll get the caterers Granny uses to help with all the cooking. They always do a good job.'

Tricia sat down on the sofa and looked at the list. 'Only sixty guests? And you want to have a barbecue? And a salsa band so you can dance on the deck outside the orangery. I think that sounds grand, you know. And such fun. What about the dress?'

'I'd like to wear your dress, Mum,' Vi said. 'Can I?'

'Of course,' Tricia said, feeling suddenly overwhelmed. 'That would be lovely.'

'It won't make you sad?' Vi asked, looking worried.

Tricia put her hand on Vi's cheek. 'No, darling, it won't. It will bring me back to the happiest day of my life. But are you sure you want that style? Puffed sleeves and that wide skirt with layers of flounces. Looks a bit like a meringue. It was all the rage in the nineties, but fashions have changed since then.'

'I know but I've always loved it,' Vi declared. 'You looked like a fairy-tale princess in the photos I always thought.'

'When you were eight, yes.' Tricia smiled and shook her head. 'Now you might think it's hideous. But I'll find it and we'll have a look. You can always buy something new if you change your mind. We have plenty of time.'

'Two and a half months,' Vi said. 'So we need to get started on all the details and send out the save the date emails and then the invitations and order the flowers and talk to the caterers and... well, check with Lily if she can give us the orangery for that one day.'

'Very true.' Tricia folded the list and put it in the handbag. 'Lots to consider and discuss. I'm sure Granny will have some of her own ideas, too, so we should be prepared for that.'

Vi looked suddenly worried. 'Yes, she will. We have to let her do some of the organising or she'll be upset.'

'We'll play it by ear,' Tricia said, feeling only slightly apprehensive. 'But apart from all that, I want to go to the cottage and take a peek at it before Granny's dinner. We have time to take a walk over there beforehand.'

'Why? You'll get the keys in a few days.'

'I know,' Tricia said. 'But I just want to see it before I tell Sylvia I'm the new owner.'

'Okay.' Vi nodded and got up. 'Maybe you can go on your own? I want to call Jack and then have a quick shower and change out of these jeans.'

'Grand.' Tricia rose, gathering up her bag. 'I'll see you up there, then.'

'Brilliant.'

Vi disappeared up the stairs while Tricia left the house and started up the avenue to the manor house. She then took a path to the left which would lead her to the cottage. She couldn't wait to see it in real life. Even though she knew it well, she hadn't been to that part of the garden for many years. Now, as time had passed, she had come to cherish the memories rather than trying to forget, and it was sweet to remember the happy times. It made her feel good to think about them.

Tricia saw the roof of the cottage above the trees before she arrived there. She walked faster, feeling a dart of nostalgia as she arrived at the front garden which had once had an herbaceous border full of flowers of all kinds. Peonies, roses, marigolds, daisies and hydrangea bushes had provided a colourful display and Tricia had often come here to pick a bunch for the dining table in the summer. But now the garden was overgrown and only a few roses and daisies remained, poking their heads through the tall weeds. Her gaze drifted to the house itself which had been newly whitewashed and the thatch replaced with slate ten years ago, the estate agent had told her. The window frames were cracked, however, and she could see broken panes here and there.

She knew the cottage had a kitchen–diner, a spacious living room and a bedroom and a box room downstairs. There was a further bedroom in the attic space with a window in the gable end of the house. The bathroom was in the lean-to and would have to be updated.

Tricia could imagine that the house would have been a lovely family home for the gardener and his wife in the early days. The cottage was built in 1869 so there would have been many families living here, one after the other and the house and garden would have been teeming with children. She had always had a feeling it was a happy house, and Fred had said the same when they'd come here to look at it just after Violet had been born. It felt at the same time like yesterday and a very long time ago. The memories came tumbling back as she stood there at the gate looking up at the cottage.

5

___

'What are we doing here?' Tricia asked as their walk ended outside the cottage.

'You'll see,' Fred said, and opened the gate. He took her hand and pulled her into the front garden that was still well tended. 'The last tenant left six months ago and now there will be no more resident gardeners. Dad is going to hire a gardening firm from Dingle to look after the grounds from now on. So the cottage is up for rent.'

'Oh?' Tricia asked, mystified. 'We were going to do it up when we were first married but then Lily arrived, so we forgot about it. But now here we are again. Are you thinking what I'm thinking?'

'Maybe I am,' Fred said with a teasing grin.

Tricia smiled back at her handsome husband, taking in his tall frame, thick copper-coloured hair, sparkling green eyes and the beautiful smile that lit up his face. Fred was always so cheerful, always ready to crack a joke or play a trick when you least expected it. They had been married for over ten years and Violet was two years old, and had just started to talk in real sentences. Tricia loved the old manor and was very fond of her parents-in-law, Liam and Sylvia, with whom they got on so well. But they were never really on their own even though the house was very big. They had dinner together in the formal dining room every evening as one big family. Fred's parents still stuck to old traditions and although Tricia loved the old house and the beautiful rooms, it felt strange, even after ten years, to live like this, with his parents so close. She knew Fred felt the same, and now as she stood in the kitchen of the cottage, she had an inkling that he might be planning for them to have a space of their own.

'I know what you want to do,' Tricia said as she looked around at the old cupboards, the wood-burning range and the sink with its wooden draining board. 'It wasn't quite the right thing for us when we were just married but now it feels right. I love the idea.'

Fred turned from inspecting the range. 'You do?' he said, looking suddenly very happy. 'But this house needs a lot of work to get it liveable. And it's not as comfortable as Magnolia and never will be.' He took her hand. 'I know it's small, but the girls would love to play in the garden and we could put up swings and maybe put in a small swimming pool or something in the back garden. We could have chickens and ducks and they could play farmers. What do you think?' There was such hope in his eyes as he looked at her with love and a yearning for them to do something together. They had been so busy all these years, Fred with running the farm and the estate with his father and Tricia with her three daughters and her part-time job as an accountant. Doing up the house would give them a chance to be together more.

Tricia nodded and went over to kiss him. 'I think it's a lovely idea. A place where we can be together on our own away from everyone. We can do it up slowly and make it just the way we want. It'll be like a little hideaway. And the girls will love it too. But...' She paused. 'What will your parents think? Will they let us buy the cottage to do what we want with?'

'I'm sure they will,' Fred said, looking nearly sure. 'We'll still be close by.'

'We'll ask them at dinner,' Tricia suggested. 'I mean, we'll be doing them a favour doing up the house ourselves. I can't wait to get started. You know how I love getting my hands dirty. The garden will be a great project, and then we'll paint all the rooms colours that Sylvia would never choose, and I can make curtains and we'll get furniture at the flea markets all over Kerry. Oh, Fred, it will be so much fun. And our very own home at last.'

'Terrific,' Fred said and hugged her close. 'I knew you'd be keen to do this. And you know what?' he added after a long pause. 'There might be something hidden here that could be very valuable.'

'Like a treasure?' Tricia had asked, laughing at his mysterious expression.

'You never know,' he had said and then kissed her, making her forget everything except their love for each other.

They had floated the idea to Liam and Sylvia over dinner and after some persuading, they had agreed to let Fred and Tricia buy the cottage as a project to do up as a place for them to be together.

But it had all come to nothing in the end after that fatal boating accident.

Tricia felt tears sting as she stood in the overgrown garden remembering that day. But then she pulled herself together and felt that she now had the chance to realise their dream. Fred would be happy she was doing it. It was the best way to cherish his memory. And he would be there in some way as she made the little cottage come alive again.

With her mind full of plans about what she could do with the cottage, Tricia walked towards the manor house. She could see people going in and out of the large entrance door and assumed they were the tenants of the senior apartments. It was nice to see the manor being so busy after many years of the building being half empty, with Sylvia the only occupant. It had been a sad and lonely house then but now it was full of people who had been given a chance to be independent in their old age while being near to amenities they might need.

Tricia went around the back to the courtyard and Sylvia's private quarters and rang the bell outside the green door that used to be the back entrance. Now it led to a bright hall, and then into the kitchen–diner, all redone and modernised without losing its old-style country charm. Tricia had come here for Christmas since the house was restored, except for that year when Sean had been so ill.

She gave a start as the door was opened by Sylvia, who greeted her with a cheery, 'Hello, Tricia, how lovely to see you again.'

Tricia walked inside and kissed Sylvia on the cheek. 'Hello. Nice to see you, too, Sylvia. How are you?'

Sylvia, dressed in a white silk blouse and navy slacks, stepped back and smiled. 'I'm very well, thank you. You look good. I can see you've had a good rest after all you've been through.'

'Yes, I feel much better now,' Tricia said. 'You look amazing, too,' she added, wondering how this woman managed to appear decades younger than her eighty-five years. Sylvia's face was lined but she glowed with good health, and her thick grey hair was cut in a short style that suited her strong features and brown eyes.

'You're very kind,' Sylvia said. 'Youth isn't on my side any more, I have to admit.'

'Ah sure, age is only a number, as they say.' Tricia peeked into the kitchen. 'Are the girls here yet?'

'No, it's just you and me for the moment. Come in and we'll have a drink and chat before they arrive.' Sylvia led the way to the alcove in the bright kitchen where the large round table was set for six people. 'It'll be a girls' only dinner,' she said. 'You and me, the girls and Nora. I thought as you've just arrived it would be good for you to meet the whole family in one go.'

'Oh, that's great.' Tricia pulled out a chair and sat down at the table. 'I've been in touch with Lily and Rose, of course. I haven't seen Nora since Christmas so it'll be great to catch up with her. We used to be close friends back in the day. But...' Tricia paused, trying to gather up enough courage to break the news to Sylvia. 'There is something I have to tell you before everyone's here.'

'What's that?' Sylvia sat down opposite Tricia. 'Come on, let it out. You look as if you're about to explode. I can take whatever bad news you're about to share.'

'It's not bad news at all,' Tricia protested. 'It's good news. For me, anyway. You see, I'm the one who bought the cottage. The gardener's cottage, I mean.'

Sylvia looked at Tricia. 'That's what you call news?' She shook her head and smiled. 'I was sure you were the buyer. That's why I accepted the offer so fast.'

Tricia stared at Sylvia. 'How did you know? Did Vi say anything?'

'No, not at all, she wouldn't if you told her not to. Nobody told me. I just figured that out all by myself. And I think it's perfect. For you and me and the girls. And...' She paused and blinked away tears. 'For Fred's memory. He would love for you to do it up and live there.'

'I know,' Tricia whispered, surprised and happy that Sylvia understood. It hadn't always been like this when Fred was alive. There had been tensions between them and Tricia had always felt Sylvia watching her, expecting her to do something wrong. It could be a comment about the way Tricia brought up the children, or something to do with etiquette during a dinner party or even the way she dressed. Tricia had always felt she didn't quite come up to scratch in Sylvia's eyes. But now, after all the years that had passed, she seemed happy that Tricia was doing something in Fred's memory, which was wonderful.

Tricia had expected some tough questions. She'd wondered if Sylvia would ask why she wanted to leave Dublin in such a hurry, and she hadn't been looking forward to telling lies. Tricia sighed with relief as the anticipated interrogation didn't happen.

Sylvia squeezed Tricia's hand for a moment. Then she got up and went to the fridge and took out a bottle. 'Let's have a glass of bubbly to celebrate.'

'Maybe we should wait for the others?' Tricia suggested.

'We'll have a glass now and then another when the girls arrive.' Sylvia shot Tricia a mischievous smile while she expertly opened the bottle, sending the cork up to the ceiling. Then she filled two champagne flutes and carried them to the table. 'It's prosecco, so not strong at all,' she said as she handed Tricia one of the flutes.

'Lovely.' Tricia held her flute up and smiled at Sylvia. 'Cheers!'

'Here's to your new life at Magnolia Manor,' Sylvia said with a fond smile as they clinked glasses. 'May it be as happy as possible.'

'Thank you.' Tricia felt a surge of affection for her former mother-in-law. Sylvia was a real trooper. If she had misgivings about Tricia living so close and competing for the affections of her granddaughters and their children, she didn't show it.

'I assume Violet already knows since she was with you in Dublin?' Sylvia remarked.

'Yes, and I'm staying with her at the gatehouse while I organise the cottage.'

'Good idea. How do you feel being back?' Sylvia asked. 'How are you coping with all the memories?'

'Very well, to my surprise,' Tricia replied, touched that

Sylvia would ask. 'I think that because of all the time that has passed, I'm beginning to cherish the memories. Fred and I had such a happy time here even if it was cut short.'

Sylvia nodded. 'That's good. Better to face the past and feel grateful to have been happy than to be sad. We have to cherish the memories and feel blessed to have had those wonderful times.'

'Exactly.' Tricia paused. 'I even went swimming off the pier just after I arrived. I really enjoyed it.'

Sylvia looked suddenly alarmed. 'You were at the pier? Swimming?'

'I was. Loved it.' Tricia smiled. 'No need to worry. It's perfectly safe there. No currents or anything and the raft is still there. But...' She stopped as she remembered what she had seen. 'Oh, I meant to ask you. There was a rib on the shore beside the pier. With diving equipment. Does it belong to Henri?'

'No. Henri isn't here much,' Sylvia said and got up from her seat. 'He works remotely from France these days.'

'So who owns that rib? Someone who's diving in the bay?' Tricia asked. 'Why would anyone dive there? What would they be looking for?'

'I don't know anything about that,' Sylvia said, her back turned to Tricia. 'Could be anyone. Lots of people scuba dive around here. It's becoming quite a popular hobby.'

'Okay,' Tricia said, deciding to drop the subject. But she had a strange feeling that it wasn't just 'anyone' who was diving in the bay. Was Sylvia also harbouring secrets she wasn't willing to share?

6

The girls arrived all at once, preventing Tricia from asking any more questions about the rib she had seen. In any case, she forgot about it for the moment while she greeted her elder daughters, who she hadn't seen for many months. They all formed a group hug, squeezing each other tight, chatting and laughing. Tricia hugged Lily and Rose in turn and then pulled away to look at them in wonder. They were, to her, all so beautiful. And so different. Lily, with her dark hair and large brown eyes, was the image of Sylvia; Rose had the same blue eyes and blonde hair as Tricia, and Vi with her red hair, green eyes and freckles so heartbreakingly like her father. But Tricia saw something of Fred in all her girls, in their expressions, smiles and voices. It was at once comforting and melancholy.

'Mum, it's so lovely to see you.' Lily let go of Tricia after placing a kiss on her cheek. 'And Vi said you're here for good. Why didn't you tell us?'

'I wanted it to be a surprise. How are my lovely grandchildren?' Tricia asked.

'In great form, if a little exhausting,' Lily replied. 'Naomi is growing up to be a real bossy-boots and Liam is good at charming everyone, especially older ladies.'

'I can't wait to see them,' Tricia said. She turned to Rose. 'And darling Sophie?'

'A bundle of joy at the moment,' Rose said with a fond smile. 'Four is a lovely age.'

'You were gorgeous at that age,' Tricia said and hugged Rose again. 'I'm so happy to be here with you all.'

'So are we, Mum. But where are you going to live?' Rose asked, pulling away from the hug.

'It's a secret,' Vi said, looking smug.

'Not any more,' Sylvia announced from kitchen counter, where she was filling more glasses with prosecco. 'Tricia has bought the cottage.'

'The gardener's cottage?' Rose asked. 'So you're the mystery buyer?'

Tricia smiled. 'No mystery. But yes, it's me.'

'Oh, Mum, that's the best news. But why didn't you tell us?' Lily handed out the glasses of prosecco to Rose and Vi and they all sat down at the table.

'No reason,' Tricia said with a glance at Sylvia. 'I just wanted to make sure it all went smoothly before I said anything.' She smiled at her daughters. 'But now I'm here to stay. I'm going to do up the cottage little by little and get it just the way I want it.'

'I'm sure Dominic will be willing to help,' Lily said. 'He's always said he'd love to get his hands on that place to do it up.'

'Well, now he can.' Tricia grinned happily at her eldest daughter, whose husband was an architect, builder and handyman all in one. His firm had done most of the restoration work on Magnolia Manor. 'But my cottage will be small potatoes compared to what he usually does. In any case, I want to do a lot of it myself, like painting and minor repairs. Dom can do the big stuff.'

'He'll love it,' Lily said. 'Give him a ring tomorrow and you can discuss dates and any details of what you want to do.'

'I'm not getting the keys until Wednesday,' Tricia said.

'You can have them straight away if you want to go in and take a look,' Sylvia cut in as she got up from the table to answer the doorbell that had just rung. 'That'll be Nora,' she added while she walked into the hall.

'Hi, everyone,' Nora said as she came in. 'Sorry if I'm late.'

'You're just in time for a drink,' Sylvia said, handing Nora a glass while Tricia got up to hug her old friend.

'Lovely to see you again,' Nora said and hugged Tricia back. 'Welcome back.'

'Thank you, Nora.' Tricia smiled at Nora, noting how good she looked. With her strong features, thick greying hair, lovely brown eyes under black eyebrows, she was a handsome woman with great warmth and charm. Only a few years older than Tricia, Nora had been a great support after the tragedy, helping Tricia to cope and being a second mother to the little girls who had just lost their father and grandfather. She had also provided practical help, cooking and keeping things tidy, organising the funeral, answering the phone and talking to all kinds of people who called to the house. Tricia had often wondered what they would have done without Nora and Martin, her husband. They had remained friends and kept in touch all through the years after that.

'Now that you're here, you'll have to catch up with the old gang,' Nora said. 'We still have our book club meetings once a month.'

'More like a wine club than anything to do with books,' Sylvia remarked with a wink, handing Nora a glass.

'We do discuss literature, though,' Nora said with pretend primness. 'And we go to see a movie sometimes too. It's all about culture, really.'

'Sounds like fun. Can't wait to catch up with everyone. Cheers, Nora,' Tricia said and clinked her glass against Nora's.

'Cheers.' Nora smiled and took a sip and then sat down between Vi and Tricia. 'How's my little movie star?' she asked. 'I hear Jack proposed. Congratulations, pet. Show me the ring.'

Vi held up her hand and showed Nora her beautiful ring. 'Isn't it lovely?'

'Fabulous,' Nora said. 'He has good taste.'

'That's not the only news,' Vi said. 'There's something else to announce as well. I'm going to be shooting in Limerick in an Irish production very soon so I can commute home practically every day depending on the shooting schedule.'

'Oh, that's excellent news, sweetheart.' Tricia turned and looked at her daughter. 'What kind of part is it?'

Vi grinned. 'You're looking at Inspector Colleen O'Dea, the new female sleuth in a detective series that might run for a long time.'

'That's wonderful,' Tricia exclaimed. 'I'm so happy for you.'

Vi beamed at her mother. 'It's very exciting. Limerick is only an hour or two from Dingle, too, so it's perfect timing.'

'Congratulations,' Sylvia interjected. 'Now we have another thing to celebrate.'

'So when's the wedding?' Nora asked. 'Have you set a date yet?'

'Yes,' Vi said, glancing nervously at Sylvia. 'We want to get married on the twenty-second of August.'

'What?' Sylvia, who was carrying a platter with roast chicken, potatoes and vegetables to the table, nearly lost her grip. Nora rushed to help her and they managed to put it all on the table. Then Sylvia turned to Vi, who was cowering at the other side of the table. 'You picked the date? Without telling me?'

'I told Mum,' Vi said. 'And we were going to tell you tonight, which we just did.'

'Well, thank you very much,' Sylvia snapped. 'I suppose you're planning to hold the reception in the ballroom as well?'

'No...' Vi glanced at Tricia. 'We're having a small wedding and the party is going to be in the orangery, if Lily agrees. We thought we'd have a barbecue if the weather is nice and...'

'Fab idea,' Lily exclaimed, looking excited. 'Of course you can have the orangery. I'll do it up with decorations and flowers and make it super cute. How many guests?'

'We think about sixty,' Vi replied. 'Just family and close friends. And no dressing up, except me, of course,' she added with a giggle.

'Sixty guests? And a barbecue? Not what I'd call suitable for a Fleury,' Sylvia remarked, looking put out. 'Did you know about this, Tricia?'

'Well, some of it,' Tricia confessed. 'I think it's—'

'Terrible,' Sylvia interrupted. 'A small wedding? With a barbecue? For a Fleury wedding? What will people think?'

'I don't care what "people" think,' Vi said, making quote marks. 'It's our wedding and this is what we want to do.'

'And you didn't consider me at all when you put together this plan?' Sylvia asked.

'But it's not about you,' Tricia said hesitantly, feeling she couldn't stay quiet any longer. 'It's about Vi and Jack and the most important day of their lives.'

'That's why it has to be a fitting event for a Fleury bride,' Sylvia retorted.

'But Granny...' Lily started.

Nora got up and put food on plates and handed them around. 'Maybe we could eat and then calm down a bit and discuss this? No need to argue on an empty stomach.'

'Thank you, Nora,' Sylvia said and took one of the plates. 'I'm not arguing, I'm just sharing my thoughts. And I'm a little shaken by what I just heard, that's all. Vi's wedding could be my swansong, my last hurrah and the final big party that I'll organise. You all know how much I've enjoyed doing all the big events in the family.'

'We know that, of course,' Vi said. 'Granny, you're the best, most popular hostess in Dingle. But this time, it's about me and Jack. He wants our wedding to be casual and fun, not a big splashy do. I'd hate to disappoint him.'

'So instead you're disappointing Granny,' Rose remarked.

'I'm not...' Vi started, glaring at Rose. 'This is going to be our day, mine and Jack's. It'll be something we'll remember for the rest of our lives. Can't you understand that?'

'Yeah, but you have to consider other people, too,' Rose argued.

'Please calm down, Rose. Let's eat and then talk,' Tricia suggested. 'Nora's right. We're all hungry and the discussion about the wedding can wait until later.'

'Good point,' Lily said. 'But I still want to say that I love Vi and Jack's plans for a wedding in the orangery. But let's eat and enjoy this lovely dinner.'

'I'm with Granny, just so you know,' Rose cut in before she dug into her food. 'A big glamorous wedding at Magnolia Manor that could be featured in a magazine would be fantastic publicity for the events side of our business. We could get an exclusive with *OK!* magazine for the photos. You might consider that side of things, Vi.'

'No, I won't,' Vi said, still glaring at Rose. Then she started eating without another word.

Tricia looked around the table at the sullen looks between her daughters and the stern disapproval in Sylvia's eyes. The welcome home dinner had turned into a battlefield with Lily, Vi and herself on one side and Sylvia and Rose on the other. She glanced at Nora for help but Nora just rolled her eyes, shrugged and started to eat, taking a sip from her glass of prosecco. This was terrible for Vi, who had been so happy about her engagement and the fun wedding she wanted.

They all ate in silence for a few minutes. Tricia was trying to see a solution when an idea came to her. 'I know what we can do,' she suddenly exclaimed. 'Something that's not quite a wedding but still a great party.'

'What would that be?' Sylvia asked, one of her eyebrows lifting.

'An engagement party,' Tricia said, now firing on all cylinders. 'A big, glam event where we all dress up and get a lot of attention just for the one night. And we could do it as soon as Jack arrives. No need to plan for weeks, we'll just invite everyone and it can be all over Instagram and all kinds of other places, whatever you want.'

Vi smiled, looking at once much happier. 'That's a great idea, Mum. And we could have a band and dance and serve posh food and all that jazz.' She stopped for a moment and then grinned. 'I have it! We could do a *Great Gatsby* theme. How about that? With jazz music and everyone dressed in that nineteen twenties style. Wouldn't that be fun?'

'Brilliant,' Lily said, looking excited. 'That would be amazing. We could have it in the afternoon so we won't disturb the tenants of the senior apartments. A tea dance like they did in the old days. But with champagne.'

'The ballroom and gardens are booked solid for weddings all through July,' Rose said. 'So I don't think...'

'Then we'll have the party during the week,' Tricia cut in. 'In the late afternoon. How does the calendar look for the next week or two, Rose? For a midweek do, I mean.'

'That could be doable, I suppose,' Rose admitted.

'A lot of people in town are away on holiday during July,' Sylvia interrupted. 'Most of my friends have already left for the summer.'

'So what?' Tricia countered. 'They will at least get the invitation by email and can decide if they want to interrupt their holiday or not. I bet a lot of them will do anything to come to this party.'

'Nobody will want to miss it,' Nora remarked.

'So can we do it?' Tricia asked, looking at Sylvia. 'An engagement party for Vi and Jack in the next two weeks or so?'

'I suppose it's possible,' Sylvia said, looking only slightly mollified. 'This takes the spotlight off the actual wedding, of course. So Violet and Jack can have their small ceremony and we can call it a secret wedding or something. With photos posted when they've left for their honeymoon.'

'Perfect,' Vi said, beaming a smile at her grandmother. 'You're the best virtual assistant, Granny. You can do all the Insta stuff. And we'll send photos from the honeymoon in Cornwall.'

'So romantic,' Lily said with a happy sigh. 'And all so perfect, Mum. You're a genius. Don't you think, Granny?'

'I wouldn't go that far,' Sylvia said. 'But we came up with a good solution, yes.'

'High praise indeed.' Tricia smiled, knowing she had won this time, even if Sylvia now pretended it was all her idea. The wedding would be another matter, but she was sure Sylvia would accept most of Vi and Jack's wishes now that she was allowed to throw a big party in the ballroom, even if the *Great Gatsby* theme wasn't really what she might have planned.

'Phew,' Nora whispered in Tricia's ear as the girls and Sylvia chatted on about the engagement party. 'You did a great job, even if the glory will be all Sylvia's.'

'I don't care,' Tricia whispered back. 'If Vi and Jack are happy, that's all that matters.'

'Of course. Better to sit back and enjoy it,' Nora said.

A thought suddenly struck Tricia. 'Sylvia said it could be her last hurrah. What did that mean? Is she ill?'

'Not at all,' Nora said, grinning. 'She's been saying that for the past twenty years when she wants something to go her way. She's as fit as a fiddle.'

'Oh, phew.' Tricia laughed. 'I'm glad she's the same feisty Sylvia. Not always easy to handle, but we still love her, don't we?'

'Of course we do,' Nora agreed. 'And hey, Violet told me you've bought the cottage. That was quite a big step for you.'

'I know but I felt in my bones that I had to come and live here. My grandchildren only see me occasionally and that's not a good way to be.'

'It will be hard work to make the cottage comfortable,' Nora remarked. 'But the structure is good and the roof is in good nick.'

'I realise that,' Tricia agreed. 'And I can put up with just the basics for the summer while the work is going on. I like being outdoors anyway, as you know.'

'Yes, I remember. You and Fred were always doing all that swimming and hiking and cycling.' Nora looked suddenly awkward. 'I'm sorry. I hope that didn't make you sad.'

'No, not any more.' Tricia put her hand on Nora's arm. 'I like remembering the happy times. And I can't wait to see old friends again.'

'They'll be happy to see you too,' Nora replied. 'You seem so much stronger now, ready to face life again.'

Tricia nodded. 'Yes, I think I am. It's perhaps the realisation that at my age, I have no time to waste. If I'm to live a full and happy life, I have to count my blessings and move on. Make the best of every single day.' She laughed. 'That sounds far too positive for me. I must have drunk too much of that prosecco.'

'Have some more,' Nora suggested. 'I like the new light-hearted you.'

'Yeah, why not.' Tricia smiled and nodded while Nora filled her glass. She shot a look at Sylvia across the table, expecting a cold stare, but all she got back was a benign smile. What a relief.

Sylvia had been sidetracked and was happy to organise yet another event and might this way keep her hands off Vi's wedding. All Tricia's problems in Donegal felt far away and it seemed as if all the rumours would never catch up with her here, where she was safe in the bosom of her family. All was well and Tricia could look forward to stepping into her new home very soon. She couldn't wait for her new life to start.

7

The sale of the cottage went through without a hitch on Wednesday. Tricia rushed over to the estate agents to pick up the keys, excited to get into her new home. Then she drove back to Magnolia Manor and parked outside the cottage, happy beyond words to finally step inside. She guessed the house would be damp and dirty after years of neglect. Cleaning it up would be the first step and then getting her son-in-law Dominic to come and go through whatever renovation work needed to be done. She knew the structure was sound and the roof good. The original thatched roof had been replaced with slate, which was sad but meant the insurance was not a problem. The change meant a loss of the old-world charm but there was less danger in case of fire.

When she arrived at the cottage, Tricia took the keys from her bag and entered the garden. She waded through the high grass and then stood at the front door, its red paint peeling in large flakes. There was a hand-shaped brass knocker which made her smile as she inserted the large key into the keyhole. It turned with slight difficulty, the door stiff, emitting a loud creak as Tricia pushed it open, and then, finally, she stood inside a tiny hall that smelled only a little musty.

The door to the corridor was open and Tricia turned left into the living room and stood for a moment looking around in wonder. The dirty, neglected room she had expected was instead bright and clean, the wide oak planks on the floor polished and the fireplace clear of any old timbers or soot. There was a smell of soap and beeswax and the window was open to the sunny back garden. The remnant of a lace curtain fluttered in the soft breeze and a thrush sang in the apple tree just outside the window. It was so lovely and peaceful it made Tricia feel quite tearful.

But who had been in here to clean the house? Nora? Or... There was only one way to find out. Tricia fished her phone from her pocket and called Sylvia's number. She answered straight away.

'Tricia? I hope all is well and you got the keys?'

'I did and I'm here in the cottage,' Tricia replied. 'I was expecting it to be damp and dirty but it looks like someone has been cleaning the place from top to bottom. Was it you?'

Sylvia laughed. 'Not me but the cleaning firm we use at Magnolia. I wanted to hand over the property in as good a nick as possible. Didn't seem quite correct not to have it cleaned for the new owner. Take it as a housewarming present from me.'

'Oh. That's the best housewarming gift ever. Thanks a million,' Tricia said. 'That really makes it feel a much happier place, I have to say.'

'There's still a lot of work to be done before you can live there,' Sylvia remarked.

'I know but I'm not afraid of a bit of hard work,' Tricia replied.

'Good for you. But now I have to sign off. I'm doing the invitations for the party and then trying to contact the caterers. Lots to be done,' Sylvia said, sounding important.

'Of course. I won't disturb you any more. You're brilliant to organise this party.' Tricia knew heaping praise on Sylvia was the best way to stay in her good books. 'You're the most amazing party organiser.'

'Well, it's hard work but I think I'm on top of it,' Sylvia said.

'Of course you are. Thanks again for having my new house cleaned,' Tricia said. 'See you soon.'

'Yes, if I have the time. Bye, Tricia.' Sylvia hung up.

Tricia smiled and put away her phone. That exchange had told her old age hadn't changed Sylvia. She was still strong, opinionated, stubborn, but deep down very kind. Tricia had had to eat humble pie on many occasions when she and Fred were just married, but she had felt it was worth it as she and Fred were so in love. And now, so many years later, that rivalry between them was gone, even though she was sure there would be arguments and differences of opinion.

Tricia knew the girls all loved their darling granny and she had to admit that Sylvia had been their rock all through the girls' teenage years and given them a kind of stability that Tricia had not been able to provide. Sylvia had insisted that they should still go to Coláiste Íde, the boarding school for girls near Dingle that she herself had attended. Fred had put the girls' names down when they were born, but after his death, Tricia had been worried that she couldn't afford the fees. Then Sylvia had stepped in and set up a trust fund and it was all organised without Tricia having to pay a cent. Sylvia had also made sure Tricia and the girls spent their summer holidays at Magnolia Manor which meant they felt more at home there than in the flat in Dublin. This had meant that Sylvia and her granddaughters had a special bond which could never be broken. It had been hard for Tricia to accept all the financial help from Sylvia but she had known she had no choice. Now she had to get closer to her daughters after her long absence and get to know her grandchildren.

Better to take things slowly than try to change things and create even more tension. If we're all going to get on and live together in harmony, I'll have to take a step back now and be prepared to agree to things that might not be exactly the way I'd like it. That wasn't too high a price to pay for her new life with her daughters and grandchildren. She was still their mother and that was something Sylvia could never compete with.

As soon as Tricia had pocketed her phone, it rang again. It was Nora. 'Are you in?' she asked.

Tricia laughed. 'Yes. And Sylvia had the place cleaned before she handed over the keys. I'm in the little sitting room now so I haven't inspected the rest yet. I want to establish if I can live here after I order some furniture.'

'Well, you like camping,' Nora said. 'So it shouldn't be a problem.'

'That's true,' Tricia said. 'But with advancing years, I've come to like a bit of comfort.'

'What advancing years?' Nora laughed. 'I'm a little older than you and I'm still flying.' She paused. 'Except I do like a comfortable bed and a hot shower these days.'

'Me too,' Tricia admitted.

'I'd better leave you to inspect your new abode,' Nora continued. 'I just wanted to call you and see if you'd like to come out with me tonight? There's trad music at that pub up Green Street where we used to hang out. Some of the girls from my book club are going. A girls' night out for us oldies. Should be good craic.'

'I'd love to,' Tricia replied, happy to have been asked.

'Great. Martin will drive us and pick us up afterwards so we can have a jar,' Nora said. 'Can you be ready at eight o'clock or so?'

'Of course,' Tricia promised. 'That sounds like a great night out.'

'Grand. We'll pick you up at the gatehouse,' Nora said.

Tricia said goodbye to Nora, excited at the thought of going out and meeting some of her old friends, and making new ones. It was a long time since she had had a night out like that. It made her feel young again.

But now she needed to explore the house further and make a list of what she needed to do to at least be able to live here for the summer. She could manage with just the basics for now. Jack was coming home at the weekend and Tricia wanted to leave the young couple alone. Who wanted a future mother-in-law in the house when they had just got engaged and were planning a wedding?

Tricia left the living room and walked down the corridor to the kitchen, which was spacious and in fairly good nick. There was a wood-burning range, an electric cooker and a fridge. The old, scarred kitchen table would need to be scrubbed down and the three wobbly-looking chairs replaced. The linoleum on the floor was scuffed and worn but it would be easy to replace that with something modern. It would do for now, even though the old porcelain sink and wooden draining board were not very enticing. She would just have to manage and do everything little by little.

The bathroom was even more rundown than the kitchen, with a bathtub that had a hand shower and a washbasin that had a huge crack in it. At least the toilet worked and she could cope with the rest. The little window had a view of the sea if she stood on tiptoe and the green tiles on the floor were quite beautiful. It would eventually be a sweet little bathroom once it was done up.

The large bedroom was the best room in the whole house, with a wooden floor, a large window overlooking the back garden and a cute cast iron fireplace that looked as if it would work. Tricia immediately imagined being in bed on a winter's night with a fire glowing in the grate. She would buy a comfortable bed with a slatted base, a good mattress and get an iron headboard that would go with the early Victorian-period feel. She could see herself cuddled up under the duvet, reading a book and feeling snug and safe.

Tricia inspected the box room which was just that: a room for boxes. Not much to be done with it except keep it as a storage room – or maybe a guest bedroom for her grandchildren. She'd decide later.

At least she knew for now that she would be able to live in the house as soon as she had some bedroom furniture, kitchen chairs, a sofa, easy chairs for the living room and curtains and blinds for all the windows. And she could definitely sell it and make a small profit. Standing in the home for the first time, she felt hopeful that the cottage could indeed solve all of her problems. She thought of Sean's family, and the angry words she had exchanged with his nephew Terence and shivered. Everything was going to be fine, she reassured herself, trying to be positive. She just needed a little more time.

Just then, Tricia remembered that there was another bedroom in the attic. Deciding to just take a look at the room, she gingerly climbed the stairs holding on to the banister, hoping it was strong enough to hold. But even though it creaked loudly, it seemed solid enough and she arrived at the top without any mishaps. She'd ask Dominic to check it when he came to inspect the cottage.

Having arrived in the attic room, she looked around in the dim light and discovered it was larger than she had thought and that the pitch of the roof was quite high and could be a nice guest room sometime in the future. That could certainly add value to the property. It gave her a few more options. Except for an old pine wardrobe, the room was empty of furniture. The small window in the gable end had a view over the walled garden and the apple trees in the old orchard. The room could be turned into a cute bedroom with wallpaper and matching curtains, a rug on the old planks and old-style bedroom furniture. She lingered in the room for a moment, breathing in the smell of old timbers and apples that might have been stored here once. This could have been her and Fred's bedroom if... *If the accident hadn't happened,* she thought, feeling his presence as if he stood beside her. *What fun we would have had doing this house up together... But I will do it on my own and live here remembering the happy days...*

Content with what she had found, Tricia walked back to the car and picked up her phone as soon as she was inside to call Dominic. They decided to meet at the cottage on Monday.

'I think I can camp here as soon as I have some furniture,' she told him.

'Are you sure?' Dominic asked. 'I can imagine that there is a lot to be done. What's the rush anyway? I'd say Vi and Jack don't mind you staying with them for a while longer.'

Tricia laughed. 'That's what they *say*, but not what they really think. I lived with my parents-in-law all through my first marriage. The manor is a big house, but it was still quite tricky. I always felt quite crowded and there was little privacy. We couldn't even have a decent row without everyone knowing about it. And their cottage is much smaller. No, I don't want to put them through all that.'

'You're very understanding and considerate,' Dominic said, sounding impressed.

'Ah, not really. I want my own space, too, you know,' Tricia remarked. 'I'm chomping at the bit to get this cottage restored. There is so much I want to do and I can't wait to do it.'

'You'll be one of those impatient clients,' Dominic joked. 'But I'll do my best to have it done sooner rather than later. I've put a few jobs on hold so I can concentrate on your house.'

'You're a star, Dominic Doyle,' Tricia exclaimed. 'A real mother-in-law's dream.'

Dominic laughed. 'Ah sure, it's all Lily's doing. She's a

Fleury girl. When they say "jump" we men say "how high?" We should warn Jack before it's too late.'

'I'm sure he already knows,' Tricia replied with a laugh.

Tricia took a long time getting ready for her girls' evening out. Having spent a while picking an outfit, she finally decided to go casual. After all, it was only a pub evening and not some glitzy party. She told herself sternly to act her age and picked her best jeans and a light blue linen shirt with a navy sweater thrown over her shoulders. Mascara and a little lipstick completed her look, and she was ready to go. Martin's car pulled up outside the gatehouse and Tricia quickly kissed Vi goodbye and ran down the steps, looking forward – with just a little trepidation – to the evening ahead. It felt a little like a school reunion as she hadn't met her old friends for a very long time.

Martin got out to give Tricia a hug. 'Welcome home, Tricia,' he said. 'I hear you're going to be a neighbour.'

'Thanks, Martin.' Tricia hugged him back. 'I'm really looking forward to the next chapter in my life.'

'You look great,' Nora told her as she got into the back seat. 'Rested and glowing already after just a day here.'

'I'm so happy to be here,' Tricia said. 'And excited to start my new life. I've ordered a few things from IKEA and once they arrive, I'll move into the cottage.'

'You're very brave,' Martin said as he drove out through the gates. 'I don't think Nora would be prepared to live without a proper bathroom or kitchen. She wouldn't even let me buy a campervan.'

'Nah, that's a very male dream,' Nora said. 'The idea of sleeping in a van doesn't appeal to me at all.'

'Nor me,' Tricia agreed. 'I prefer sleeping in a house, even if it's rundown. I know it'll be a little bit rough at the start, but sure it's summer and warm and I'll be in my own house. I'll be working hard on whatever I can do myself, so I'll probably fall into bed completely exhausted every evening.'

'Let me know if you need a hand,' Nora said.

'Thanks, Nora, I'll probably give you a shout. It'd be fun to work together.' Tricia glanced out the window and saw they were nearly at their destination. It was a pub called Mulligan's and she had often been there years ago with friends and later with Fred. 'Here we are,' she said as Martin pulled up outside. 'Thanks for driving us, Martin.'

'No bother,' Martin said as Nora gave him a quick peck on the cheek. 'Have fun, girls. Let me know when you want me to pick you up.'

Tricia laughed as she followed Nora into the pub. 'Girls? I haven't been called a girl since I was seventeen.'

Nora shot Tricia a smile over her shoulder. 'About time someone did, then.'

'Maybe you're right,' Tricia said, laughing as they entered the pub. She was suddenly shaking with nerves, feeling as if everyone was looking at her. But then she realised she was wrong and that despite a glance here and there, people were generally more interested in their friends and ordering drinks. As she pushed through the crowd following Nora, she regained her confidence and started to look forward to the evening. This was the first night of her new life as a single woman, although a little long in the tooth. Coming out like this, meeting new people was the best way to forget the troubles she had left behind. She only hoped the rumours about her would never spread this far south.

8

'Hey, I see our friends over there,' Nora said. They walked towards the table where a group of three women, around the same age as Tricia, were waiting. They all got up to greet the new arrivals.

'Hi, Tricia.' A woman with greying dark hair grabbed her hand. 'Remember me?'

'Of course I do, Mary,' Tricia said. 'We used to meet up with our kids at the beach and the playgroup. How lovely to see you again.'

'And you,' Mary said. 'You know Nora, of course, but you might not have met Maggie and Colette.'

A tall redhead held out her hand. 'Hi, Tricia. I'm Maggie. I moved here after you left. But I heard so much about you.'

'Me too.' Colette, who had a headful of white curls and deep brown eyes, shook Tricia's hand. 'I'm from Cork. Been here over twenty years but I'm still a blow-in.'

'So am I,' Tricia said with a grin. 'I blew out and now I've blown in again.'

'Fabulous to see you back,' Mary said. 'I remember the fun we had way back then.'

'Oh, yes,' Tricia said as the memories of her friendship with Mary came flooding back. 'We used to leave the kids with Sylvia and take off for lunch and shopping in Killarney. And Kildare Village later on as well.'

'Those were the days,' Mary said. 'But hey, let's sit down and have a drink before the music starts. What will you have, Tricia?'

'A glass of Guinness, please,' Tricia replied. 'And I'll get the next round.'

'Great,' Colette said. 'We're already on the first round except for you. And Nora, of course. What will you have?'

'The same as Tricia,' Nora replied.

They all sat down and then drinks arrived and they started to chat, getting to know each other and finding out about Tricia and her plans. They all agreed that it was very brave of her to take on the cottage and offered to help with whatever they could.

'You might be sorry you said that,' Tricia quipped. 'I'll need all the help I can get. It's going to be a very busy summer for me with the cottage and my daughter's wedding in August, which will also take up a lot of time.'

'But you have to take a break and have a bit of fun,' Maggie suggested. 'We've all made a pact to enjoy ourselves as much as we can this summer. Except for Nora, we're all single for one reason or another, and we're all in our early to mid-sixties, but we're not dead yet, are we?'

'Certainly not,' Mary said. 'I lost my husband ten years ago and it was tough for a long time.'

'I was so sorry to hear that,' Tricia interjected. 'John was such a lovely man.'

'He was. And you wrote to me and said the kindest things.' Mary patted Tricia on the arm. 'It was a great comfort. But now I feel ready to get out there again. Not to catch a new husband but maybe just to find someone to go to the movies with or something.'

'I know what you mean,' Maggie agreed. 'I went through a very painful divorce after twenty years of marriage. Not that I want to go there again. I'm done with marriage. But it would be nice to have a boyfriend.' She looked at Colette. 'You were never married, were you?'

'No, but I've been in relationships that didn't work,' Colette said with a sad little sigh. 'I just picked the wrong types, I suppose. I don't regret not being married, but living alone is beginning to feel boring. So why not have a go?'

'Have a go – how?' Tricia asked, both intrigued and amused. 'Not that I'm looking for anyone, of course. I think I'm done with all of that. I want my own space and to live on my own terms from now on. I cared for my late husband for two years until he died.'

'And you lost the love of your life when you were so young,' Mary filled in. 'I remember how sad we all were for you when you lost Fred. It must have broken your heart.'

Tricia nodded. 'Yes. It was hard and the feeling of loss will never go away completely. Grief never ends but you can heal and move on. That's what I'm doing, anyway.' Tricia blinked away tears and took a swig of her Guinness to hide her distress. Then she looked around the group. 'But I'm curious. What are your plans for finding that occasional boyfriend?'

'Not me,' Nora said, waving her hands. 'I have all the male companionship I need.'

'You married a saint,' Mary said. 'And we're all jealous. So we'll count you out of our plan, of course.'

'Out of what plan?' Tricia asked, her curiosity mounting.

'We're going speed dating,' Colette replied.

'Speed dating?' Tricia burst out laughing. 'That's hilarious.'

'It's not a joke, though,' Colette said. 'It's for mature single men and women. On Friday night in the community hall.

Then there's finger food, wine and dancing to sixties music. You have to be over sixty to attend and we all qualify big time.'

'You want to come?' Maggie asked.

'Sure, why not?' Tricia said, feeling reckless. 'It's just a bit of fun, isn't it? Meeting people, having a laugh.'

'Well, yes,' Maggie agreed. 'No serious stuff at all. Except maybe we have to be kind to the old boys even if you don't like any of them.'

'They're a little lonely, you see,' Mary remarked. 'I think men find it harder to live alone than women do.'

'I think that's true,' Tricia agreed. But she didn't feel like meeting anyone new and wondered how she could politely refuse. 'I'm not sure it's my thing, though. I'm not interested in meeting anyone.'

'Oh, please, Tricia. I'd love you to come,' Maggie pleaded. 'It would be nice to have someone with me. I'm not feeling very confident about going to something like that on my own. I know Colette is going but I'd love to have someone else to prop me up if things don't work out.'

'Well, in that case, I don't mind coming with you,' Tricia said, touched by Maggie's insecurity. 'If you need a little support. It'll be interesting to see how it works anyway.'

'Oh, great.' Maggie looked relieved. 'I'll pick you up and we can go together. You can just watch from the sidelines and have a drink with us afterwards.'

'Great,' Tricia said. 'It sounds like a fun event anyway.'

The conversation moved to another topic, and her thoughts drifted while the others chatted on. She tried to imagine how she felt about getting into yet another relationship. *No, not again*, she said to herself. *I've had enough of that kind of thing. I'll go along to the speed dating just for fun all the same. It will be nice to make friends with women my age and to support Maggie, who seems a little nervous about it.*

'How come you left Dublin so suddenly?' Mary asked. 'I thought you had a nice little flat there or so I heard from Sylvia.'

'Oh, eh...' Suddenly drawn back into the conversation, Tricia, squirmed, trying to find a plausible explanation. 'I wanted to spend the summer here to be with the grandkids. And then Vi announced she and Jack are getting married so that was an added reason to come here and settle down for a bit.' She hoped Mary would stop asking questions. It reminded her of the legal problems she had left behind. She had hoped it wouldn't catch up with her but if people started asking questions, it would be difficult to avoid revealing what was going on. But to Tricia's relief, Mary seemed to accept her explanation and didn't pursue the subject. They all began talking about other things while Tricia tried to maintain a cheerful façade.

Nora's voice broke into Tricia's musings. 'How about that, Tricia? I've never done it but it would be fun to have a go.'

Tricia blinked. 'Do what?'

'Karaoke,' Maggie said. 'There's a pub in Killorglin that has started that kind of thing. We could all go together just for the craic.'

Tricia laughed and shook her head. 'You're all mad. But hey, why not? I'm rubbish at singing but that's not important, is it?'

'Of course not,' Maggie said. 'It sounds like fun, though. I've always wanted to do it.'

Nora finished her drink and looked at the far side of the pub. 'I think the band is ready to start.'

'But we have time to order another round,' Tricia said and waved at a waiter. 'What'll you have?'

They ordered their drinks which arrived just as the band started up and then they were silent, listening to the music, smiling and clapping in time with the jigs and reels while some people got up and danced. Tricia looked around the group of her new and old friends and felt a growing sense of contentment and belonging, something she hadn't experienced since she had left Kerry all those years ago. She knew then that she had been right to come back here to her roots. The memories, sad or happy, could no longer chase her away.

Later, in the car on the way home, Tricia thanked Nora for inviting her to join the group of friends. 'It was such a fun evening,' she said. 'What a nice gang. They made me feel so welcome.'

'I could see that you were enjoying yourself,' Nora said from the front seat. 'And they liked you immediately. Of course you knew Mary already but not Colette and Maggie. They're a bit mad but great company. I think you'll have fun with them.'

'I'm sure I will even if some of their suggestions were a little daring. Especially the speed dating. But sure why not? As they said, we're not dead yet. Not that I'm looking for a man or anything. I'm over that kind of thing. Except...' She paused. 'Wouldn't it be nice to have a boyfriend just for company now and then? I mean, like Sylvia with Arnaud. They aren't always together but when they are they're very happy.'

'Seems to work for them,' Nora said, turning to smile at Martin. 'But I have the best man any woman could ask for.'

'You're very lucky,' Tricia said.

'We both are,' Martin cut in.

'Of course,' Tricia agreed. 'I think you're the best-matched couple ever.'

'Like you and Fred,' Nora said. 'Such a tragedy that it had to end so soon.'

'Yes, it was. But I still feel privileged to have known him, and I was so lucky to meet Sean,' Tricia said. 'I'm enjoying the happy memories at last and not feeling so sad any more. The cottage happened just at the right time. I'm going to make it live again and that's where Fred will be. Our grandchildren will enjoy the house and garden and it will be the best thing I've ever done.'

'You're so brave, Tricia,' Nora said, turning to squeeze her hand. 'Fred would be proud of you.'

'Yes, I think he would,' Tricia replied, tears welling up in her eyes. 'He will be with me every step of the way.'

'He will,' Nora said as they neared the gates to Magnolia Manor. 'I'm so glad you came back, you know. I've missed you.'

'I missed you too,' Tricia replied. 'It's great to be together again.'

Martin pulled up outside the gatehouse. 'Here we are.'

Tricia opened the door. 'Thanks again for being the chauffeur tonight, Martin.'

'No problem,' Martin said. 'I was happy you girls had a good time.'

'Sleep tight,' Nora said. 'See you soon. Give us a shout if you need any help.'

'I will,' Tricia promised. 'But I'll be talking to Dominic at the cottage on Monday and we'll draw up a plan. Then we'll see what I can do myself. Goodnight, you two. Thanks for a lovely evening, Nora.'

When Martin had driven off through the gates, Tricia walked up the steps to the front door of the gatehouse. There was a light on in the hall and the spare bedroom upstairs. Vi must have left them on before she went to bed. Tricia mounted the stairs, smiling as she thought of the conversations in the pub. Speed dating and karaoke? Seemed a little strange to do that at her age. But why not? She wasn't that old yet. Who knew what would happen? Life suddenly seemed to be full of promise and the way forward full of exciting things to do and people to meet.

Tricia's phone rang as she was getting ready for bed. It was Nora.

'I hope I didn't wake you up,' she said. 'I just wanted to tell you something I saw the other day that worried me. I didn't want to talk about it in front of Martin. He thinks I'm being silly. And I don't want to upset Sylvia. But...' Nora stopped.

'Go on,' Tricia said.

'Well, there is something going on near your cottage. I saw people walking on the beach below the house just before you arrived.'

'Tourists?' Tricia suggested.

'No. They weren't tourists, I'm sure of that. They seemed to be looking out across the bay with binoculars and taking notes. I thought I recognised one of them, but I can't be sure. Anyway, I thought you should know and maybe call the Guards if you see anyone acting suspiciously. It's happening on Magnolia property after all and they were trespassing.'

'Oh.' Tricia thought for a moment. 'That's a little worrying. Maybe it has something to do with the rib I saw pulled into the reeds beside the pier when I went down for a swim the day I arrived.'

'Could be,' Nora said. 'Maybe you should talk to the Guards about it. Just so they know something is going on.'

'I might,' Tricia said. 'I'll keep a lookout anyway.'

'No need to tell Sylvia,' Nora said. 'But it's late and I'm sure you want to go to bed. We'll talk later. Sleep well.'

'Goodnight, Nora,' Tricia said and hung up. *What is going on?* she wondered as she got into bed. *I'd better have a chat with the Guards tomorrow. Nora told me not to worry Sylvia about this.* But then she remembered Sylvia's face when she mentioned the rubber dinghy and the diving gear she had seen. Did Sylvia already know what that was all about?

9

Tricia thought long and hard about what Nora had said the following day. Then she decided not to contact the Guards right now. She didn't want so sound like a hysterical woman who was worried about a few people on the beach. Of course they were trespassing but there was no proof anyone was doing anything illegal, especially if Sylvia knew about it. Tricia had a feeling she did but either didn't want to talk about or had agreed to keep it quiet. Whatever was going on, it seemed better to say nothing for the moment and try to figure it out for herself. Besides, she didn't particularly want to draw any further attention to herself. She'd wanted to keep a low profile as long as possible in case Terence was still looking for her.

Tricia thought back to the reading of Sean's will. Terence's face. His accusations and threats, and then that gossip in the local newspapers. That had all come from him. Those newspapers were not widely distributed and everything had died down after the first flurry of headlines. But there had been glances and whispers everywhere she went. Added to that was the worry of being charged with a crime. Terence seemed to hold all the cards at the moment. She wasn't ready to face him again, not yet. As an afterthought, she googled her name to see if there was anything further about her in the local news – or even nationally. But nothing came up and she breathed a sigh of relief.

She sent an email to her solicitor to check that everything about the sale of Sean's farm was going ahead as planned. He replied that everything was in order and that the legal problem might be resolved with a bit of luck. Tricia said a silent prayer that he was right and decided not to worry and simply enjoy the doing up of the cottage, spending time with her grandchildren and having fun with her new group of friends.

Maggie, the fun redhead, picked Tricia up from the gatehouse on Friday night. 'Hiya,' she said when Tricia got into the car. 'Are you ready for the speed dating?'

'As ready as I can be,' Tricia replied with a nervous laugh. 'Not sure I know what I'm doing. Except to give you some support. I have absolutely no interest in dating or meeting men.'

'Of course you don't,' Maggie said. 'But I'm so glad you decided to come with me. I don't think I'd have the nerve to walk in there on my own.' Maggie eyed Tricia's red cotton shirt and beige chinos. 'You look great, though. Not a day over fifty.'

'So do you,' Tricia said. 'Much younger than me, actually.'

'Thanks. I hope some of the old guys will agree with you.' Maggie started the car and they rolled slowly through the gates.

'Old guys?' Tricia asked. 'I thought they'd be around our age.'

Maggie grinned. 'Yeah, they are. And we're old too according to our kids, but women are better at thinking themselves young.'

'I'm not sure I agree with you,' Tricia said. 'It's very individual and not really related to gender, I feel.'

Maggie shrugged. 'Could be. But I certainly don't feel old. My body is a little saggy here and there, of course, and my red hair is thanks to my hairdresser these days. But as long as I have my health and have a laugh from time to time I'm not going to complain. And tonight is not about being serious, is it? It's about meeting people and having fun.'

'Of course,' Tricia agreed, feeling a slight buzz of excitement mixed with fear. What had she got herself into? She had only come to support Maggie, who she liked a lot already. Meeting men or dating was far from her mind and she hoped she wouldn't attract any attention. In fact she wasn't even interested in that kind of thing any more. She didn't even know what speed dating was all about.

'It's not as scary as you think,' Maggie said as if reading Tricia's thoughts. 'You get five minutes with each man and then another one takes his place. During the five minutes you're supposed to tell him a few facts about yourself and then he does the same. It all lasts about half an hour and then we all have drinks and some finger food and chat. It's very nice, really. And no obligation to meet any of the men if you don't like any of them.'

'Well that's reassuring at least,' Tricia remarked.

They parked beside the community hall and hurried inside as a rain shower suddenly smattered against the car.

'Typical,' Maggie panted as they rushed in through the door. 'Now my hair will be all frizzy.'

'It looks fine to me,' Tricia told her as she looked around the hall where people were already sitting at tables dotted around.

A woman with grey hair came up to them and asked for their names. Then she handed each of them a Post-it sticker with their name on it from a stack she was carrying and told them to put them on and to sit at any free table. 'We're about to start,' she said. 'You get five minutes with each date and then the men change tables and you stay put. Have fun,' she added before she went to another new arrival. Tricia had been about to tell her she didn't want to participate in the speed dating and that she was only there for Maggie, but the woman was now busy with other participants.

'Oh, well, I might as well play along,' Tricia muttered and put the sticker on the front of her shirt and sat down at an empty table near the end of the row.

'Good luck,' Maggie said before she went to find a table. 'Hope you find the man of your dreams.'

Tricia laughed. 'I'm not here for that as you know. But I hope it goes well for you.' They gave a start as a bell rang loudly and the speed dating started.

A man in a plaid shirt with grey hair in a ponytail sat down in front of Tricia, smiling broadly. 'Hello, my name is Brendan and you're...' He peered at her sticker. 'Tricia? So tell me about yourself.'

'Eh... well, I've just arrived here from Dublin and my daughters and grandchildren live here.' She went on to say she was actually from Dingle and that she loved swimming and walking. Then Brendan took over, telling her about himself and that he lived in Dingle town and had a shop that specialised in fishing gear. Then the bell rang again and another man sat down at her table and then another and another until Tricia felt quite dizzy and hoped it would all be over soon. She found it hard to remember anything any of the men had told her but they had all been nice and a little shy, some even saying, 'Welcome to Dingle.' None of them had really appealed to her even though they were all nice.

'One more date and then we'll mingle,' the organiser announced as the last man slid onto the chair opposite Tricia. She looked at him and her heart nearly stopped when she realised who it was. *Is this really happening? It can't be...* she thought, wondering if this was some kind of weird dream.

Before her was a man she knew very well. A man with black hair streaked with grey and large hazel eyes. Cillian O'Malley, Fred's best friend. She hadn't seen him for years but it was as if they had parted only yesterday. *Oh no*, she thought, *not him, not now, not here. What am I going to do? We didn't part on good terms and he might still carry a grudge. It's been over twenty years, but still...* She felt cold sweat breaking out and her throat was suddenly so dry she couldn't utter a word.

They stared at each other in shock for a moment while Tricia tried to find something to say. But Cillian beat her to it.

'Long time no see,' he said, still staring at Tricia as if he couldn't believe his eyes. He seemed as shocked as she was. 'How long has it been? Twenty-five years?' he asked.

'Something like that,' Tricia said, her voice hoarse.

'So... how are you?' he asked.

'I'm fine,' Tricia replied, still so shaken by seeing him again she found it hard to get the words out. 'But what about you?' she finally asked. 'What are you doing here?'

'Me?' Cillian smiled. 'Oh... I'm here on a job and to connect with my roots and maybe take a little trip down memory lane. And... well, this dating thing just happened by accident and I came on a whim. Didn't know I'd meet you here, though. What about you? What are you doing here?'

'A bit of the same as you,' Tricia said, trying to regain her composure. 'I came to this thing to support a friend, not to find a man or anything. I just recently arrived back to Dingle after a long time away. I'm starting a new chapter of my life in old surroundings. My daughters are all here and my grandchildren and...'

'You've come home,' he said quietly.

'I suppose I have in a way,' Tricia agreed. 'After all these years.'

'You look different,' he said.

'Older,' she filled in with a wry smile.

Cillian shook his head while his eyes twinkled. 'No, not that. Older yes, but aren't we all? But you haven't changed much except for the look in your eyes. A happy, hopeful look.

So different to what I saw when we said goodbye all those years ago. Then you were... angry and sad all at the same time.'

'I'm sorry about that. I wasn't very nice to you.'

He shrugged. 'No. But I did understand. Eventually.'

'I do feel better now. About everything,' she added.

'That's good to hear,' he said, his eyes warm as he looked at her.

The bell rang, startling them. 'Time to mingle,' a voice ordered.

Tricia smiled. 'We'd better obey. Anyway, I could do with a drink.'

'We can talk later,' Cillian suggested, getting up. 'Nice to see you, Tricia.'

'Nice to see you, too,' Tricia said as he walked away. He shot a smile at her over his shoulder and then he disappeared into the crowd.

Feeling shaken after the sudden meeting, Tricia got up and walked to the bar, where people were gathered, chatting and sipping wine. Meeting Cillian like that had given her a jolt. A few years after Fred had died, the two of them had met in Dublin. And sparks had flown. But it was still too soon after the tragedy. She had felt as if Fred was standing between them and she was somehow cheating on him, even though he was gone. It had taken her more than ten years before she had felt she could fall in love with someone else. And then Sean had been there, offering her love, companionship and a safe haven at his nice farm in Donegal. She had wanted to go far away from everything that reminded her of Fred. Lily and Rose were at university and Vi at boarding school, all happy, at the beginning of their adulthood away from home. She had been ready to go north to a new place where she could start afresh.

With Sean, she had been finally at peace and content, even if the passion and romance hadn't been anything like what she had experienced with Fred. But she couldn't expect to feel like that for anyone else ever, so Sean provided a different life on a farm with sheep and cows and all kinds of other animals. It had been a peaceful time full of new experiences until Sean had become ill and then died. Tricia had been deeply grateful to him for taking care of her. She missed him terribly but her grief was nothing compared to the devastation and loss she had felt when Fred had died.

And now she was back in Kerry and had planned to start a new adventure, one that Fred had wanted them to do together. She felt she was picking up his mantle and that this new venture would help her heal at last. Would Cillian stir up feelings she thought were dead? She felt he wouldn't succeed in disturbing her peace. She was stronger and older now and so much time had passed. She was determined to go forward on her own, to live here with her daughters and their families without distractions. *I won't let Cillian or anyone else rock my boat*, Tricia thought as she joined Maggie and Colette, who were waiting to talk to her near the bar.

Maggie handed Tricia a glass of white wine. 'Here, have some plonk while we share our experiences. How did you get on?'

'Oh, they were all very nice,' Tricia said. 'And one of them was even someone I know – or knew,' she added.

'Was that the good-looking man at the end of the session?' Colette asked.

'The archaeologist,' Maggie filled in. 'He's here on some kind of job, I heard. I was hoping he'd end up at my table. But he seemed to be heading straight to you without looking at anyone else. Did you arrange to meet again?'

'No,' Tricia replied, looking around. 'He said "see you around" or something like that. I thought he'd be mingling with everyone and we'd meet up here at the bar.'

'Maybe he left,' Colette said. 'I think I saw him heading for the door. Is he a bit shy?'

Tricia shook her head. 'No, Cillian isn't the shy type. He might not have felt like staying.' She sipped her wine while the others looked expectantly at her.

'So what did you talk about?' Maggie said.

'Nothing much,' Tricia replied. 'There wasn't enough time to say a lot.'

Colette sighed. 'No. I think the idea was just to give us a sample and then we'd mingle and meet up with whoever we found interesting.' She smiled at a tall man who had just joined the group. 'Hi there. Brian, was it?'

The man smiled at Colette. 'Yes. I enjoyed our little chat.' They fell into a conversation, exchanging more facts about themselves.

Maggie looked at Tricia and smiled, leaning forward. 'Will we leave them to get to know each other better?' she muttered.

Tricia nodded. 'Okay,' she whispered back.

'Did you meet anyone else that took your fancy?' Maggie asked. 'Except for the silver fox from your past.'

'Not really,' Tricia replied. 'What about you?'

'Well...' Tricia paused. 'There was this guy who asked for my number and said he'd call. But I'm not holding my breath as I see him chatting up another woman over there. How about calling it a night and heading home? It was a nice evening and all that but I've had enough of the wine and sausage rolls.'

'Me too.' Tricia put her half-finished glass on the bar counter. 'I'd be happy to leave if you are.'

They waved at Colette and made their way through the crowd, smiling at the men they had met and saying it was a fun evening and it would be nice to meet up again – or words to that effect. Then they walked out of the hall into the cool, still evening as the sun slowly sank behind the hill across Dingle Bay and a lone seagull emitted a plaintive cry as it flew across the darkening sky.

Maggie took a deep breath and looked up at the sky. 'Oh, this place... Isn't it so soothing and healing?'

'It truly is,' Tricia agreed. 'I'm so happy I came back. Aren't we blessed to live here?'

'We are.' Maggie put her arm through Tricia's and they walked slowly to Maggie's car, chatting about the evening, the lovely weather and the people they had met during the speed dating event.

'I'd have a go again,' Maggie said as they got into the car. 'Not because of meeting men but because I'm a bit lonely and it's great to be with people our age who have lived as long as we have and been through a lot but come out of it still laughing.'

'You're right,' Tricia said. 'Nothing like being with people who danced to Abba, smoked cigarettes when it was still fashionable and wore those crazy nineteen seventies clothes thinking they looked fabulous.'

Maggie laughed and started the car. 'Yes, the bell bottoms and the weird colours. And then the big hair and shoulder pads in the eighties. I used to binge watch *Dallas* and *Dynasty*.'

As they drove out of Dingle and up the dark road to Magnolia Manor, Tricia's thoughts drifted to her surprise meeting with Cillian. He had just left without a word and she wondered why. Was he paying her back for her behaviour over twenty years ago? She knew she had been unfair but it had been a very difficult time for her. Now she felt differently. But maybe he would never forgive her. She pushed the thoughts away and tried to look forward and concentrate on her new life and her project. Better to put a little distance between her and Cillian for the moment – or maybe for good...

10

Tricia stood in the living room of the cottage with Dominic while they went through a list of jobs. It was longer and more complicated than she had thought.

'You need to dryline the whole place,' he said. 'And rewire, of course. Then I would suggest storage heaters here in the living room and the kitchen. They work on the night-time setting which is a lot cheaper.'

'How does that work?' Tricia asked.

'The bricks inside heat up during the night when rates are cheaper and then they release the heat during the day. Very effective. They'll keep the rooms warm during the day and evening.'

'Sounds good,' Tricia said.

'You could put smaller heaters in the bedroom and bathroom. Do you want to heat the box room too?'

'I suppose so,' Tricia said after a moment's reflection. 'I can just turn it on whenever I'm in there.'

'Okay.' Dominic started to walk down the corridor. 'Let's take a look at the bathroom.'

'It needs a complete update,' Tricia said, walking behind him. 'But maybe I can manage for now and do it later?'

Dominic opened the door to the bathroom and peeked inside. 'Hmm. Well, if you don't mind coping with the old plumbing and a cracked basin, I suppose you could do it later.'

'The toilet flushes and the bath doesn't leak,' Tricia said. 'There's a hand shower and I can put a small plastic basin inside the wash hand basin.'

'The linoleum on the floor here and in the kitchen are a bit worn but that is easy to replace,' Dominic said. 'You could just spruce it all up a bit, paint the walls, put in one of those bathroom wall heaters and redo the floor for now. Then replace everything when you want.'

'Great,' Tricia said. 'There's hot water from the immersion, so that's all I need for now.'

'Except a new immersion tank,' Dominic said with an apologetic smile. 'It doesn't work at all and the insulation is torn. You need a new one with proper insulation.'

'Okay.' Tricia sighed and added it to the list. 'What else?'

'Well... The windows could be replaced. If you have double glazing the house will be much warmer.'

'I'll do that next year,' Tricia muttered. 'I know it should be done now, but I want to try to keep costs down. I'll just get the broken panes replaced for now.'

'Of course,' Dominic agreed. He looked at the staircase leading up to the attic. 'What's up there?'

'A room that will eventually be a bedroom,' Tricia replied. 'But I'll leave that until later. There's nothing up there except an old wardrobe that looks as if it was from the time the house was built.'

Dominic looked intrigued. 'A wardrobe from 1869? That's interesting. Anything in it?'

'I haven't looked but I don't think so,' Tricia said. 'Who were the first people to live here?'

'Mary and John O'Grady,' Dominic said. 'They were the couple who built this cottage.'

'Really?' Tricia asked. 'How do you know?'

'It's in the records in the archives,' Dominic replied. 'And their initials are carved into the bricks above the fireplace. M, J, O'G, 1869.'

'Wow,' Tricia said. 'That's amazing. I'll have to look at that. I thought I'd plaster over the bricks but now after what you told me, I won't.'

'You shouldn't,' Dominic agreed. 'I think the bricks look nice on the chimney breast. I'd just put a shelf made of oak underneath and then have it as a feature.'

'Great idea.' Tricia consulted her list. 'So, what do we have here? Rewiring, dry lining, heaters, a new immersion... Those are the most urgent things to do, would you say?'

Dominic nodded. 'Yes. The rest can wait until next year, if you think you can cope with the outmoded bathroom and can do the painting yourself.'

'I can, but even so all this will cost a fair amount of money,' Tricia said with a sigh.

'I'll try to keep the costs down,' Dominic promised. 'You won't need a project leader so the electrician and plumber are all that's required. In fact...' He paused, looking thoughtful. 'As a matter of fact, there's this guy who's a kind of Jack of all trades. He can do everything, is very neat and tidy and doesn't charge an arm and a leg. Retired builder, actually. He could do everything for you. Electricity, plumbing, the lot. Does it as a hobby these days. Better than sitting in a chair reading books and annoying people, he says.'

'That sounds great,' Tricia said, feeling suddenly more hopeful. 'Maybe I can meet him here and have a chat? Just to go through everything without committing myself.'

Dominic nodded. 'Yes. Great idea. I'll get him to contact you. His name is Ted O'Reilly. He might be free to do what you need. If he is, that'll free up a lot of time for me. I just need to come and inspect the work and tell Ted what to do. Then we can do the fun stuff together.'

'Wonderful.' Tricia smiled at her son-in-law. 'That way I won't take up too much of your time as you must be very busy.'

'I am but I would put your cottage first, of course,' Dominic said with a warm smile. 'Lily would not be pleased if I didn't give you high priority.'

'I know. But if this Ted can do a lot of the work, then I'll be out of your hair.'

'Talk to him first and then we'll decide.' Just then, Dominic's phone rang. He fished it out of the pocket of his jeans and looked at the screen. 'A client. I have to take this and then I must go. I'll get Ted to call you.'

'Okay, thanks,' Tricia said as he walked away, talking into his phone.

She looked at him through the window as he got into his car, knowing he had been such a good sport taking time to advise her. She hoped this Ted O'Reilly Dominic had mentioned would turn out to be a good fit. A retired builder who now was restoring houses as a hobby? She couldn't wait to meet him. She mentally crossed her fingers, hoping he would help her realise her dream. Then she looked at the list and sighed, wondering if her dream might be too impossible to fulfil. Could she make a profit from the cottage later on if she had to do so much expensive work?

Well, whatever happened, she'd camp here for the summer and then rethink her situation...

Ted O'Reilly called that evening and they scheduled a meeting at the cottage the next day. Tricia liked his jovial tone and warm voice and felt a surge of hope. 'It's quite a tall order,' she said apologetically. 'It might not be possible to do it at all.'

Ted laughed. 'I sense a big challenge. That's very interesting. I like impossible tasks. I'll do my best to make it possible. See you tomorrow, Tricia.'

Tricia said goodbye, more cheerful after the brief conversation. Ted had sounded both enthusiastic and eager to do the work. She looked forward to meeting him tomorrow to hear his views on the work. It would take her mind off her meeting with Cillian at the speed dating event, which had been bothering her ever since last Friday. But she was meeting her new gang again soon and then there was a beach picnic with Lily, Rose and their children next Saturday. Her life had not been this full of excitement for a very long time. If only it wasn't for that niggling worry about the legal issues she had left behind, Tricia would feel her life was complete. But until that was resolved, she wouldn't have any peace of mind.

11

When Tricia arrived at the cottage the following morning, she saw a blue van parked outside. A man with thinning grey hair sat in the driver's seat drinking from a water bottle. He got out as soon as he spotted Tricia and walked towards her, holding out his hand.

'Tricia? I'm Ted. Nice to meet you.'

Tricia smiled at the man and shook his hand. 'Hi, Ted. Thanks for being so punctual.' He had brown eyes, a big nose and his beard was close-cropped, showing a dimple in his left cheek when he smiled. Of medium height with a slight pot belly and broad shoulders, he was not the best-looking man she had ever met but his charm made up for the lack of looks. He was dressed in a tweed blazer that had seen better days over a navy polo shirt and baggy jeans. She liked him immediately.

'Happy to be here on such a nice morning,' he said. Then he rubbed his hands together. 'So let's take a look at this cutie, then. I mean the house, not you,' he added.

Tricia had to laugh. 'That's what I thought. I haven't been called cutie since I was seven.'

'I wonder why,' Ted said before he walked to the front door and opened it. 'Mind if I step inside?'

'Of course not.' Tricia followed him to the door. 'Let's go through everything.'

'Perfect.' Ted fished a notebook and a pen out of his pocket as he went into the house. 'I'm ready. Being old fashioned I'll write everything into my little book here.'

They started in the living room and Tricia told him what Dominic had said were the most urgent jobs. 'Rewiring, dry lining, heaters to be installed and perhaps also repair of some of the floors.'

Ted bounced on the planks. 'This floor seems solid. I like the wide planks and the grain. Old and very nice. Polish them a bit more and they will look very nice.' Then he went over to the far side of the room and put his hand on the wall. 'Cold,' he said. 'Dry lining a must in here. All over the house, I should think, or the cost of heating will go through the ceiling.'

Standing by the fireplace, Tricia nodded. 'Yes, that's what I think too.'

'Good.' Ted slipped on a pair of reading glasses and scribbled something into his notebook. 'What's next?'

'The kitchen,' Tricia said and led the way down the corridor and opened the door to the kitchen.

Ted followed her in and looked around. 'Nice room. But the floor could do with a new lino. I'd need to lift it up to see what's underneath but I suspect some old flagstones that might need to be replaced with some kind of tiling. I'll take a look when I start the job.' He peered at her over his reading glasses. 'If you decide to hire me, of course.'

'That depends on your fee and what schedule we can agree on,' Tricia replied, although she knew he would be her best bet. Dominic was so busy and Ted seemed to be keen to take on the job.

'Oh, I'm as cheap as chips,' Ted said cheerfully. 'I only take on jobs when I like the vibe of the house. And I do like it here. This house has a very warm feel to it, don't you think? A kind of soul, if that doesn't sound too cheesy.'

'Not at all,' Tricia said, happy he shared her feelings about the house. 'I know what you mean and I feel it too. The cottage needs a little love and attention and it will be a real home to me.'

Ted looked at her for a moment. 'Yes, I think you're right. You and the house are a good fit.'

Tricia smiled. 'That's nice to hear. So, there's just the bedroom and box room and then there's the attic room but I'll leave that alone for now.'

'Okay.'

They inspected the bedroom and box room and then they went upstairs to have a quick look at the attic room. 'It would make a lovely bedroom,' he said, looking out the window. 'Nice view of the sea from here. I can see all the way down to the pier and a bit towards Dingle town.' He turned to Tricia, who was standing in the middle of the room. 'What's going on out there in the bay?'

'What do you mean?' Tricia asked, moving closer.

'There's a boat out there and someone seems to be getting into the water in diving gear.'

'What? Where?' Tricia looked out the window as Ted shifted to the side.

'Out there. That boat that looks like a fishing boat,' Ted said, pointing.

Tricia looked out over the bay and then she saw what Ted meant. A small boat was sitting at anchor just off the raft she had swum to last week. Not the rib she had seen, but a real boat. There were rings on the water where the diver had disappeared under the surface. 'I see what you mean,' she mumbled. 'I saw a rib with a diving suit and oxygen tank pulled up on the shore the other day. I wonder what's going on?'

'Is that bit of water within Magnolia Manor property?' Ted asked.

'I don't know,' Tricia said, puzzled. 'I must ask Sylvia.'

'Mrs Fleury? She probably knows what's going on. Nothing escapes her eagle eye,' Ted said with an amused smile. 'Formidable woman.'

'She certainly is,' Tricia said as she backed away from the window. 'I couldn't see clearly what they were doing on that boat, but I'll bring my binoculars next time.'

'Probably just some kind of marine survey,' Ted suggested.

'Could be,' Tricia said, despite her niggling feeling that it was something a lot more than that.

'So this room could be made nice eventually,' Ted continued. 'But as you said, it can wait.' He looked at his notes for a while, muttering to himself. Then he looked at Tricia. 'So... All things considered, I think I can do the lot, except the wiring. I don't do electricity, you see. Plumbing, yes, because then you'll only get wet if things go wrong. But I leave electricity to the experts. Don't worry, I know someone who can do it for a reasonable price.' He put his glasses on his head. 'He'll also install the new immersion tank and wire that.'

'Sounds great,' Tricia said. 'So... when can you start?'

'I haven't given you my quote yet,' Ted said, grinning. 'But I doubt if anyone can undercut it.'

'I suspect you're right,' Tricia cut in. 'So I'd like to confirm that you're hired.'

Ted brightened. 'Are you sure now? I mean, you might like to consider other options.'

'I don't have any other options. So you can start making plans.' She knew instinctively that this man, who looked to be around her age, would do his very best to turn her cottage into a comfortable home. He was kind and understanding and seemed to love the house. He was also someone she knew she'd get on with. She had felt at ease in his company and there had been no undertones or mansplaining from him at all. With him there would be mutual respect which was important as she would be working alongside him painting and decorating.

Ted looked a little surprised. 'Oh? I got the job? I am to work on this little gem?' He held out his hand and grabbed hers in a warm handshake. 'Thank you, Tricia, for trusting me. You won't be sorry.'

'I know I won't,' Tricia said. 'But I do hope you have someone to help you. It's a lot of work for one person.'

'Especially one who's a little long in the tooth,' he suggested with a grin. 'But don't worry. I have two strapping lads to help me. College students who do this kind of thing instead of going to the gym.'

'What a good idea,' Tricia said. 'I like that. They get fit and earn money doing it.'

'Nothing makes you fitter than building work,' Ted agreed. He looked across the room to the old wardrobe. 'Interesting piece. Very old, I'd say. You could oil it and it will come up really well. Great for storage. Maybe you could move it down to the bedroom when it's been polished up a little?'

'Great idea,' Tricia said, taking a closer look at the wardrobe. It was indeed a very nice piece of furniture, made of oak with a beautiful carving of flowers on the front. 'That'll be one of my jobs when I redecorate.'

Ted moved towards the stairs. 'Well, this was a real pleasure, Tricia. I'm looking forward to getting stuck in. I'll send you a text with my quote just so you have it and then I'll get started early next week, if that suits you?'

'The sooner the better,' Tricia said as she followed him down the stairs.

They walked out of the house together into sunshine. The air was full of the scent of wild flowers, birdsong and the humming of bees. Ted stopped in the little front garden. 'You should leave this the way it is,' he said. 'It's like a meadow and all the wild flowers are great for attracting bees. Just clear the path to the front door.'

'Good idea,' Tricia agreed. 'The back garden needs a little trimming, though. I plan to have a herb garden and I should really prune the apple tree.'

'Ah well, no rush, is there?' he said. 'The house first, I think.'

'You're right.' They walked together to his van. 'Is Ted short for Edward?' Tricia asked.

He laughed. 'No, my real name is Taidgh. But my non-Irish clients couldn't pronounce it and called me Ted and that stuck.' He opened the door to the van. 'Well, it's been a real pleasure, Tricia. I'll be in touch.'

They said goodbye and Ted drove off while Tricia slowly walked back to the cottage, going over their conversation in her mind. She felt happy with what they had decided and looked forward to next week when the work would start. She knew that staying in the cottage while it was being restored wouldn't be ideal but she saw no other solution. She didn't want to stay with Vi and Jack any longer than a few days. They needed privacy and quiet during the time before their wedding. They didn't need a mother-in-law butting in on their discussions, which she was sure would happen if she stayed. She had the habit of giving advice to her daughters whether they wanted it or not.

She laughed at herself as she stepped into the cottage, thinking that she was trying too hard not to be a nuisance. Vi and Jack probably wouldn't mind her staying with them, but then Tricia felt she also needed her own space to start her new life without her daughters looking over her shoulder. *We're all so alike*, she thought, *but better to keep a distance than step on anyone's toes.* In any case, she also wanted to enjoy life and have fun before real old age set in. Her new gang of friends were on the same wavelength, even though the speed dating had been a mad thing to get involved with. She had gone with Maggie to lend her support, not to find a man, after all. But it had led her to Cillian and she had a strange feeling that it was somehow meant to happen. Maybe they'd connect again and she could make him forget her behaviour in the past. But then what? And how would they meet again? Should she simply wait for him to get in touch or call him herself? She decided to let it drift for a while. She had other things on her mind, such as the cottage and Vi's engagement party and then the wedding at the end of August. So much to be happy about without the complications of a long-lost former boyfriend.

Feeling suddenly light-hearted, Tricia walked through the rooms of the cottage trying to imagine what it would look like once it was finished. Then she went up the stairs to the attic room and looked through the window to see if the boat she had seen was still there. But the blue water of the bay was empty of any kind of vessel. Whoever had been out there had left. Tricia promised herself to get a pair of binoculars so she could study what was going on next time the boat appeared.

Next, Tricia's gaze drifted to the old wardrobe. It was a nice old piece and would look great in her new bedroom downstairs. It would only need a little beeswax and a lot of elbow grease and it would be as good as new. But how old was it? She walked over to it and opened the doors. Inside were shelves and two little drawers at the bottom. It smelled a little musty but there was no sign of mould. There were two crates on the top shelf which had possibly been used to store apples as the attic would be ideal for this kind of thing. It was cool and dry so apples would keep for a long time up here. Other vegetables, too, like carrots, onions and potatoes. But it was originally meant to hold clothes or bedlinen, so why was it up here?

As there was no answer to that question, Tricia was about to close the doors but then pulled out one of the drawers. It was empty but the other one held an old folder made of cardboard that was covered in spots of mildew. Tricia opened it and found a few bits of yellowing paper with drawings that looked as if a child had drawn them many years ago. She peered at the words scribbled at the bottom of the first page with a drawing of several stick figures. She could just about see what it said: *Mammy and the girls by Kieran.* Tricia smiled. How sweet. Some little boy called Kieran had drawn his mother and sisters.

There was only one other drawing in the folder, that of a ship in full sail on a sea of wavy blue squiggles. The faint text said: S.S. *Carmen in Dingle Bay, 1879.* Fascinated, Tricia stared at the little drawing, amazed at how old it was. Whoever had drawn the picture – Kieran? – must have been sitting at the window looking out at sea where this ship was arriving on its way into the harbour.

Tricia closed the folder and put it back in the drawer. That's where it had been put by someone all those years ago and there it would stay. She thought of Fred's words all those years ago: *'There might be something hidden here that could be very valuable.'*

As she prepared to leave, she glanced yet again out the window, imagining some child sitting there looking out and seeing this ship, maybe dreaming of sailing away on the high seas, looking for adventure. She could nearly feel the presence of the little boy. This house held so many stories that she would never know. But the feeling of peace in the room told her that whoever had lived here in the past had been happy. She decided to take a look through the archives of Magnolia Manor that Rose had catalogued very soon. Maybe she'd discover who that little boy was and what had happened to him. Could the wardrobe help her pay for the renovations? It might be a valuable antique. But most of all she wanted to find out more about the original occupants of the little house. *Maybe*, she thought, *I can ask Cillian to help me? After all, he is an archaeologist and should be able to tell me how to look for clues about the past. A good excuse to suggest we meet...*

12

Despite her resolve not to let her run-in with Cillian affect her, Tricia couldn't stop thinking about him. She remembered the good times, when they had been on dates, and hadn't been able to stop talking. Sometimes she had managed to forget her sorrow and simply enjoyed Cillian's company and the way he made her laugh. She had to admit she had felt attracted to him then, even if it had been impossible for her to get any closer to him. And now, they had met again and she didn't quite know what to do about it. She knew she had to contact him so she could nip her feelings in the bud. And she had her mystery to solve. But how would she get in touch? She didn't have his phone number nor did she know where he was staying, but she was sure she could find out by contacting his sister who she knew lived near Nora's house. So when Nora called in to the gatehouse a few days later to say hello on her way to see Sylvia, Tricia decided to act.

'Hi,' Tricia said as she opened the door and found Nora standing there. 'Great to see you.'

'Hi there,' Nora said. 'I just thought I'd drop in to see how the speed dating went.'

'Oh, well,' Tricia started. 'It was fun. And interesting. Also a little startling. But come in and have a cup of coffee and I'll tell you all about it.'

'Thanks, just a quick one, then,' Nora said and stepped into the hall. 'I'm on my way to help Sylvia with the invitations to the engagement party but thought I'd pop in to get all the news.'

'Lots to tell you,' Tricia said and led the way to the kitchen. 'Sit down while I make the coffee. Vi is in Limerick for that new TV series she told us about. The details are very hush-hush right now so I'm not allowed to tell you everything. But I will as soon as I can.'

Nora sat down at the kitchen table. 'I can't wait to hear. But tell me about Friday night. Maggie said you met an old flame. Who was it?'

'Cillian O'Malley.'

'What?' Nora blinked and stared at Tricia. 'You're joking.'

'No, it really was him.' Tricia put a pod into the Nespresso machine and pressed the button. 'Hang on until the machine finishes. It's a bit noisy.' She made two small mugs and carried them to the table and sat down. 'Help yourself,' she said and gestured at the sugar bowl and milk jug.

'I take it black.' Nora grabbed a mug and took a sip. 'So tell me,' she said.

'Well, nothing much happened,' Tricia started. 'But I nearly fainted when I saw him. I was stunned, to be honest. So was he, I think. So we sat there, staring at each other, trying to think of something to say. He was there by accident, he said and then we only had five minutes to chat and he said he'd see me later, but then he disappeared and I haven't seen him since.'

'Oh.' Nora looked startled. 'But... I mean... How did you feel? Must have been a shock to see him.'

'To put it mildly.' Tricia poured a dash of milk into her mug. 'We stared at each other like two rabbits caught in headlights. I think I stammered something and he asked me how I was and said I looked good, or something.' She looked into her mug and thought for a while. Then she looked at Nora. 'I was happy to see him,' she said. 'Shocked but happy. I want to see him again. Just to talk. It's nothing to do with Fred. More with me and a kind of connection I've always felt with him. We dated for a while in Dublin about twenty-five years ago, but it didn't lead anywhere. It was too soon for me.'

'I had no idea he was in town,' Nora said. 'How does he look? A lot older?'

'He looks the same as ever, even if the black hair now has grey streaks,' Tricia replied. 'There's no mistaking the wide shoulders, the broken nose, square jaw or those big hazel eyes. I often wondered why he never had the nose fixed when he stopped playing rugby,' Tricia continued. 'And I thought he had left Ireland for good.'

'Looks like he's back,' Nora said. 'He's an archaeologist, isn't he?'

'Yes,' Tricia said, as the memories of Cillian O'Malley came back to her. 'He worked on digs all over the world. I haven't met him for over twenty years but I did google him a while back because someone I knew in college asked about him.'

'Maybe he's digging somewhere around here?' Nora suggested. 'There is so much to discover around Kerry. Megalithic tombs, Iron Age forts and all sorts of old ruins.'

'Could be,' Tricia said. 'We didn't talk much about his work.' Cillian and Fred had been close friends and had been both at school and at Trinity College together. But Fred had come home after completing his BA degree and Cillian had stayed on to do first a masters then a PhD in archaeology. 'Cillian often stayed at Magnolia Manor for his summer holidays even after Fred and I were married.'

'Yes, I remember that,' Nora said. 'The three of you had such fun together.'

'Yes we did,' Tricia said. 'We'd often met up to go hiking in the mountains or camping trips along the Wild Atlantic Way. We were like the Three Musketeers,' she said. 'Cillian used to worry about crowding us but we loved having him join us on our adventures.'

Nora looked thoughtful. 'Did it upset you to see him again?'

'Well...' Tricia thought for a moment about how she had felt about coming face to face with Cillian. Nora didn't know that they had met in Dublin a few years after Fred's death and started seeing each other quite often, just as friends.

But then, when Cillian seemed to want more out of their friendship, she had pulled away. Even though she found him madly attractive, her mind and heart had been too full of memories of Fred. She was still raw after the tragedy. She knew then that she wouldn't be ready to start a relationship with anyone for a very long time. If ever. She had also been worried it might upset Sylvia that she was dating Fred's best friend. That was an added reason to pull away.

She knew Cillian was hurt when they had parted and they had not been in touch ever since. Then a few years later, she had met Sean and they had married and she had moved to Donegal and his farm. 'I wasn't upset,' she said after a moment's deliberation. 'Just a little startled and nostalgic, perhaps. We actually went on a date or two after Fred passed.'

'Oh,' Nora said, taken aback. 'I had no idea you had dated. It wasn't long after Fred's death that the girls were all settled at school and you moved to Dublin for work.'

'Yes,' Tricia said. 'It was when I moved to Dublin to find a job so I could start supporting the girls.' Tricia had bought her small apartment once she had enough money to afford a mortgage. The girls' boarding school fees were paid from Sylvia's trust fund, but all the extra costs had to be found after that. Tricia remembered how hard she'd had to work to find the rest.

And then there were the school uniforms and sports equipment and books and the orthodontist and all the expense that always arises with teenagers. 'But it was all worth it, me moving away, and their time at school, wasn't it?' Tricia asked Nora. Sometimes she had wondered if she'd made the right choice.

'Of course it was. They're wonderful young women,' Nora filled in. 'It was a tough time for you but you came through it.'

'Oh, we had good times too,' Tricia argued. 'Lots of fun outings and weekends when we just hung out and watched movies and ate pizza. And then Sylvia had them for the summer holidays and I got to have a break. It was during one of those summers that Cillian and I met and started to see each other.'

'It must have been nice for you both to talk about Fred and all the memories you shared,' Nora suggested. 'Cillian missed Fred terribly. They were best friends since college and real soul mates.'

'I know.' Tricia finished her coffee and put the mug on the table. 'But as we were still mourning him in different ways, we couldn't really comfort each other.'

'Maybe he wasn't looking for comfort?' Nora said.

'But I was,' Tricia filled in. 'That was the problem. I didn't give him a chance to show me who he really was and what he felt about me.'

'But now you want to give him that chance?' Nora asked.

'Not really,' Tricia said, looking away from Nora's probing gaze. 'I'm just looking for some kind of closure. After what I've been through, I really don't want to get into any kind of romance. That chapter is closed for me.' She paused and looked back at Nora. 'In any case, the reason I want to see him is that I want his help to do a little research into the history of my cottage. I'd love to know all about who lived there before and why the cottage was built where it was. I know I can look into the Magnolia archives but that doesn't tell the whole story.'

Nora nodded. 'That's a good idea. To ask him to help, I mean. That'll make you connect again doing something together.' Her phone pinged and she pulled it out of her pocket. 'That's Sylvia wondering when I'll be there.' Nora got up. 'I'd better go. I'll get Cillian's sister to give him a message to get in touch.'

'Brilliant,' Tricia said. 'That's exactly what I wanted. How did you know?'

'I read you like a book,' Nora quipped. 'Thanks for the coffee. See you soon, pet.'

'Thanks for your help.' Tricia got up to see Nora out. 'I'll keep you posted.'

'What about the cottage and all the work you're going to do?' Nora asked as she got into her car. 'Is Dominic going to do it?'

'No, someone called Ted O'Reilly,' Tricia replied. 'Retired builder who does stuff like that for a hobby. Very nice man.'

'I know him. Lives in Anascaul.' Nora started the engine. 'He'll do a good job.'

'I hope so. He's starting next week. Hey, let me know if Sylvia needs any help with the party. She's being very secretive about the arrangements.'

'She just wants it to be *her* show and nobody else's. I'd better go. Bye.'

Nora drove off, waving through the open window.

Tricia laughed and shook her head. Typical of Sylvia to take over all the arrangements for Vi and Jack's engagement party. But at least it would take the spotlight off the wedding so the young couple could get a free hand arranging it the way they wanted.

Then her thoughts drifted to Cillian and what Nora had said. It was true that Tricia had been looking for comfort from Cillian, forgetting he was also grieving for his best friend. *How selfish I was, only thinking of my needs and never considering his*, she thought. *Can I ever make up for it, or is it too late?* She hoped not and that maybe, even if they would not connect romantically, they could be friends again the way they were when Fred was alive. Whatever happened, she was ready to take the risk, even if it would open old wounds.

Tricia didn't have to wait long to see Cillian. He rang that evening, telling her he got her number from Sylvia.

'I told her we had met up and she thought it would be a good idea if I called you,' Cillian explained.

'Oh, great,' Tricia stammered, a little shaken by hearing his voice. 'I was going to try to get in touch with you anyway. But you beat me to it. I've been busy with the work at the cottage, washing down walls, prepping it for painting.' She had been startled by his contacting her like this and wondered for a moment if he had called her only because Sylvia had suggested it, or for another reason.

'Great minds think alike,' he said, sounding amused. 'You've been busy. I hope I'm not disturbing you?'

'No, I was just watching the evening news.' Tricia turned off the TV and sat back in the sofa, tucking her feet under her. 'I'm glad you rang. I was asking Nora if she had your number.'

'We both want to meet up, it appears. At least I do. How about you?'

'Yes, I think that would be good,' Tricia said, feeling only a little calmer. 'We need to talk. Are you staying nearby?' She tried to steady her nerves while she waited for his reply, wondering at the same time why he wanted to see her.

'I'm staying in my campervan that I parked behind my sister's house. Not ideal as she's not thrilled to have me there. Cramps her style a bit to have an old weirdo around the place and a campervan parked in her neat and tidy garden. You might remember what she's like.'

'I do,' Tricia said, trying not to laugh. Cillian's sister Orla, as far as Tricia remembered, was very particular about appearances and her house and garden were always neat and perfectly tended. A campervan outside her house would not be what she wanted the neighbours to see. 'I wouldn't call you an old weirdo, though.'

'She does,' Cillian quipped. 'And worse. I've heard her on the phone to her friends. I think I'll have to move somewhere else soon or there'll be war.'

Tricia couldn't help laughing now. 'That's hilarious. But you'd be welcome to park your van at the cottage I've just bought. Only there will be a lot of noise as I'm having it done up.'

'I heard,' Cillian said. 'You bought the gardener's cottage from Sylvia. How did that happen?'

'By accident,' Tricia replied. 'A happy one, really.'

'That's good to know.' He paused and then cleared his throat. 'So... how about us meeting up somewhere? Lunch? Dinner? A drink, or...'

'Or...' Tricia thought for a moment. She didn't feel like meeting him this first time at a public place and not in any way that could be interpreted as a date. Then someone would notice them and the gossip would start. 'Hey, why don't you come to my cottage tomorrow?' she asked on an impulse. 'I'll be there trying out some different colours for the rooms before I start to redecorate. I got these little sample pots from a paint shop in town. You might help me choose.' She knew he must remember how she and Fred had been planning to do it up. Maybe this would be a chance to come to terms with the past, to show him that she had healed from her grief and was cherishing the happy memories. She was going forward and she wanted him to know it.

'Oh, okay.' Cillian sounded surprised. 'That'll be fun. I'd

love to see inside that house. I remember how...' He stopped. 'Well, you know.'

'Yes.'

'You're very brave,' he said in a soft voice. 'It must be tough at times to be there with everything you must have been through.'

'Not the way you think,' Tricia said. 'I'm doing this for me. And for Fred too.'

'He'd be happy you're finally realising that dream you both had. Must be a good feeling.'

'It is.'

Cillian was silent for a while. 'I'll be there tomorrow. What time?'

'Lunch time?' Tricia suggested. 'I'll bring sandwiches.'

'Great. I'll cycle over as the weather seems to be holding. See you then, Tricia. And thanks for inviting me into your space.' He hung up before she had a chance to ask what he meant.

But then, when she thought about it, she knew. Her space, her memories of Fred were personal and private. She hadn't shared them with anyone, keeping them in her heart all this time. Lily and Rose had childhood memories of their father, special to them. Vi didn't remember him at all as she had only been two years old when he died. That must be difficult for her but she seemed to have come to terms with it. Sylvia had been a great help, going through photo albums with Vi and sharing her own memories of Fred with her youngest granddaughter. That was something Tricia hadn't been able to do so she knew she owed Sylvia huge thanks for helping out. *I must talk to Vi about her father*, Tricia thought, feeling guilty. *I must not let my own sorrow get in the way. And now that I feel more positive and stronger, I can tell her what a wonderful man he was and how proud of her he would be.*

But before she talked to Vi, she would be meeting Cillian at the cottage. She was glad she would now have a chance to make amends for the cold shoulder she had given him in the past. They would start with a clean slate and leave the past behind them and maybe become friends like before. But that would demand a lot from them both.

13

After breakfast the following morning, Tricia prepared for the day ahead that might be full of tension. She had promised Cillian sandwiches so she took a look in her fridge to see what she could put together. There was cheese, a jar of pickles, mustard, ham and tomatoes. Perfect. Tricia remembered how Cillian used to love pickles and mustard with practically everything. So she made a couple of sandwiches using the sourdough bread from the bakery. Then she found two blueberry muffins in the breadbin that she had bought for Vi. Promising herself she'd replace them, Tricia put them into the picnic basket, adding two apples from the fruit bowl. Then she put two bottles of beer into a cool bag and made coffee to put into a thermos flask she found in a cupboard.

It all reminded her of picnics she had prepared for the three of them when they were off hiking or just going to the beach. What a strange feeling it was to do this. Nostalgia mixed with a tender feeling of continuing a tradition she had thought she had left behind. But this time there would only be the two of them. Fred was gone – really gone. She no longer had that sensation of him standing between her and Cillian and she hoped it would stay that way. In its place was a kind of nervous anticipation and something else. Was it hope of a new beginning for them both? Just as friends for now, but it was a good start.

Tricia stopped in her tracks for a moment, wondering if she was getting into something that she would find hard to handle. Then she told herself sternly to enjoy this moment, this day and stop worrying about what might – or might not – happen.

The clouds scudded across the sky, the sun playing hide and seek, peeping out now and then only to disappear again as Tricia walked over to the cottage carrying her bag. It was nearly time for lunch. She had spent most of the morning preparing the picnic and then agonised about what she would wear, trying on different trousers and tops before settling for jeans and a navy shirt. After all, she was not going on a date, just having lunch with an old friend. A friend with whom she shared so many memories and who she still found attractive despite what had happened between them in the past.

She saw a bike leaning against the fence as she approached the cottage. Then Cillian, similarly dressed in jeans and a plaid shirt, came into view at the door, partly obscured by the large shrubs.

He smiled as she opened the little gate. 'Hi there. Good to see you again.'

She returned his smile, her heart suddenly skipping a beat from pure joy at being here with him. 'Hi. Nice day too.'

'All the lovelier with you in it.' He took the bag from her. 'Is this lunch?'

'Yes, and a few little pots with paint samples and some bits of wallpaper I thought I might try.'

'Oh, great. Can't wait to see this lovely place. I was never inside it even though Fred often talked about it.'

As she came closer, she noticed a slight apprehension in his eyes as he mentioned Fred's name. 'Oh, yes, he was quite obsessed with it. He was so excited to start doing it up.' Tricia opened the door. 'And now it's my obsession.'

'Life is strange,' he said as he followed her inside. 'And hard and wonderful and heartbreaking and then great again. Until the next disaster.'

'I know.' Tricia looked at him over her shoulder, feeling a strange connection as their eyes met. 'But this is going to be my happy place, so no sad thoughts are allowed.'

'Got it,' he said. 'I see you haven't changed. Still the bossy-boots. Just like all the Fleury girls.'

'I'm only a Fleury girl by marriage, just like Sylvia. But she seems to have picked up the mantle from her in-laws.'

'Oh, I think the Fleury boys pick feisty girls to marry. That's how the tradition keeps going.'

'I'm glad you think so.' Tricia went into the kitchen. 'Put the bag on the table and then I'll show you around as you've never seen the inside of this house.'

'Yes, that'll be great.' Cillian did as he was told and Tricia led the way out of the kitchen, glad of the distraction of the house. She had no idea why he wanted to see her and she felt awkward and shy in his presence. She decided to talk about the history of the cottage and stay with that subject in order to hide her confusion. After all she had wanted his help with researching the house.

They walked into the living room together and Tricia stopped beside the fireplace. 'The exposed bricks on the chimney breast will stay the way they are because I like them. But also because of the initials of the first occupants of the house are cut into one of the bricks,' she said, pointing up. 'See those letters? M and J and O'G. Mary and John O'Grady and the year 1869.'

Cillian peered up at the letters, as he stood beside her. 'Fascinating.'

'My son-in-law Dominic suggested I put an oak plank as a mantelpiece underneath, which I think is a great idea.'

'Or you could try to find a piece of driftwood,' Cillian suggested. 'I think I saw a big, long branch on the beach after the last storm. Polished by the waves, it has a kind of silver hue. It would make a great display. Not a plank but flat enough on one side to make a kind of shelf.'

'That sounds perfect,' Tricia said. 'Do you think you could find it for me?'

'I'll go and look for it,' Cillian offered.

'You mean you saw it on our little beach?' Tricia asked as an afterthought, wondering what he had been doing there. 'Down there beside the pier?'

'That's right,' Cillian replied, looking suddenly awkward. 'I was walking there the other evening. Sylvia told me years ago that I could come and go whenever I wanted. I often go there on a summer's day whenever I'm here for a visit, just to look at the view and see the birds. It's a place full of memories for me.'

'Me too,' Tricia said. 'I went for a swim there my first day back here. I felt as if I was laying to rest the ghost of all the sad things in my past.'

'That was brave of you.' Cillian came closer and took Tricia's hand. 'I did that a long time ago. It was finally time for you to let go.'

'Yes,' Tricia said, as the warmth of his hand both comforted her and made her slightly breathless. 'It took me a long time but now I feel free and a lot more hopeful.' She looked at him for a moment, noticing the lines in his face, the crinkles around his eyes. All those little flaws and details made him look handsome in a seasoned, lived-in way, as if his life had been full of both sorrows and joy. 'Have you had a good life?' she asked. 'So far, I mean.'

'It has had its ups and downs.' He let go of her hand. 'I've had my heart broken twice, never been married, except to my job,' he added with a wry smile. 'Perhaps that was the problem. I was never able to stay in one place for very long, having a restless soul and itchy feet.'

'That would be a little problematic for most relationships,' Tricia remarked. 'Not to mention quite uncomfortable for you. The itchy feet, I mean.'

Cillian laughed. 'You make it sound like athlete's foot or something. But let's leave my love life alone for a moment and discover the rest of this charming house. I hope you're not going to change it too much when you do it up.'

'No, I won't,' Tricia replied. 'Just a little freshening-up here and there. In this room, I'm going to put bookcases in the alcoves on either side of the fireplace, paint the walls and put up curtains, that's all.'

'Do you still read as much as you used to?' Cillian asked. 'I remember what a bookworm you were. You even brought books on our hikes and let Fred and I go off while you sat and read halfway up a mountain.' He laughed softly.

'I still love reading,' Tricia replied. 'But these days I prefer light, feel-good books. Nothing too sad or dramatic or scary. I've had too much of that in real life.'

'Of course you have,' Cillian said, looking at her with great empathy. 'Nothing wrong with a little escapism from time to time.'

They continued on through the house while Cillian agreed with most of her ideas and suggested a few things she hadn't thought about. They finished the tour and then they went into the back garden and sat on two rickety garden chairs Tricia found in the shed. She went to the kitchen and got the picnic, handing Cillian a bottle of beer and a sandwich. He took a bite and told her it was truly delicious. 'It's like the sandwiches we used to have when the three of us were out hiking.'

'I remember how you used to love pickles,' she said. 'But Fred didn't.'

'He was more of a mustard and mayo guy,' Cillian said with a grin. 'We used to argue about what to put into sandwiches. And you had a job trying to please everyone.'

'That was when I was trying to be perfect,' Tricia retorted, handing him a bottle opener. 'More fool me. I should have let you make your own lunch.'

'Of course you should have.' Cillian took the cap off the bottle and took a few sips, wiping his mouth with the back of his hand. 'But you were dealing with two boys that had been spoiled by their mammies. We expected women to do stuff for us.'

'I know.' Tricia drank from her bottle and nibbled on her sandwich. 'But that was then. Things are different now. Women don't try to please as much as we used to. In fact, these days I try to look after myself.'

He squinted at her against the sunlight. 'You're doing a good job. When I came face to face with you at that silly speed dating event, I was blown away by the way you glow.'

'That was blushing from embarrassment,' Tricia said, smirking. 'I was feeling foolish to be found at such an event by someone I know.'

'You mean a place you wouldn't want to be seen dead at? I could see you enjoyed yourself, though.'

'It was fun, actually. And nobody seemed to take it seriously. I didn't meet anyone who seemed sad at all. Maybe a little lonely but that goes with getting older, I think.'

'Are you sad and lonely?' Cillian asked, studying her.

Tricia shrugged. 'Sure, I'm sad sometimes. I miss Fred and I miss Sean, my second husband too. He was a lovely man, you know. I found it hard to lose him and to find myself all alone. But I'm not as lonely here as I was in Dublin. Now I have my girls and my grandchildren and Sylvia and Nora and a few friends, both old and new. Life is easier and a lot more fun because of them.'

'That seems to make you strong, too,' Cillian said. 'A real challenge for any man who might be interested in knowing you better.'

'Why would that be a challenge?' Tricia asked, beginning to enjoy the admiration in his eyes. 'Are strong women some kind of threat?'

'No but they're very hard to impress.'

'We're a lot more demanding than before, of course,' Tricia agreed. 'It takes a strong man to take on the modern woman.' She returned his probing look with one of her own, challenging him to respond. She knew he was flirting with her and she was secretly enjoying it. He was very attractive and there was a new vibe between them that had nothing to do with old memories. *What am I doing?* she asked herself. *I must stop leading him on, even though this flirting is fun. It makes me feel young and attractive again but I can't let him think I'm interested in starting anything. I'm done with all of that.* 'I'm only joking,' she said to break the tension. 'You don't need to impress me. We're just old friends meeting up again after many years.'

'Of course we are.' Cillian finished his sandwich and drained his bottle of beer. 'But enough of this banter. I'd like to see more of this house.'

'You've seen most of it.'

'Not upstairs. What's up there?'

'Just a room that I think was either a bedroom or just used for storage. There's a nice view of the bay from the little window. But it seems to have some kind of history.' Tricia got up from the chair. 'I was actually hoping you could help me find out more about the people who built this house.'

'That sounds interesting.' Cillian handed Tricia the wrapper from his sandwich and got up.

'I have coffee and muffins but we can have that later,' Tricia said as she tidied away the remains of their picnic.

'Okay. Let's go upstairs. It's such a great little house so I want to see every nook and cranny.'

'It's a true gem,' Tricia agreed. 'I want to make it come alive again and be a real home.'

'I think you will,' Cillian said as they walked into the house. 'It's as if it's been waiting for you.'

Tricia smiled, happy that he felt the same way she did. It was comforting to be together like this, chatting and joking like in the old days. *It's true what they say*, she thought. *Real friends can be apart for a long time and then be just as close when they meet again.* Cillian didn't seem resentful of the way she had drifted away the last time they met; at least he hadn't mentioned it. Tricia decided to leave it alone and not try to apologise. If he truly understood, there was no need to bring it up.

She caught up with him at the top of the stairs and followed him to the window, the floorboards creaking as they walked.

Cillian opened the small window and looked out. 'That's a lovely view. It would be even better in the winter when the trees are bare.'

'Yes, probably,' Tricia agreed. 'I didn't think of that. I'm going to put some kind of window seat here so I can look out and see what's going on out there.'

Cillian didn't reply, but kept looking through the window. 'I had no idea it was possible to see the whole bay from here,' he muttered as if to himself.

'Neither did I,' Tricia said. 'I didn't even know the cottage had an upstairs until I got the keys and went up here.'

He turned to look at her, and she joined him by the window. She suddenly remembered the divers she had spotted. 'I saw a boat out there the other day and a diver getting into the water. Ted said it had to be some kind of marine survey.'

'Who's Ted?' Cillian asked.

'The retired builder who is going to restore the cottage. Dominic gave me his name.' Tricia smiled as she thought of

Ted. 'Not that retired, as a matter of fact. He's doing building work as a hobby now. He seems keen to do this house.'

'I'm not surprised,' Cillian remarked. 'If I were a builder, I'd be very keen to turn this house into a home again.' He turned back to the view. 'So you saw divers out there?'

'Just the one person getting in the water. But I'm guessing Ted was right. This area has a marine wildlife that's quite unique.'

'Very true. I'd say it would be teeming with marine life of all kinds.' Cillian looked around the room. 'This would be a nice bedroom, or even a little sitting room eventually. So what made you interested in the house's history?'

'I found these little drawings.' Tricia went to the wardrobe and opened it. 'In here.' She found the folder and took out the two drawings, handling them with care. 'They're very old, so don't touch them.'

Cillian looked at the drawings as Tricia held them up one by one. 'Amazing.' When she showed him the sketch of the ship, his eyes widened and he leaned forward gazing at it as if he didn't believe his eyes. 'S.S. *Carmen*...' he mumbled, touching the drawing with the tip of his finger. 'A sailing ship with goods from Spain...'

'Yes.' Tricia closed the folder, wondering why he was suddenly so pale. 'Seen through the eyes of a child who must have looked through the window over there and watched it arrive.'

'Over a hundred and fifty years ago...' Cillian looked as if he had seen a ghost. 'It's nearly spooky. And...' He stopped.

'And what?' Tricia asked, intrigued. He had looked shaken as he read the caption of the drawing. And seemed to be about to say something but then held back.

Cillian looked away. 'Nothing. I was just so taken with the drawing. Like a message from the past. And then that name... Kieran.'

'Wasn't there an artist called Kieran O'Grady?' Tricia asked, as a thought suddenly hit her. 'The one whose work hangs in the National Gallery in Dublin?' Tricia kept looking at Cillian as it dawned on her what it could mean. 'This drawing might be worth a lot of money then, do you think?'

'Possibly,' Cillian said, still looking uncomfortable.

Tricia suddenly felt awkward for mentioning money. Cillian had spent his life preserving the past, and he obviously valued that over everything else. He had always been so passionate about his work, she remembered that from his studies, poring over textbooks late into the evening, and talking about old letters and ornaments he was working with when they spent time together in Dublin.

She wouldn't normally think about selling a piece of Kerry's history. But she might need to hire a good lawyer to help defend her if Sean's family acted on their threats. All the problems she had left behind in Donegal would one day come to the surface. This could be the lifeline she needed.

She watched Cillian, in deep thought, all the memories of the past months suddenly flooding back into her mind like a recurring nightmare.

Sean had left her everything, but Terence had made it clear he contested the will. He had accused Tricia of manipulating Sean during his last few months, making him sign a codicil that gave her a larger slice of his estate than she was entitled to.

'Sean was confused and borderline demented,' Terence had stated. None of this was true, but she had no way of proving her innocence. Sean had been perfectly sane when he signed the papers and had been adamant that this was what he wanted. The fact that he had made her executor of the will was an added problem, the nephew maintained, telling everyone in the neighbourhood about his suspicions. There had even been a few articles about the case in the local press, mentioning Tricia and her assumed wrongdoings in a very accusatory way. That was why she had needed to flee Dublin.

It was all nonsense and she would have dismissed it as such if it hadn't been for a letter from her solicitor. It wasn't about the codicil to the will but about a document she had presented to the bank that proved to be 'borderline illegal', as Terence had put it. If this came out, it would add further fuel to the flames of the gossip, he had warned her.

She had thought she could make a profit on the house, but with the work it needed, that didn't feel like it would happen anytime soon. If this little drawing turned out to be the early work of a famous artist, it could set her up for life if she sold it. And she could simply tell Terence to keep Sean's whole estate. She could wash her hands of the whole thing. And protect her family.

She looked again at Cillian as all these thoughts raced through her mind. How could she tell him how much she needed the money? That she might have to put her own needs first? She opened the folder again and looked at the drawings. 'Could be very valuable,' she mumbled to herself.

'Maybe. But don't show that drawing to anyone for the moment,' Cillian said with an odd look in his eyes. 'Promise me you won't.'

'Of course,' Tricia replied. She looked at him and wondered what was going through his mind. He seemed desperate to leave, suddenly jittery and nervous, his fingers tapping on the windowsill. What was it about the drawing that had shocked him so much?

14

As she looked at Cillian, Tricia tried to tell herself that his reaction was just his archaeologist mind working overtime. He was probably just very excited and needed time to take it in. 'These are so touching, whoever drew them,' she said, bringing Cillian back to the drawings. 'If I knew more about the people who lived in this house in the past, I could find out who that little boy was. But apart from the Magnolia archives, I wouldn't know where to look.'

'I'm not sure about that. My experience is with digging out graves and remains of houses from thousands of years ago. I think your only hope is to look in the manor. There doesn't seem to be much left to discover in the actual house,' Cillian said, seeming to have recovered from whatever it was that had made him look so shocked.

'I suppose you're right.' Tricia put the folder back in the drawer. 'I'm going to keep this here and not tell anyone. It's my little treasure and it belongs to the house.' She felt slightly guilty for lying to him. She might still need to sell it, but she didn't want to tell Cillian that yet. He had seemed so upset by what he had seen in the drawing and she didn't want to make things worse. Perhaps she could find another solution to her problems.

'Yes, you shouldn't let anyone see it,' he said.

Tricia nodded. 'No, not yet anyway, so it will stay between us.'

Cillian moved closer and gazed into Tricia's eyes. 'I'll keep your secret. I'm really touched that you shared it with me.' He paused for a moment, his eyes tender. 'Trish, I...' Then he stopped and pulled away. 'Meeting you again and now, being together here is doing something strange to me.'

Tricia felt her heart contract. That old nickname that only he had used brought her back to the time he had tried and failed to get closer to her. She had been wrong to reject him but she hadn't been ready. And now she couldn't cope with anything more than friendship after all she'd been through. Romance had been far from her mind when she came here. She took a step back. 'Cillian, we had something. A close friendship that was very precious to me. But we can't be more than friends. We're not teenagers and I am still trying to cope with everything. It's not the right time for me right now.' The words were out before she could stop them.

He nodded, looking sober. 'I understand. But that last thing you said gives me a tiny ray of hope all the same. Would I be right?'

'Maybe. That other time all those years ago, I was still grieving, still so raw. But now I feel free and ready to look forward. That's all I can say for now.'

He nodded. 'That sounds good to me. No pressure.'

'Good,' she whispered.

He leaned forward and kissed her lightly on the cheek. The brief touch of his lips made her blush. He looked suddenly serious. 'You have a lot on your plate right now. This house, your daughter's wedding and that mad party next week that Sylvia has invited me to.'

Tricia stared at him. 'She invited you?'

He laughed. 'Yes, she did. She said as I was such an old friend of the family, I should be there to celebrate Fred's daughter's engagement.'

Tricia put her hands on Cillian's chest. 'She's right. You should be part of family celebrations such as this one. You've been away for a long time, so we didn't know where to find you when Lily and Rose were married. But now that you're here, you should come.'

'I'm not sure. It said a *Great Gatsby* theme in the email. Not my kind of thing at all.'

'Nor mine, really.' Tricia smiled and rolled her eyes. 'Yeah, it's going to be a mad party. We got Sylvia to organise it so she would forget about the actual wedding. Vi wants it to be small and intimate and friends and family only. Sylvia wanted to do a big celebrity wedding and there was a huge argument about it until I suggested the engagement party and she jumped at the chance to do a big bash and the *Great Gatsby* theme. She has invited half the town to it.'

'Typical of Sylvia. She was always the party princess. I suppose I'll have to go. Maybe I could dress up as Al Capone or something.'

'Haha, yes. That would be terrific.' Then Tricia shot a serious look at Cillian. 'But I don't want anyone to know we've been spending time together. I think Sylvia could be upset. You were Fred's friend after all, and—'

Cillian nodded and took Tricia's hand. 'It's okay. I won't say anything.'

'I just know you're very dear to me,' Tricia said quietly.

'That's good. Maybe I won't go to the party,' he suggested. 'I'm sure to give it all away when I see you all dolled up in a nineteen twenties outfit.'

'Oh, no, you should go,' Tricia argued. 'You'll just have to try not to notice me. I would love for you to get close to my girls, especially Vi. I want you to tell her about Fred and all the things you did together when you were students. She'd love to know more about him. She doesn't remember him as she was only two years old when he died. That's her greatest sadness. Not that she can't remember the accident and that awful time afterwards, but that she has no memories at all of her father. It's as if a part of her is missing.'

'Poor girl.' Cillian's eyes were full of empathy. 'Of course I'll talk to her about Fred. And to Lily and Rose too.' He shook his head. 'Fred's girls. I haven't seen them since they were kids. I should have got in touch as soon as I arrived, but I've been so busy with this...' He stopped.

'With what?' Tricia asked. 'You haven't told me what you're doing here. Where is this dig you're working at?'

Cillian looked suddenly worried. 'I'm sorry, Trish. I can't talk about it. I've been told that we have to keep it secret for now or we get a lot of people going to the site looking for treasure. You know how quickly rumours start around here.'

'Yes but...' Tricia started.

'I know I should be able to tell you and I should trust you to keep a secret,' Cillian said, looking awkward. 'But then I'll put a burden on you and you might accidentally say something without meaning to. So it's better for me to keep it to myself for now. Please don't be upset.'

Tricia realised he was right. She might blurt something out without thinking, so it was best for her not to know. Plus, she had her own secrets to keep. 'Oh, okay.' She smiled reassuringly. 'I understand what you're saying, even if I'm dying with curiosity when you say there might be some buried treasure. I read in some newspaper about a find in Donegal a while back. A thousand-year-old grave that contained jewellery made of gold and silver worth a fortune. Such beautiful pieces of Celtic design. That dig had to be manned by security guards until the objects could be removed from the site. They're now in the

National Museum in Dublin. I can imagine how awful it would be if pieces like that ended up in the wrong hands.'

'That's it.' Cillian looked relieved. 'I'm glad you understand. When are you planning to move in here?'

'In a few days. As soon as I get the furniture delivered.'

'But you can't live here until the house has been rewired,' he argued. 'It's not safe now.'

'Oh.' Tricia stepped away from him. 'I didn't think of that. Could I live here without using electricity maybe?'

'I doubt it,' Cillian replied. 'It's not very comfortable to live without electricity. How are you going to cook a meal or have a shower, for example?'

Tricia sighed. 'Oh, okay, I get your point. I'll just have to be patient and tell Vi and Jack that they'll have to put up with me for a bit longer.'

'I'm sure they won't mind.' Cillian smiled at Tricia. 'I have to go back to work. See you soon, I hope. Bye for now.' He walked out of the attic, running nimbly down the stairs and out the door.

Tricia stood there for a while as the front door banged shut, thinking about what had just happened. She touched her cheek, still feeling Cillian's soft lips and the prickle of his beard. It had seemed like the right time for them to meet again and now there was no feeling of rejection or hurt. Just a sweet friendship that connected them to Fred. She knew Cillian had itchy feet and a restless soul so he might want to move to somewhere else when the autumn set in. But she didn't care how long it would last or even if she wanted it to. This was now and life was so short, why not grab this little bit of happiness and enjoy it however long it would last? Her experiences had taught her that anything could happen, good or bad, in an instant and life would never be the same after that.

I have to live in the moment, she thought as she slowly went down the stairs, *take happiness as it comes and grab it and hold it as long as I can. Who knows what the future will bring? Cillian is such a nice man, but all I want from him is friendship, which he seems to accept. It feels so good to talk to him about Fred.*

But there were so many things niggling at her new-found happiness. She tried to push the thoughts away but the questions kept coming back to the surface. Should she have lied to Cillian? Should she have told him why she might need to sell the drawings if they turned out to be valuable? That was something she still needed to find out. Would he be angry if that was to happen?

And why had Cillian refused to tell her about the work project that had brought him here? The explanation he had given her for the secrecy seemed a little lame to her. And then... there was his reaction to the drawing and what she had seen in the bay. Why had he looked so shaken by it? Their friendship couldn't deepen until all those questions were resolved.

15

The following few days were hectic and left little time for any kind of meeting with Cillian. But they managed to talk from time to time late in the evenings when they were both in bed, chatting about old memories and planning things to do together for the weeks ahead when things calmed down and they would have more time to relax.

'I'm looking forward to seeing a bit more of you,' he said one evening. 'It would be fun to go on a hike like the old days.'

She laughed. 'Yes but let's not be too adventurous. What we did when we were in our twenties could be too much for us now, forty years later.'

'Can't believe we've known each other that long,' he said. 'It's nice to remember those happy days, though. Aren't we lucky to have had them?'

'Many more to come, I hope,' Tricia said wistfully. 'Even if someone is missing.'

'I feel lucky to have had Fred in my life,' Cillian said. 'I wouldn't want to have missed knowing him, if you see what I mean.'

'That's a lovely thought,' she said softly.

'I hope it didn't make you sad.'

'No, it made me happy,' she replied. 'I don't want you to feel that you can't talk about Fred. Because when we do, he's still with us.'

'That's what I feel too.'

'I'm glad you do.' Tricia suppressed a yawn. 'Sorry, can't keep my eyes open. I was babysitting for Lily today and I took Naomi and Liam to the beach. They were running around like crazy and then they wanted to go into the water so I had to make sure they were safe. They both had their water wings on, of course, but it's still hard to keep them afloat on the waves. It was exhausting and I was like a drowned rat afterwards. Then they wanted ice cream so I had to take them to the shop and then home to get the sand off them and rinse their togs and get them ready for bed before Lily came home.'

'I'm tired just listening to that,' Cillian joked. 'How old are they?'

'Naomi is seven and Liam is four. Of course, Naomi is a real bossy-boots and was ordering me around all day.'

'Well, what did you expect from a Fleury girl?' Cillian asked.

Tricia giggled. 'I know. She's the original Fleury woman with attitude.'

'I'm looking forward to meeting them one day. Perhaps at the party,' Cillian said.

'Oh, you can meet them before that. Lily will want them to get to know their grandfather's best friend.'

'That sounds nice.' He paused. 'I can't imagine Fred as a granddad. He's forever young in my mind.'

'Frozen in time at the age of thirty-two,' Tricia said wistfully. 'Do you remember when the three of us were on that hike to Mount Brandon and we talked about growing old?'

'Oh, yes, I do.' Cillian laughed. 'He said I was already old because I had a few grey hairs and then he kept calling me granddad all through the rest of the day. But I beat him to the top and said he was the old man who couldn't keep up.'

'And I was the one who felt like the auld woman trying to compete with the two of you,' Tricia filled in. 'Boy, were you fit then.'

'We all were. God be with the days.' Cillian sighed. 'We were so young and fit and hopeful with life in front of us. Little did we know what was ahead.'

'We didn't have a clue.'

'I feel lucky to have you found you again,' Cillian said.

'We're both lucky,' Tricia said, feeling a mixture of sadness and joy. It felt good to have met him again and be so comfortable in his company. 'I have this bittersweet feeling, you know. Part of me is crying in the rain, but the other part of me is dancing in the sunlight. Isn't that weird?'

'Weird and beautiful at the same time. But that's what life is all about, isn't it?'

'Very true,' Tricia agreed. She felt a sudden dart of happiness. It was wonderful to be able to talk about Fred with someone who had known him so well and with whom she shared so many memories.

'But now I will let you get some sleep,' Cillian said. 'I have an early start tomorrow anyway.'

She said goodnight and hung up, despite her desperate desire to ask what he was busy with. The memory of their chat made her smile even if she still felt like she was lying to him. She hadn't found out anything about the drawings yet. And Cillian hadn't mentioned it either.

Ted sent Tricia the promised quote which she accepted and then the work could start on the cottage. Ted had all the workers lined up, including the electrician who promised to have the rewiring done within a week. They went through the whole house together and marked the positions of every light switch and plug outlet which took up nearly a whole morning with input from Ted, who offered advice and suggestions which were very helpful. Then there were discussions about dry lining of all the interior walls and what it all would cost. Ted was incredibly organised and had every single detail written down on a document he sent to Tricia by email so she could discuss it with Dominic before the work commenced. Tricia went through it all with him when she came to the house in Ventry for dinner one evening.

'That looks great,' Dominic said when he had studied the plan sitting at the kitchen table while the children ran around chasing each other. 'Ted knows what he's doing.'

'He's a darling,' Tricia said. 'I feel I can trust him with everything.'

'But you didn't move in yet?' Dominic caught Liam as he ran past and put him sitting on a chair. 'Calm down, willya? And sit still for a minute. We're trying to work here.'

'Granny Tricia doesn't work,' Liam said, fixing Tricia with his brown eyes. 'She's on her holidays.'

'Not really,' Tricia argued. 'I'm doing up my new house. And no, I haven't moved in. Cill— I mean, I didn't think it was a good idea to live there until the rewiring is finished.'

'You said Kill,' Liam remarked. 'Is that the electrician? Nora said you were reconnecting with him.'

Dominic laughed and ruffled the little boy's hair. 'You shouldn't listen when grown-ups are talking. I'm sure your granny meant something completely different.'

'I was talking about Cillian,' Tricia said, deciding it was better to drop in his name casually. 'He was friends with Fred. He's here on business and dropped in to see the cottage.'

'Cillian O'Malley?' Lily turned from the counter where she was chopping vegetables for dinner. 'Is that our dad's friend that Granny was talking about?'

'Yes, that's him,' Tricia replied, the mere mention of his name making her cheeks hot. 'We bumped into each other just after I arrived.'

'You were great friends, too, Granny said. Must have been nice to see him again,' Lily said over her shoulder. 'Liam, go and tell your sister it's nearly time for dinner. You should both go and wash your hands.'

Liam slid down from the chair. 'Okay, Mum. I'll tell her. Are we having pasghetti for dinner?'

'That's called spaghetti,' Lily corrected. 'And yes, that's what we're having. With meatballs and vegetables.'

'Yum,' Liam shouted before he ran out of the room calling Naomi.

'So you met Cillian?' Lily said. 'Must have been strange to see him after all these years.'

'It was a bit of a shock,' Tricia replied. 'Especially as he just appeared right in front of me at this speed dating thing.'

Lily laughed. 'He was at the speed dating? That's some coincidence. Like two oldies at a lonely hearts' club or something.'

Tricia bristled, feeling annoyed at Lily's joke. 'Look, Lily, you're young and lovely with a gorgeous husband and two beautiful children. I'm very happy for you. I, on the other hand, am growing older by the minute. I have been through a lot, as you know. Your father was the love of my life and I still love him – or the memory of him, in any case. Sean was also someone I loved dearly. I miss him terribly, but not as much as I miss Fred. But... I want to live again, maybe even love again before I get too old. So yes, I might join a lonely hearts' club or any kind of club where there are people like me who don't want to spend the rest of their lives alone. Cillian was there maybe for the same reason, but I doubt it. He said it was accidental, whatever that meant. He and Fred were like brothers and we share so many memories of him. That's why I was so happy to see him.' Tricia drew breath and looked defiantly at her daughter.

'I didn't mean...' Lily started.

'What *did* you mean, Lily?' Dom asked, looking annoyed. 'I think you'd better stop talking about oldies before your mother walks out of here in a huff. Tricia is a lot of things, but "oldie" is not one of them. She looks more like your older sister than your mother.'

Lily put her knife on the counter and went to Tricia and gave her a hug. 'I'm sorry, Mum. I didn't mean to say you're old or anything. I was just teasing you. Now I feel both mean and stupid.'

Tricia hugged her back. 'It's okay, sweetie. I know you didn't mean anything bad. It's just that one gets a little sensitive about things like that at my age. And I'm trying to adjust to my new life. There's so much going on and then meeting Cillian again at an event like that...'

'I bet it was a little awkward for you both.' Lily went back to the counter and resumed chopping the vegetables. 'Must have been like stepping back in time in a way.'

'It was. I thought I was dreaming when he was suddenly there in front of me.'

'But he must have changed a lot since the last time you saw him.' Lily started to fry the meatballs.

'Er, yes, of course,' Tricia said, feeling that there was no need to say anything about them dating twenty-five years ago. The girls had been in school and hadn't known who Tricia was seeing. 'So have I,' she said. 'But I would recognise him anywhere even after all the years.'

'Unless he had grown fat and bald,' Lily said. 'But I bet he hasn't.'

'No, he looks really good,' Tricia said, feeling that annoying heat in her cheeks again.

'I'd love to meet him,' Lily said. 'He must have so many memories of Dad. Things we never knew.'

'He'd love to see you, too,' Tricia said. She began to feel more relaxed about how everyone would react to her friendship with Cillian now that they might get close again. That was partly the reason she had pulled away from him all those years ago. She had been worried about the reaction to her dating Fred's best friend. But now she realised that the girls wouldn't be upset – they'd be happy to meet him and talk about Fred. 'You can meet him at the engagement party,' she said. 'Sylvia already invited him.'

'That would be brilliant.' Lily turned to Dominic. 'Go and see what the kids are up to. They're taking too long washing their hands.'

'You're right.' Dom pushed the document across the table at Tricia. 'Those figures and the work listed are all fine. I take it Ted has already started?'

Tricia nodded. 'Yes. He said he couldn't wait to begin so I gave him the go-ahead. I've never seen builders work so fast.'

'Ted loves his work,' Lily said when Dominic had walked out of the room. 'I think it's helped him get over his wife's death. When he retired, they had all these plans to travel and do things together. But then she got sick and died soon afterwards. That was four years ago, I think. I'd say he was lonely so he started working again but at his own pace. He only works on projects he loves, so you were lucky to get him.'

Tricia got up to lay the table. 'That's a sad story. Must have been hard to have had all those plans with his wife that came to nothing.'

'Yes, I'd say it was.' Lily pulled open a drawer. 'The cutlery is in here, Mum. And the glasses are in the cupboard over the sink. I'll pile everything onto the plates and we use paper napkins which are in the little shelf over there by the window.'

'Okay.' Tricia found the items and put them on the table.

'I'd better remember where everything is if I'm to help you out on a regular basis.'

'I'd be happy with any kind of help.'

Then Naomi ran into the room, dressed in pyjamas. 'Granny Tricia,' she shouted and jumped into Tricia's arms.

Tricia laughed and hugged her granddaughter, who, at seven years of age, was promising to grow as tall and willowy as her grandmother. 'Hello, Naomi. How come you're already in your jammies?'

'We got wet in the bathroom,' Naomi said with a delicious giggle. 'So Daddy thought we should get into our jammies instead of clothes. Why are you here again, Granny? Are you going to mind us tonight? Are Mummy and Daddy going on a date again?'

'No, I'm just having dinner with you and talking about my cottage with your daddy,' Tricia replied. 'And I wanted to get out of Vi and Jack's hair for a bit. They need to be alone and talk about the wedding.'

'Why were you in their hair?' Naomi asked. 'Were you giving them haircuts? Are you going to get a new dress for Great-gran's party?' she asked in nearly the same breath. 'Mummy said it's a twenties party. Is that because everyone there will be in their twenties?'

'Not quite.' Tricia took Naomi by the hand. 'Come and sit down and have your dinner and I'll tell you all about it. Where's your daddy and Liam?'

'Here.' Dominic entered the kitchen carrying Liam, who was dressed in a pyjamas with the Superman logo on the front. Not only that, he was also wearing a snorkel and mask and flippers on his feet. 'He was diving in the bathtub. That's how they both got so wet.'

'I was trying to get him out,' Naomi explained. 'It's dangerous to play in the bath all alone when you're only four.'

'It's not dangerous when you have a snorkel,' Liam said through the mouthpiece.

'Dom,' Lily chided. 'I told you not to let him play with your snorkelling gear.'

'I didn't know he was going to use it in the bathtub,' Dom argued.

'I was practising,' Liam said. 'I want to dive like the men on the boat. They're looking for a pirate ship out in the water.'

'What men?' Tricia asked. 'Where did you see them?'

Liam took off his mask and snorkel. 'In the bay when I was walking on Great-gran's little beach with Daddy yesterday. They were in a rubber boat that went *very* fast. Whoosh and they were gone.'

Lily put plates with spaghetti and meatballs on the table. 'Whoosh to the table and have your dinner, Liam.'

'Pasghetti, yum,' Liam shouted, wrenching off his flippers and wriggling out of Dominic's arms. He proceeded to run to his place and started slurping spaghetti into his mouth at an impressive speed.

Naomi rolled her eyes and sighed theatrically. 'No manners at all.' She sat down and picked up her fork. 'Come on, Granny, get it while it's hot.'

They all laughed and joined the children at the table. Tricia smiled at Liam and thought about what he had just said. 'What was that about a pirate ship?' she asked Dominic.

'Just a story we made up,' Dom replied when he had finished a bite of meatball and spaghetti. 'There's no pirate ship. I think they were taking samples of some kind from the bottom of the bay.'

'Did they really have snorkels?' Lily asked.

'I'm not sure,' Dom said. 'They were too far away for us to see them properly. But I did think it was strange that they were so far out. If they were taking samples or studying marine life, wouldn't they be closer to the shore?'

'Who are they working for, anyway?' Lily asked. 'The Department of the Environment?'

Dom helped himself to water from the jug. 'Or maybe some private company? Could they be looking for something else, though? Like mineral deposits? You never know what hides deep down on the ocean floor.'

'I'm going to ask around,' Lily said. 'People coming to my garden café might know. Nothing stays secret in this town. Mum, why don't you come and have a coffee there tomorrow? You're bound to meet some old friends there. It's getting to be a real hot spot.'

'It's the in place in town in the summer,' Dom said. 'A great place to find out what's going on in town.'

'I'd love to,' Tricia said. 'I'll pop over when I'm back from town. Vi and I are going to the vintage shop to see if we can find an outfit for the party. It's only two days away.'

'I know.' Lily sighed and pushed away her plate. 'Granny's going bananas. She pretends to be all cool and collected. But she's really up to ninety about it.'

'Why is she going bananas?' Naomi wanted to know. 'I want to go and see that. I've never seen anyone going bananas.'

'It's just a way of saying someone is really stressed,' Lily explained. 'There are no bananas involved.'

'Oh.' Naomi went back to hoovering up spaghetti from her plate.

Tricia smiled at her granddaughter, thinking how smart and cute she was, and then her thoughts drifted to Cillian and their new friendship that could become something a lot more in time. She didn't want anyone to know, it was too soon and too new. In any case, if it ended as soon as it had started, it would have been good not to share it with anyone. But how lovely it was to sit here at the table having dinner with this young family who she loved so much. She wanted Cillian to get to know them so he could talk about Fred and their student days together. It would be lovely for the children to find out what their grandfather had been like as a young man, before he had met Tricia and had a family. That was a little part of Fred that she couldn't share with them.

Then Lily's words drifted into her thoughts.

Nothing stays secret in this town.

She hadn't heard anything from Terence or her solicitors since she'd arrived. But her time was running out. She needed to find out if she could sell the drawings. She needed to get into the Magnolia archives to see if the little boy whose drawings had been put in the old wardrobe was someone famous. Or perhaps use this trip to the café to at least find out any clues as to who used to live in the cottage.

16

The café in the old orangery sat in the middle of the walled garden which, now in the height of summer, was especially lovely. The herbaceous borders were full of shrubs and flowers in full bloom; peonies competed with roses and hydrangeas, their colours vivid against the backdrop of the mellow stones of the old walls. The gravel paths had been newly raked and the lawns mowed to velvety perfection. Tricia's heart swelled with pride as she walked down the path to the orangery, where the little terrace had been furnished with small round tables under the oaks. The tables were nearly all occupied, but Tricia spotted a free one near the entrance door and headed for it before anyone else would take it. Vi was joining her when she had left the bags with their shopping in the gatehouse, so Tricia draped her scarf on the back of one of the chairs to show it was occupied.

Tricia and Vi had spent a wonderful mother–daughter morning shopping in the vintage boutique in town and had been lucky to get two perfect outfits for the party the following day. Vi had found a dark green silk shift dress that had real nineteen twenties vibes. Tricia, after going through practically the whole stock, finally struck gold with a black chiffon dress that came down to just below her knees. She added a long string of fake pearls and a velvet headband with a feather to wear in her hair. They had tried on their outfits and laughed as they saw themselves in the mirror, Vi declaring that Tricia's bobbed hairstyle was the perfect jazz girl 'do.

Tricia looked around for Lily and spotted her in the café at the till where there was a long queue of customers waiting to pay. She realised then how hard Lily worked and what a huge success she had made of the garden and the café. Waiting for the worst of the rush to be over, Tricia turned her face to the sun, her eyes closed, enjoying the warmth and the soft breeze against her skin The air smelled of flowers, and the birdsong and the murmur of many people chatting added to the feeling of calm and enjoyment.

'Tricia? Do you mind if I sit down?' a voice said beside her.

Tricia opened her eyes and discovered Mary standing there with a tray. 'Oh, hi, Mary. I'm waiting for Vi, but do sit down on one of the other chairs. The café is very busy today.'

'It always is at this time of year.' Mary put her tray on the table and sank down on one of the chairs. 'Gosh, it's warm.' She blew a lock of hair out of her eyes. 'Hey, I see a friend from town over there looking for a seat. Do you mind if she joins us?'

'Of course not,' Tricia said. 'I only want to keep one chair free for Vi. Don't know what's keeping her.'

Mary waved at a woman coming out of the café with a tray. 'Come and sit here, Theresa,' she shouted.

The woman, who was small and stocky with shiny black hair, smiled and started to walk towards them. 'I can't believe how packed this place is. Thank goodness you got me somewhere to sit.' She smiled at Tricia, put her tray down and held out her hand. 'Hi, I'm Theresa Coyle. And you're Tricia Fleury, of course. You don't know me but I know your mother-in-law Sylvia. She often comes to our salon to have her hair done.'

'Which salon is that?' Tricia asked.

'Foxy Locks just around the corner from Lidl.' Mary took a bite of her slice of carrot cake.

'Great name for a hair salon,' Tricia remarked. 'I have to say you do a wonderful job with Sylvia's hair. It's always immaculate.'

'She has amazing hair, so it's easy,' Therese said. 'And she knows what she wants.'

Tricia smiled. 'Oh, yeah, I can imagine.'

'I saw that the good-looking woman from Germany was in your salon the other day when I nipped in for a blow-dry,' Mary said. 'Did you manage to find out anything from her? She's been here since the beginning of June and I heard she's here for work.'

'Oh, yes,' Theresa said. 'Her name is Ilse. She told me she's involved in historical research and works for a German firm. No idea exactly what they do, though.'

'Historical research?' Tricia asked, suddenly intrigued. 'Like archaeology?' Her heart beat faster as she waited for a reply. Could this have something to do with Cillian?

'Something like that,' Theresa replied. 'But then when I asked what exactly they were doing here, she clammed up and changed the subject, looking as if she had accidentally revealed some big secret and was worried about it. Couldn't get a word out of her after that.'

'Maybe your friend Cillian has something to do with it,' Mary suggested, echoing Tricia's thoughts. 'Isn't he in that line of work?'

'Cillian O'Malley?' Theresa said, looking interested. 'He's that great-looking older guy, isn't he? From around here originally but he's been away a long time.' She looked at Tricia with interest. 'So you're old friends?' She looked around and then leaned forward and said in a near whisper: 'Do you know if he's single?'

Lost for words, Tricia hesitated. 'Well,' she started, 'he's not married anyway.'

'Yeah, but is he seeing anyone? Or in a relationship?' Theresa insisted. 'Is there a girlfriend or a partner?'

'We have only just met after a long time not keeping in touch.' Tricia squirmed, trying to hide how she really felt. She didn't want to admit that anything but a casual friendship was going on between her and Cillian. That would lead to a lot of gossip and discussions about their supposed relationship. 'We haven't had much time to talk about... things like that,' she ended.

'He's single, as far as I know,' Mary cut in. 'And he was at the speed dating thing, so he must be looking for company. But...' She stopped and glanced at Tricia. 'I have a feeling he and Ilse are... very friendly. I saw them in town having coffee yesterday, chatting and laughing. No idea how close they are, though. Could be just something to do with his work.'

Tricia looked at Mary while she tried to digest what she had just said. Cillian had been seen having coffee with this German woman... He hadn't said anything about this to Tricia during their chat on the phone last night. But it didn't necessarily mean anything. He could just be talking to someone connected to the project he was working on. She smiled and shrugged. 'Well, whatever. I have no idea who he's seeing – or not.'

'Oh. Okay.' Theresa looked disappointed. 'I'll just have to find out myself, then. Where is he staying?'

'He lives in a campervan,' Mary said. 'Parked at the back of his sister Orla's house.'

'Really? How come I didn't know that?' Theresa laughed suddenly. 'That must annoy Orla big time. She is so into appearances and style. Never knew a woman with such notions.'

'Hi, Mum,' Vi's voice interrupted them. She had suddenly appeared at their table and pulled out the empty chair. 'Sorry

I'm so late but Jack called to say he's on his way. He'll be here this afternoon. And he said he had a great outfit for the party. Can't wait to see what he's come up with.' She held out her hand to Mary and Theresa in turn. 'Hello, I'm Violet. Nice to meet you. Is this chair for me?'

'Yes,' Tricia said. 'The place is packed so I thought I'd keep it for you.'

'Great,' Vi said. 'But you didn't get anything to eat. It's nearly lunchtime so I'll go in and get sandwiches and water and coffee. Lily will help me get something. Won't be a sec.'

'Lovely girl,' Theresa said when Vi had gone inside. 'You must be so proud of her. I don't have any children, but if I did have a daughter, I'd like her to be just like Violet. So talented, pretty and kind. You're a lucky woman.'

'I know,' Tricia said. 'My two other daughters are also wonderful. So I feel very blessed.'

'You really are,' Mary agreed. 'But back to Ilse. Maybe she could be invited to the party? Just to make her feel welcome here, I mean.'

'And give us a chance to ask her about her work and if she and Cillian are an item.' Theresa winked at Mary.

'Yes, that too,' Mary confessed. 'But we can be discreet and just make it come up during a conversation or something.'

'Well,' Tricia started, 'maybe it's not fair to grill her if she wants to keep her work under wraps. Could be something to do with security or company policy. But asking her to the party is a good idea. I'm sure Sylvia wouldn't mind if I invite her. She loves meeting new people. Do you have Ilse's phone number, Theresa?'

Theresa nodded and delved into her handbag and pulled out her phone. 'Yes. She made the appointment to the salon on her mobile, so I'll get it from the receptionist straight away.'

Vi returned to the table with a tray loaded with sandwiches, water and coffee. 'What are you talking about?' she asked.

'Theresa mentioned that this very nice German woman is in town,' Tricia replied. 'So I suggested we invite her to the party. Very short notice, but...'

'That's already been done.' Vi put the tray on the table and sat down. 'Granny met her when she went to the hairdresser's last week and they started to chat. Granny took a great liking to Ilse and I believe she has already had dinner at Granny's.'

Mary laughed. 'I'm not surprised. There are no flies on Sylvia, always one step ahead of everyone else.'

'Such a stylish woman, always on the ball.' Theresa smiled and held up her coffee cup. 'Cheers for Sylvia, our very own Joan Collins. A cocktail in her hand and a mischievous smile on her face, that's her.'

'Great image,' Tricia agreed. 'And now we don't have to be devious and invite someone under false pretences.'

'You can be devious at the party.' Vi put a plate with a sandwich in front of Tricia. 'Here, Mum, try this sandwich. One of Lily's specials. Mozzarella, tomato and her own homemade pesto.'

Tricia took a bite of the sandwich and chewed slowly while she savoured the flavours of the pesto that married so beautifully with the creamy mozzarella and the tang of the tomatoes. 'Mmm, this is delicious,' she mumbled through her mouthful.

'I know.' Vi bit into her own sandwich. 'Lily makes the best sandwiches in town. She gets fresh bread from the bakery every morning.'

'You're making me hungry,' Theresa complained. 'I came here for a cup of coffee and decided not to have any of the yummy cakes on display. I'm trying to cut down a little on what I eat. But now that I see those sandwiches and smell that delicious pesto...'

'Lily sells little jars of her pesto in the café,' Vi told her. 'So you can buy some and then make your own sandwich at home.

Or just put it on toast without the cheese. Just as nice with fewer calories.'

Theresa brightened. 'Great idea. Thank you, Vi.' She finished her coffee and got up. 'I'm going to do just that. See you at the party tomorrow, lads. If you need any help with your hair, give me a shout. I could come to your house earlier and give you a hand.'

'Oh, brilliant,' Vi said. 'I thought I'd put mine up or do a French plait or something but I'm not great at that sort of thing.'

'I'll come to the gatehouse half an hour before the party starts,' Theresa promised. 'See you then, Vi.'

'Bye for now,' Vi said before Theresa disappeared into the café.

'I should go too.' Mary got up. 'See you at the party. I'm really looking forward to it.'

'It'll be fun,' Vi said. 'Bye, Mary. See you tomorrow.'

Tricia's heart sank – they had run off so quickly, she hadn't had time to ask her own questions about Kieran O'Grady and the drawings. And then her phone pinged. She pulled it out of her bag. 'Oh,' she said when she had read the message. 'Good news, Vi. The electrician will have finished the rewiring the day after tomorrow, so I can move in at the weekend.'

'That's great, Mum,' Vi said when she had finished chewing. 'But you're welcome to stay with us as long as you need to.'

Tricia reached out and ran her hand down Vi's silky mane of red hair. 'Oh, sweetheart, that's so kind. But I know that Jack is looking forward to being alone with you in your very first home. And, you know...' Tricia smiled as she thought of Cillian and how they could now be together without anyone knowing whenever they wanted. 'I need my own space too. I won't be far away either, so we can see each other often, with or without men.'

'Men?' Vi's eyebrows shot up. 'Are you... have you met someone? You look all glowy and happy all of a sudden.'

'Oh, er...' Tricia found herself stuck for words but then she couldn't hold it in. 'Maybe it's just friendship but there is someone who makes me feel good,' she said. 'That's all I can say right now. I've been through so much heartache and sadness, so I'm feeling a little nervous, you see.' She picked up her sandwich and finished it, avoiding Vi's probing gaze.

'Well, if someone is making you feel good, I'd like to thank him,' Vi said. 'But if you don't want to talk about it, I won't ask more questions.'

'Thank you, sweetheart.' Tricia smiled at her daughter. 'Right now you are more important than whatever is going on with me. I want you and Jack to have a wonderful summer and the wedding of your dreams. I'll be moving into the cottage the day after tomorrow but I'll be available whenever you need me and we'll plan the wedding together.'

'That's fabulous, Mum,' Vi exclaimed. 'I'm so glad to have your support. We both need it. Jack's mum is not like you. They don't have a good relationship, really, and that's sad for him. So you're very important to both of us.'

'What about your granny?' Tricia asked.

Vi sighed. 'Oh, she wants us to do it her way. She's a little bit of a control freak, as you know. But the party tomorrow should distract her from trying to run our wedding. That was a great move by you, I have to say.'

'Maybe.' Tricia wiped her mouth with a napkin and picked up her coffee cup. 'I only hope it worked. I wouldn't be too sure, though. Sylvia is not easy to fool.'

'No, but right now it has worked,' Vi remarked. 'You should see the terrace and the dining room. It's like something from a movie, all decorated with flowers and garlands.'

'Sylvia has worked so hard,' Tricia remarked. 'I asked her several times if she needed any help but she kept saying all was "in hand".'

'Typical,' Vi said. 'Granny didn't want you to get any credit.

But she is enjoying doing it all herself with a little help from Nora and Martin. She found an old gramophone in the attic and lots of old records with jazz music. We'll have to crank up that thing but it'll be fun dancing to that music. Nearly everyone has accepted the invitations and there is a great buzz in town about this event. I think it'll be fabulous.'

'And then Sylvia will announce your engagement, of course,' Tricia filled in. 'That'll be the high point of the party.'

'I know.' Vi sipped her coffee. 'The spotlight will be on us then. But that's okay. The wedding will be the main event and we'll be able to do it our own way, thanks to you.'

'Have you sent out the save the date cards?' Tricia asked.

'We did it by email yesterday,' Vi replied. 'Didn't you get one?'

'I might have missed it in the middle of all the building stuff. Ted sends me emails about it all the time. He doesn't want to clog up my texts, he said.'

'Oh. Very considerate.' Vi smiled at her mother. 'Is he the one who's making you look so happy?'

'Never you mind,' Tricia said, trying not to laugh. She picked up her phone. 'I'll check my emails now and see if your card arrived.' She quickly scanned her inbox and then saw the item. 'There it is. The twenty-second of August. Lovely virtual card, sweetheart. Well done.'

'It wasn't me, it was Jack,' Vi said. 'He did the design on some artwork app he found.' She finished her coffee and gathered up their plates and cups and put them on the tray. 'I'd better go. Jack will be home soon.'

'I'll take the tray in and put it away,' Tricia promised. 'In any case, I need to go through my emails and reply to Ted and thank him. I'm sure he was the one who got the electrician to finish so soon. And I want to see if Lily will sit down here with me when the rush is over. She needs a break.'

'Good idea, Mum.' Vi got up. 'See you later, then. Early dinner and bed so we'll be at our best for the party tomorrow.'

Tricia nodded and smiled. 'Yes, very sensible. I need beauty sleep a lot more than you.'

'Say hi to Ted.' Vi winked and then she was gone before Tricia could reply to the insinuation. But then she thought, *Why protest? If Vi thinks I'm interested in Ted, she won't suspect that my relationship with Cillian is anything more than old friends meeting up again...* Maybe it wasn't fair to Ted, but she was sure he wouldn't care. He seemed such a self-contained, confident man with a good sense of humour. He'd probably have a good laugh at the idea of being the fake love interest.

Tricia smiled to herself as she checked her emails again. There was one from Ted with a few details of minor additional costs. He also said, *The electrician found an old metal tube behind a wall panel. Rusty and dented but intact. There might be something in it so I put it on the kitchen table for you to look at.* Tricia decided to take a look at it that evening. It could contain something that might tell her more about the O'Grady family.

Then she forgot everything as she saw an email from Cillian. What he said made her throat contract.

17

Hi Trish,

just to say I miss you and that I won't be at the party after all. I have to go away for a meeting with the firm I'm working with. I have to do a presentation of all we have done so far and our future plans and also what we have found. It has to be done in order to raise funds to finish everything and we need to justify spending more money on this very exciting project. I'll be in touch as soon as I'm back from Germany.

Love,

Cillian

So it was true, then. He was working for a German firm on something that he had to keep secret. But what was it? Tricia sat there, forgetting everything around her as she tried to put the pieces together. She was certain Cillian's project was connected to the diving in the bay. Then her little grandson's words popped into her head. He had said something about diving to find a pirate ship, which of course was nonsense. But what if it had to do with some other kind of sunken ship as she had suspected? After all, Cillian had seemed very shaken by that old drawing she had found in the cottage, the one that depicted a ship called the *Carmen*. But no, it couldn't be. Cillian was an archaeologist and had nothing to do with diving or old ships. Finding the drawing now, and showing it to Cillian, was an amazing coincidence – if the two were connected at all.

Tricia shook her head trying to clear her mind. It was all so confusing, and added to that, her feelings and emotions were suddenly in turmoil. The fact that he had taken off just like that without telling her until he was gone was also a little disturbing. She had felt they were getting so close and that a warm friendship was beginning. He had said he was a restless soul with itchy feet but, blinded by her attraction to him, she hadn't paid much attention to that. Now she realised what he meant. He had gone off without as much as a goodbye, only letting her know when he'd arrived in Germany. Was this something he did all the time?

But despite her dismay, she was glad Cillian was not coming to the party. It would be too difficult not to reveal the chemistry between them. This way she could concentrate on Vi and Jack and give them all the attention they deserved. She would deal with what was going on with Cillian when he came back.

Tricia pulled herself together as she heard the gravel crunch and saw Lily approaching her table. Better to park all this at the back of her mind and concentrate on the present.

Tricia smiled as Lily pulled out a chair and sat down. 'You look a little tired, Lily-lou.'

'I am,' Lily replied. 'Today was hectic. But the rush is over now and we'll be closed tomorrow for the party. Do you have an outfit?'

'Yes, Vi and I managed to find two great dresses in the vintage shop. Possibly the last ones left. But what about you?'

'I rooted around in a trunk in the attic last week and found a red sleeveless number with sequins that I've had cleaned and mended. More nineteen forties than twenties, but it's very nice. Rose is wearing palazzo pants and a white top, which could be from any era. Granny had a dress made by a seamstress in Tralee. It's fabulous. She'll be the belle of the ball and outshine everyone. I hope Vi won't mind.'

'She won't,' Tricia declared. 'She'll be happy for Sylvia to shine this time. And she deserves it after all her hard work.'

'Yes she does.' Lily looked at her mother. 'So what else is going on? I saw you looking a little startled as you checked your phone right now. I hope there is nothing wrong at the cottage?'

'No, not at all,' Tricia replied. 'In fact, I'll be able to move in the day after tomorrow. The electrician has finished so all is safe now and Ted has done all the new pipes in the bathroom and put in a new immersion tank. The basic furniture is already there and then I have a load coming from Donegal in a few days with everything for the kitchen and my books and bits and pieces. Of course the work will still be going on for a few weeks but it's all coming together.' She smiled at Lily. 'Actually, Ted said he thought there was enough room in the box room for a bunk bed, so the kids will be able to stay the night with me whenever you and Dom want to get away.'

'Ted seems to be like a real gem,' Lily remarked. 'What a good idea to put in a bunk bed. That'll be such fun for the kids. And great for us too. I think Rose and Noel need to get away more than we do, though. So Naomi and Sophie could have a girls' sleepover with you when you're ready.'

'That sounds lovely.' Tricia smiled. 'You have no idea how wonderful it is for me to be here with all of you. And to feel needed and wanted. That's all I could ever wish for.'

'And someone nice to go out with from time to time?' Lily

asked with a cheeky smile. 'I have a feeling that Ted the builder is the cause of that happy look in your eyes.'

'Oh, not really,' Tricia protested, laughing. 'He's been a true friend in need, but that's all he is. I'm so happy with my new home and making all these plans, that's all.'

'Okay,' Lily said. 'I won't ask any more questions about any gentlemen friends. I'm just enjoying the new you. We all are.' She got up and took the tray with all the cups and plates that was still on the table. 'I'll take this in and then I'll go home and see to the kids. I promised them that we'll go swimming before dinner. Dom said he'd be home early and then we'll be all set for the party tomorrow. Great that it's on a Thursday and then we can all relax afterwards.'

'Well, it was that or not at all as there are two weddings at the weekend,' Tricia remarked. 'The reception rooms are all booked out for the whole of July and August. Rose has done a good job with that part of the business.'

'She has,' Lily agreed. 'I have to get going. See you tomorrow at the party, Mum,' she said before she walked away with the tray.

Tricia looked at Lily's retreating figure, thinking that both she and Rose were working a little too hard. They needed some 'me' time now and then and Tricia promised herself she'd see that they got it. She would have weekends with the children once the cottage was ready, which, with Ted's help, would not take too long. In a few weeks she could have them all for sleep-overs and have fun picnics with them on the little beach.

Looking forward to all the fun times with her grandchildren, Tricia decided to go straight to the cottage to thank Ted for all he was doing to make all that happen and to take a look at that item he had found. She would try not to think about Cillian until he came back. With him gone, it would give her the time to investigate the drawings she'd found without having to hide anything from him.

． ． ．

When Tricia arrived at the cottage a little later, work was in full swing. Ted's pick-up truck was parked outside the door and she could hear hammering and banging from inside. There was also a small van with the Dingle Electrical logo on the side. Two young men were carrying sheets of insulation from the truck through the door so Tricia had to wait until they had gone through. Then she entered the cottage and breathed in the smell of paint and plaster and new wood. She stuck her head through the living room door and found Ted and his men preparing the walls for the insulation. The wall around the window was already finished with new plaster, ready to paint.

Ted, standing in the middle of the room instructing the workers, turned around. 'Hi there, Tricia. As you can see we're hard at work here. You can soon take out your paint pots and get started.' His brown eyes twinkled as he smiled at her. 'I bet you can't wait.'

'You're right.' Tricia laughed. 'My fingers are itching. I love painting and decorating. I did up our old farmhouse in Donegal all by myself,' she said proudly. 'And I did a great job, even though I say so myself.'

'Of course you can say so yourself,' Ted replied. 'Be proud of what you achieve, is my motto. I'm a bloody good builder and I'm not afraid to say it.'

'That's terrific,' Tricia said, charmed by his smile and that twinkle in his eyes. This nice man had been through as much sadness as she had but he seemed still so cheerful and happy in his skin. 'I'm going to be less shy about my achievements from now on.'

'Excellent,' Ted said. 'Hey, I was just about to take a little coffee break. Why don't we sit down in the sunshine? I have a big thermos with coffee and a packet of Hobnobs in the truck. I'd be happy to share it with you. I want to give the lads a chance to have a rest, too. They've worked so hard. We usually have a tea or coffee break around now, except they seem to prefer a beer sitting in the truck with their phones.'

'Good idea,' Tricia said. 'I just had coffee at Lily's café, but I don't mind another one. I need to see that old thing the electrician found, too. We can look at it together while we're having coffee. I have to confess that I'm partial to a Hobnob.'

'Then it's my lucky day,' Ted said. 'I was going to pick up a packet of ginger snaps, but something told me the Hobnobs would be a better choice. Now I know why. Must be the universe trying to tell me something. I won't be a tick. I'll just get the lads to secure the insulating panels.'

'We can sit in the back garden on the old garden chairs,' Tricia suggested. 'I'll see you out there.'

Ted made a thumbs-up sign and went to speak to his workers while Tricia walked away into the kitchen. On her way, she noticed the new switches and outlets that the electrician had put in. It was wonderful to see that at least the rewiring was nearly finished, which made her feel that her dream would come true very soon. Even though her idea to sell the house for a profit had been shattered by the cost of the renovations, it felt good to be moving into what she felt would be her forever home, a home she wouldn't have to move out of until she was old. She would be close to her daughters and their families which was a huge comfort to her. She walked into the kitchen, her mind full of plans for the painting and decorating she was going to do in the house herself once the building work was finished.

She turned her attention to the kitchen table and the item that had been put there. It was an old rusty metal tube with a lid at the top made of what looked like leather. There was something about it that made her pick it up and try to open the lid. But it was stuck. She noticed an inscription painted on the side in black that said: *KOG 1889.* Could that be Kieran O'Grady? Excited, she tried again to prise open the lid but broke a nail and had to give up. 'Ouch,' she said and went to the tap to run water over her sore finger as Ted walked in carrying a thermos and a packet of biscuits.

'What's up?' he asked.

'I broke a nail trying to open that old thing.' Tricia dried her finger on her jeans and pulled off what remained of the tip of her nail. 'Never mind. Maybe you have some kind of tool that could open it?'

Ted inspected the metal tube. 'Yes, of course I do. I think this needs just a little pulling with...' He nodded. 'I know what to do. I'll get my toolbox.' He came back moments later with a pair of pliers. 'Let's try this.' He proceeded to tug at the lid with the pliers and after a bit of pulling, managed to open it. 'Here we are,' he said and handed Tricia the open tube. 'Smells a bit mouldy, but I can see that there is something inside like wads of papers or something. You have smaller hands so maybe you could fish it out? But be careful and don't cut yourself.'

'It's worth a broken nail or two.' Tricia carefully pushed her fingers into the tube and immediately felt the edge of something. 'It's thicker than paper.' She managed to get a good grip and carefully pulled the item out of the tube. 'It's a canvas,' she said, breathless with excitement. Then she opened the roll and spread it out on the table. 'Oh,' was all she managed as she discovered what the item was.

Ted looked over her shoulder. 'My goodness,' he said. 'How beautiful.'

18

They looked in awe at the oil painting that Tricia had just unrolled. It was a portrait of a woman sitting at a window overlooking a beautiful garden. She had brown hair that hung in a plait over her shoulder. Her gaze through deep blue eyes was both gentle and contemplative, as if she was lost in thought.

'Stunning,' Tricia murmured, profoundly moved by the beautiful painting. Then she looked at the bottom right-hand corner and saw the signature. '"*Mother* by Kieran O'Grady",' she whispered. Then she remembered Fred's words again. When they had been looking around the cottage, Fred had said something about a hidden treasure but she had thought he had meant something else, something to do with them and how they felt about each other. Could this be what he was talking about?

'*The* Kieran O'Grady?' Ted asked, looking awestruck.

Tricia nodded. 'I think so. I'm beginning to believe that he grew up here, in this cottage.'

'But I thought he was from Tralee,' Ted said. 'At least that's what I read in a leaflet at the National Gallery the last time I was there. I'm a huge fan of his work.'

'Me too,' Tricia said. 'And I also thought he was from

Tralee. But I have a feeling...' She stopped and looked at Ted. 'I really must look up the O'Gradys in the Magnolia archives. Not the family archives, but the records of the staff of the estate. There must be some information there.'

'Of course you should,' Ted said. 'But if I were you, I'd put away this canvas until you can have it looked at by an expert. Don't tell anyone about it until you know who painted it. If it's a true O'Grady, then it could be worth a small fortune.'

Tricia looked at Ted in shock. This was what she had been hoping for. The drawings wouldn't be worth much, but this painting was another matter. It could be worth a fortune and solve everything. 'Of course you're right.' She looked at the painting again and then started to carefully roll up the canvas. 'I'll take it with me and keep it in my bedroom at the gatehouse until I can get to Dublin to have it looked at.'

Ted nodded. 'Good idea. I wouldn't tell anyone if I were you. For the moment, anyway. Take a photo of it with your phone and then you can send it to someone at the National Gallery or Trinity College, someone qualified to examine it.'

Tricia fished her phone from her pocket and took a photo of the painting and then rolled it up again. 'I won't put it back into that dirty old tube, though.'

'I have a cotton bag in the truck,' Ted said. 'I'll go and get it and then we'll have that coffee. I have a feeling you need to recover from the shock.'

Tricia smiled and nodded. 'Yes, I think you're right. I feel a little shaky right now.'

'I'll be back in a minute,' Ted said and left to fetch the bag while Tricia went out into the garden carrying the rolled-up canvas under her arm. Had she really just found a painting by a famous artist? If she sold it, she could tell Terence he could keep Sean's estate, and all her problems would go away. She sat down, flooded with relief, knowing she couldn't tell Ted what this meant to her, even though she was desperate to share it with someone.

Ted was back moments later with a cotton bag that seemed a good fit for the painting and they both went out into the sunshine. Then Ted pulled out one of the chairs. 'Here, sit down while I get that little table over there.' He walked over to the shed where he took a small round wrought iron table and carried it over to the chairs outside the kitchen door. 'There.' He put the packet of biscuits on the table and opened the thermos. 'The table is a bit rusty but it'll do for now.'

'I'm going to fix the table and chairs up.' Tricia took a mug with coffee that Ted handed her. 'I'll just sand off the rust and paint it and the chairs white,' she said. 'I love the style. Must be from the nineteen twenties, at least.'

'Possibly.' Ted opened the packet of biscuits and held it out to Tricia. 'I can't wait to see what you do with the place. I'm sure it'll be great. Just as good as your old home in Donegal.'

'But very different,' Tricia said, glad of the distraction. 'That was done in a kind of farmhouse style. I want to do the cottage in a seaside kind of style with a cosy look in the living room.'

'Do you miss it?' Ted asked. 'The farm in Donegal, I mean.'

Tricia thought for a moment while she nibbled on a Hobnob. 'Not really. I mean I was sad to leave but I would have been sadder to stay. Too many memories of someone who is no longer alive.' She met Ted's warm gaze and suddenly found herself telling him about Sean and his illness and how she had spent two years nursing him and all the trauma of winding up his estate after his death, leaving out the legal problems and the accusations that she had tricked Sean to change his will. 'I didn't want to say it, but I felt a huge sense of relief when he passed away. Both for him and for me. We were both finally free, and he wasn't suffering any more. He was a lovely man and we had some very happy years, so I'm concentrating on remembering the good times and trying to put the bad times behind me.' She looked at Ted, willing him to understand, feeling she might have shocked him with the revelation that she hadn't grieved the way a widow should. But he'd be even more shocked if he knew about that document she had signed that was now with her solicitor. She had pushed it out of her mind but now it reared its ugly head in her mind as she talked about Sean and his final days. 'It doesn't always work, though,' she added.

Ted nodded and sipped coffee from his mug. 'I know what you're saying. You gave your all to your husband for a long time. And now you want to live and be happy even if the sad memories come back from time to time. I don't see anything wrong with trying to forget.' He paused for a moment, his eyes sad. 'Sarah, my wife, was ill for a long time, you see. When I retired, we had made plans to travel and do a lot of things together but then she became ill and it all came to nothing. Like you, I looked after her during her illness and then she passed away in her sleep. I was happy for her then. I miss her but I felt that she set me free, as if she had said the words out loud. "Be happy, Ted," I heard Sarah say in my imagination and then I decided that I would try my best to do that.'

'And you succeeded?' Tricia asked.

Ted smiled wistfully. 'Well, that sounds weird but I actually am quite happy now. It took me a while but now it's easier.'

'That's good to know. I'm sure it was hard at first.' Tricia thought back to Sean. She knew he had wanted her to have the farmhouse, and that Terence was wrong in his accusations about her. Should she fight to keep it, because that was what Sean wanted? She had been happy to find the painting, a potential solution to her problems, but there were Sean's final wishes to consider too. But he was gone and she had to look out for herself and be with her family. She was sure Sean would understand why she couldn't stay in Donegal for the rest of her life.

'It was but I have learned to live in the moment,' Ted said, his voice cutting into Tricia's thoughts. 'I enjoy the little things.

Like sitting here with you and feeling the warm sun on my back. Doing up your house. Eating a Hobnob,' he added, taking a huge bite of the biscuit in his hand. He returned Tricia's gaze. 'You lost your first husband when you were so young. That was your real tragedy. But he lives on in your three daughters. I'm sure you see a little bit of him in every one of them. And your grandchildren.'

'Of course I do.'

Ted nodded. 'Good. But enough about grief and sadness. I just told you I'm a bloody good builder. Tell me what you're good at. Come on,' he urged when Tricia hesitated. 'Let it out. Be proud of what you can do and let the world know. Modesty is so last year.'

Tricia laughed. His good humour, added to that cheeky look in his eyes, was so contagious. 'Okay,' she said. 'I'm really good at maths and accounting. I can look at a column of figures and add them up in no time. I'm also a terrific painter and decorator and a hell of a babysitter. I can get even the crankiest toddler to go to sleep in a few minutes. Oh, and I'm a very good swimmer.'

'Impressive,' Ted said, looking slightly awestruck.

'This is fun,' Tricia said. 'I didn't know how good it feels to boast like this.'

He grinned. 'That's another thing to add to the list.' He slapped his knees and got up. 'But now I have to get back to work. Did you come to check up on me?'

Tricia smiled. 'No, I came to thank you for all you've done already, especially getting the electrician to finish the rewiring. I can move in during the weekend.'

'Won't it be a little... ahem, basic, though?' He looked doubtful. 'I mean, you don't have much furniture except for the IKEA bed that needs to be put together and the sofa in the living room.'

'I have a load coming from Donegal on Monday, so then I'll have more than enough,' Tricia replied. 'I'll manage.'

'I don't doubt that for a second.' Ted took the mugs and the thermos from the table. 'I'll leave the Hobnobs here in case you want some more.'

'No, take those, too,' Tricia urged. 'I don't need to fill up on biscuits right now. I have to get into my dress for the party tomorrow and it's already a bit of a squeeze.'

'I'm sure you'll fit into it without a problem,' Ted remarked. 'You'll be a huge hit at that party. I wish I could see you dance.'

'You're not going?' Tricia asked, feeling a pang of disappointment.

'No. I was invited by your lovely mother-in-law, but unfortunately I have another commitment.'

'It would have been fun to dance the Charleston with you,' Tricia said. 'But maybe another time.'

'Not for the Charleston,' Ted remarked. 'Or any other dance except perhaps a bit of jiving. I used to be good at that in my youth about a hundred years ago. But now I bid you farewell, lovely lady. See you next week when you've moved in. I'll leave the Hobnobs for you as a housewarming gift.'

'Thanks,' Tricia said. 'I won't touch them until after the party. See you soon, Ted.'

'*Hasta la vista*,' Ted said and went back into the house.

Tricia smiled as the kitchen door shut behind him. She had enjoyed the coffee and the chat with this charming, empathic man who seemed so happy in his own skin. She had felt herself forget her worries as he told her about his wife and then made her boast about her accomplishments which she found funny. She felt she had gained another new friend and it was nice that it was a man who had been through a similar sadness to her own.

But now it was time to get back to the gatehouse and get ready for the party. Tricia grabbed the packet of Hobnobs and put it into one of the kitchen cupboards on her way out. She'd have them with a cup of coffee when she moved in at the weekend. There were busy times ahead that she looked forward to with great excitement. The only fly in the ointment was Cillian's odd behaviour. And what to do about both the drawings and the painting Ted had found. She needed to give it all some thought. Should she face the accusations and contest Terence's claims? Or go against what she had promised Cillian and get both the drawings and the painting valued? Then that might all be resolved by the time Cillian came back. But could she trust him and get used to the way he was? Always rushing off, never staying in one place for too long?

19

There was a great buzz at the gatehouse as they got ready for the party. As promised, Theresa, the cheery hairdresser, arrived half an hour early to do Vi's hair, giving her an intricate chignon that looked both elegant and timeless. She then applied a straightener to Tricia's blonde waves turning it into a straight bob which went beautifully with her outfit. She also helped her to secure the headband with the feathers and her twenties look was complete. Vi and Tricia then did a twirl in front of the tall mirror in the hall while Jack put on his white tux and gelled his hair back, adding a fake black moustache because he hadn't had time to grow one. Then, laughing and chatting, the three of them walked up the avenue to the manor, then around the corner to the terrace, from where the tinny sound of music from the old gramophone could be heard. The weather was perfect for an outdoor party behind the house with warm sunshine and a soft breeze from the sea that could be seen glinting in the distance.

Most of the guests had already arrived and had gathered on the terrace where a long table, covered by a white damask table-cloth, had been laid with platters of finger food and glasses of champagne. Everyone had made a huge effort with dressing up and Tricia felt as if they had stepped back in time.

Sylvia, dressed in a knee-length dress covered in silver sequins, stood on the top of the steps greeting everyone as they arrived. She kissed Tricia on both cheeks and then did the same to Vi and Jack. 'You all look wonderful,' she declared. 'And Violet and Jack, you are such a beautiful couple. I'm so proud of you.'

'You look amazing, Granny,' Vi exclaimed. 'That dress is magnificent.'

'The queen of Magnolia Manor,' Jack said and kissed Sylvia's hand.

'Thank you,' Sylvia said, looking more than pleased. 'You're very kind. But now you must help yourself to food and drink and we'll start the dancing. At least you young ones will. I'll just sit and enjoy watching you all having fun. Arnaud will be here in a moment to help serve the champagne. After a little bit of dancing, we'll have more food, then the cake and the formal announcement of your engagement.'

'Hello,' a voice said behind them. Tricia turned and discovered a pretty woman with jet-black hair cut in a razor-sharp bob and grey eyes under thick, dark lashes. 'I'm Ilse,' the woman continued and held out her hand. 'And you must be Tricia and this gorgeous couple Violet and Jack.'

'Well done,' Sylvia said and kissed the woman on the cheek. 'You got everyone's name right. Welcome, Ilse. So glad you could make it.'

'So nice of you to invite me,' Ilse said in perfect English only slightly laced with a German accent. 'I'm delighted to meet your family at last.' She looked around at the people gathered on the terrace. 'Isn't this fun? Everyone looks incredible.'

'So do you,' Tricia said, admiring Ilse's grey silk shift that came to just over her knees. 'Love the black beads.'

'Thank you.' Ilse ran her hand down her long necklace that

hung to her waist. 'I picked them up in that second-hand shop. They had a great stock of vintage accessories.' She turned to Arnaud, who had just joined them. '*Bonjour*. You look just like Cary Grant in that tux.'

Arnaud laughed and ran his hand over his thick white hair. 'Except for the difference in hairstyles. But thank you.' He kissed Ilse on both cheeks. 'Lovely to see you again, Ilse. You look perfect for the theme of the party.'

Rose and Lily arrived together at that moment, both looking beautiful in their own different ways. 'Hi,' they said in unison and then burst out laughing.

'That must have sounded weird,' Rose said, still giggling. 'We don't usually talk as one like that.'

'We don't usually get on either,' Lily remarked, poking her elbow into Rose's side. 'Do we, darling?'

'No, we don't,' Rose quipped. 'We like to entertain our nearest and dearest with our bickering. But we thought we'd behave today.'

'Good luck with that,' Vi said with an ironic smile.

'We're giving it an hour,' Lily said. 'What's your bet?'

Arnaud kissed them both and stepped back, smiling. 'Adorable both of you, even if you start fighting.'

'Thanks, Arnaud,' Lily said. 'But remember that if we do, it'll be all Rose's fault.'

'Oh, never mind, you both look fabulous.' Tricia studied her elder daughters with great pride. Lily's red dress suited her to perfection, bringing out her big brown eyes and dark, glossy hair. Rose, so like Tricia, had recently cut her blonde hair into a pixie style and it went beautifully with her white top and palazzo pants. 'Love the trousers, Rose.'

'Aren't they great?' Rose did a twirl. 'They might have been very daring in the twenties, but I think I would have worn them anyway.'

'Of course you would,' Lily retorted. 'The twenties would

have been your era and you'd have been a famous flapper and a total scandal queen.'

'Oh, yes, I would,' Rose said, beaming. 'What fun that would have been.'

'Thank goodness this isn't then,' Sylvia said drily. 'I'd have hated to watch you and have to sort out any scrape you'd get into.' She smiled at Ilse. 'Now you see what I mean when I said the girls were a handful.'

'I love them already,' Ilse said and held out her hand to Lily. 'Hi, I'm Ilse. I was looking forward to meeting you all. Sylvia is very proud of you, you know.'

'When she's not smacking our hands for being bold,' Rose filled in and shook Ilse's hand after Lily. 'Hi, Ilse. Nice to meet you. And now you have to tell us about yourself and the work that brought you here.'

Ilse looked suddenly uncomfortable. 'Well... ahem... It's a long story and I'm not really allowed to talk about it yet.'

'Oh, please, girls. Stop being so nosy,' Sylvia exclaimed. 'Let's enjoy the party and Vi and Jack's big day. Come this way, Ilse.' She took Ilse by the arm and started to propel her towards the table. 'Champagne for you all, except those who are driving. And I'll introduce you to everyone.'

'Wonderful,' Ilse chortled. 'I came in a taxi and I love champagne. Let's party,' she called over her shoulder as she walked away with Sylvia by her side.

'Good idea,' Tricia said.

Jack took Vi by the hand. 'Let's dance, sweetheart. That music is strangely contagious. I suddenly feel an urge to do the Charleston.'

'You have to open the ball, of course,' Tricia said. 'Otherwise nobody will want to start dancing.'

'Of course we will.' Jack pulled Vi onto the terrace and they started to dance a wild Charleston to the scratchy sound of the old record player while everyone gathered around them. Then, suddenly they were all on the middle of the terrace, trying their best to copy Jack and Vi, everyone laughing.

Tricia watched them all and then Dominic, who had just arrived, pulled her with him, telling her to kick her legs up. 'Come on, Tricia, show them how it's done,' he urged. She tried her best and then found herself moving with the music, doing the Charleston as if by magic.

'Gosh, this is fun,' she panted when they stopped. 'Even though the sound from that old thing is terrible.'

'The rhythm is hypnotic, though.' Dom wiped his brow with a handkerchief. 'But now I feel like a glass of bubbly, don't you?'

'And some food,' Tricia said. 'This is supposed to be a tea dance but I know that Sylvia is offering a buffet a little later and then we'll have the announcement and a cake. Or I should say *the* cake.'

Dominic let out a laugh. 'Oh, yeah, it's a monster, Lily said. Can't wait to see it.'

Tricia was right. When the dancing petered out and the guests had cleared the plates with finger food, a buffet was laid out along with more champagne and mocktails for those who were driving or not drinking alcohol for whatever reason. Then, when everything had been devoured, Sylvia, who was standing at the table beside a huge cake with white icing decorated with pink marzipan hearts, tapped her glass with a fork and called for 'Attention' at the top of her voice. 'I have an announcement,' she said. 'A big one that concerns two young people. As you might have seen on some social media, Violet and Jack have just got engaged and that is why we are here celebrating today. So please raise your glasses to them.'

Everyone held up their glasses and said, 'Violet and Jack,' in unison and then there was a long applause. 'And to Sylvia, the hostess with the mostest,' someone shouted when the applause died down. 'This party is the best ever.'

They all toasted Sylvia and then there was more applause. Violet and Jack cut the cake together and soon the slices were distributed to everyone on the terrace.

'Delicious cake.' Ilse sat down beside Tricia on the balustrade with a piece of cake on a plate. 'Those big cakes are normally not that good but this one is amazing. Isn't Sylvia great? To organise this party and then she says the wedding will be fabulous too. Violet is going to wear her dress and everything. How romantic.' She took a huge bite of cake.

Tricia's mouthful of cake suddenly got stuck in her throat and she started to cough violently to dislodge it. Ilse slapped her on the back and then the bite flew out of Tricia's mouth and she could breathe again. 'Sorry,' she said when she could talk. 'I tried to swallow too fast, I think. What was that you said?'

Ilse looked confused. 'About Sylvia? I said that she will be arranging the wedding and that Violet will wear her grandmother's dress. Sylvia told me all about it when I had dinner with her and Arnaud recently.' Ilse cut another bite out of her cake with her fork.

Tricia stared at Ilse. 'What else did she say?'

'Oh, just that the wedding is going to be small but very beautiful and that the date hasn't been fixed yet.' Ilse smiled and took yet another bite of cake. 'I'm looking forward to seeing it all in the media, though.'

'The media?' Tricia asked.

'Yes. Magazines and so forth,' Ilse said, waving her fork. 'Sylvia said there'll be some features in the press. Can't wait to see it. They're such an adorable couple. You must be so happy for them.'

'Of course I am,' Tricia said while she secretly seethed with anger. How dare Sylvia tell Ilse, a complete stranger, all about Vi and Jack's wedding? And how dare she say that it would be featured in the press? None of that was true. 'But you know, all the details are not fixed yet. And I think they want the wedding to be family only with no media coverage.'

'Maybe,' Ilse said. 'But I bet the press will want a foot in the door.' She smiled. 'That's not for me to say, of course, not being family or a close friend or anything. Except I heard so much about you and the girls from Cillian. He told me all about how he and their father were close friends and all that. And now you are all meeting up again, I believe. Such a touching story.'

'Yes,' Tricia replied, suddenly wanting to get away from this woman with her knowing smiles and insinuations. 'So you and Cillian work together?' she asked in order to take the spotlight away from her own connection with Cillian. 'Something to do with an archaeological find, he said. All to do with a sunken ship out in the bay, I believe.' Tricia cringed slightly at telling lies but she felt that if she pretended to know, Ilse would feel safe to tell her more.

Ilse stared at Tricia, her eyes wide. 'He told you?' she whispered. 'But he can't have. It's confidential.'

'I know, but he's an old friend and we're nearly like family,' Tricia replied, mentally crossing her fingers behind her back.

'Oh. I see. Well...' Ilse hesitated. Then she shook her head. 'No, I can't say any more.'

'But you're a colleague of Cillian?' Tricia asked, changing tack. 'You're an archaeologist like him?'

Ilse shook her head. 'Not really. My work is not as academic. I'm more of a... technician. Anyway, Cillian will be back soon and I'm meeting him for dinner in Dingle next week. I'll ask him to tell you about the project then. He'll have been briefed about it at headquarters in Germany and if they're happy with what we have found so far, they might agree for us to talk about it. But now I must go and chat with the nice people Sylvia introduced me to. See you later.' Ilse smiled and slipped away into the throng of guests who were now gathering to help themselves to what was left of the cake.

Tricia looked at the back of Ilse's head with a feeling of having tried to catch a fish that kept getting away. So Cillian was having dinner with Ilse when he came back? Ilse had a glint of coyness in her eyes and Tricia wasn't sure she could be trusted, or even if what she had said was true. She turned as someone grabbed her arm. It was Maggie, looking excited.

'Hi, Tricia. You look fabulous. All I managed was this lace nightmare I found in my granny's trunk.' Maggie gestured at her black dress that went down to her ankles. 'Not really nineteen twenties, but I gave it a lash all the same. How's the house coming on?'

'Great,' Tricia sad. 'I'll be moving in during the weekend. It will be a little basic at first but I'm dying to start decorating.'

Maggie nodded. 'Brilliant. Let me know if you need any help. I'm a dab hand with the old paintbrush, you know.'

'I will,' Tricia promised. 'I'm sure I'll be screaming for help later on.' They joined the group around Vi and Jack as Vi showed off her ring and everyone congratulated them. While she looked on, Tricia thought about what Ilse had said. So Sylvia was pretending to be organising the wedding? And Vi was going to wear Sylvia's wedding dress and not Tricia's? She suddenly felt she was up against a wall of conspiracies and that Sylvia, looking so demure as she smiled at everyone, was planning to hijack the wedding that Vi so wanted be her own.

Well, two can play that game, Tricia thought. *I just have to be diplomatic and pretend I'll go along with it.*

20

Tricia pushed the controversy with Sylvia about the wedding to the back of her mind as she packed her bags and loaded them into the car with the help of Vi and Jack on Sunday. She had hidden the painting in one of her suitcases and had also sent the photo to a curator at the National Gallery in Dublin but hadn't got a reply yet. Cillian had been on her mind ever since his message to her but the painting and what to do about it was her major concern at the moment. There was no harm in finding out more about the painting, and she could decide what to do later. Tricia figured that since Cillian had left just like that, he had lost his right to tell her what to do. Her resentment at his absence was growing by the day.

Vi pushed the last bag into the boot and closed it with some difficulty. 'There. That's all, I think. But if you've forgotten anything, you don't have far to go.' She paused and looked at Tricia with concern. 'Are you sure you should move in so soon, Mum? You won't be very comfortable until all the work is done. You can stay here as long as you like.'

Tricia smiled and touched Vi's cheek. 'You're so sweet. But I want to move in now and start working. I know it'll be like camping for a while but it's summer and warm and I'll have a roof over my head – my roof, the very first roof I've owned all by myself.'

'You have the flat in Dublin, though,' Vi argued. 'That's all yours, isn't it? And didn't Sean leave you anything?'

'Yes, of course he did,' Tricia started, not wanting to reveal too much. None of her daughters had asked her about Sean's estate after his death. 'But the flat is not a house and I don't own the roof,' Tricia replied. 'The apartment in Dublin is just a base, a place to spend the night from time to time. I can't imagine how we all fitted in it when you were growing up and I was working in Dublin. But that was just during the shorter breaks. The rest of the time you were either in boarding school or at Magnolia Manor. It was just you and me during term time and you were so small. It was a home then, but now I don't feel I want to go back there.'

'That makes sense,' Vi said and patted Tricia on the arm. 'Good luck, Mum. Let me know if you need anything.'

'I will. Thank you, darling.' Tricia got into the car and drove away while Vi waved goodbye. As she looked at her daughter's figure in the rear-view mirror, Tricia suddenly felt a huge sense of freedom. Not that she didn't want to spend time with her daughter, it was just that she was now heading to a new beginning and a life all on her own terms and her very own space. It felt a little frightening but also exciting and she promised herself not to let anyone dictate how or where she should live ever again.

A week later, Tricia was astonished at how much she had achieved. In the living room, the walls had been drylined and painted, and the bookcases set up in the alcoves. There was a sofa in front of the fireplace, a rug in warm colours on the sanded and polished wooden floor and even two prints with

seascapes from an art shop in Dingle on either side of the
window which was hung with a sage green wool curtain to
block out cold draughts in the winter. But now, on this Sunday
morning, the window was open, letting in the scent of flowers
floating in on the warm breeze which mingled with the smell of
fresh paint.

In the distance, Tricia could hear the waves lapping onto
the sand of the little beach and she felt a sense of peace and
tranquillity as she wandered barefoot, still in her dressing gown,
across the floor, warmed by the sunlight streaming in. She
turned on her little radio to Lyric FM to listen to a Chopin
piano concerto while she sat on the sofa sipping tea and
munching on a cinnamon bun for breakfast. Not the healthiest
of meals, but she felt like treating herself on a Sunday morning
like this, when she had worked so hard all week.

Cillian had not been in touch since he went to Germany
and she wondered why. Was he back, and if so, why hadn't he
called her? His behaviour was erratic and she wondered if he
was suddenly as hesitant about their relationship as she was.
She realised that she had no right to feel he should tell her the
truth about his work, when she kept her own secrets so close to
her chest. But then, what hope was there for them if they
couldn't trust one another?

She looked around the room, looking forward to finishing
the walls by putting her books on the shelves of the bookcases
and hanging more pictures. A big load had been delivered from
the farm in Donegal, mostly crockery and utensils for the
kitchen, bed linen and also a few framed prints and oil paintings
she and Sean had chosen together. It had felt a little sad to
unpack those things but she was also happy to have the memen-
toes from her life with him, which had been mostly happy and
full of lovely moments to remember. The old painting which
might – or might not – be by a famous Irish artist was safely
locked away in one of Tricia's suitcases that she had put behind

the immersion tank where nobody would think of looking. She hadn't heard from the National Gallery but as it was the holiday season she assumed the curator must be away and she'd hear once she was back to work.

The sound of someone walking on the gravel outside the front door made Tricia sit up. Who could that be? Probably one of the girls calling in to say hello. They had been so sweet: Lily brought food from the café as she guessed that Tricia would have had little time for cooking; Rose had brought her daughter, Sophie, for a visit and the little girl had run around the house, climbing the stairs and then in and out of the back door to the garden and finally climbing onto Tricia's knee to wrap her arms around her grandmother for a hug. 'Not the best help,' Rose had remarked, 'but I thought you might need a break and that you'd want to see Sophie.' Tricia declared that she always wanted to see Sophie and they had a lovely few hours together – Tricia even teaching her four-year-old granddaughter to paint a wall, which she hugely enjoyed.

As there had been no sound of a car just now, Tricia assumed the visitor had to be Vi, possibly to ask Tricia to come over for lunch. Maggie and Nora had called around, too, bringing potted plants as housewarming gifts. But it couldn't be any of them as they would have arrived by car. It could only be Vi, Tricia decided.

Tricia walked to the front door and opened it wide. 'Well, I suppose you're...' she started but stopped and stared in shock at the visitor who was not Vi, but Cillian, carrying a piece of drift-wood on his shoulder. 'Oh,' Tricia managed, pulling her dressing gown tighter around her. 'It's you.'

'Sure is.' Cillian grinned and put the piece of driftwood on the ground. 'I brought this up from the beach. Do you remember I said I thought it would make a great mantelpiece for your living room?'

Tricia backed away from the door. 'Okay, thanks,' she said,

still trying to recover from the shock of seeing him there all of a sudden, even though he had been on her mind. 'Bring it inside while I get dressed. I didn't expect anyone, so I'm just pottering around and relaxing after a hectic week.'

'Sorry to interrupt your lazy morning,' Cillian said, looking guilty. 'And also sorry for not letting you know I had to go away for business, but it happened so suddenly, I didn't have a chance to...'

'To what?' Tricia asked, still standing in the hall. She folded her arms and glared at him. 'To send me a single message since you left? Well, don't worry. I got your message loud and clear,' she said, trying to keep her anger out of her voice. 'I don't know if I want to beat you over the head with that thing or hug you,' she added in a jocular tone as the silence grew thicker.

Cillian looked shocked. 'I'm sorry.'

Tricia immediately regretted snapping at him but her resentment had been building up since he hadn't been in touch. 'Okay,' she mumbled, not knowing what else to say.

'I should have texted you. Or called you,' he continued. 'I'm used to only thinking about myself, I guess.' He held out his hands to her in a gesture which made her anger disappear. 'I'm sorry for taking off like that and not getting in touch, I know it was wrong. Do you think you could find it in your heart to forgive me?' He smiled ruefully. 'Feel free to bash me over the head if that's what you want to do.'

Tricia felt herself soften. It wasn't all his fault. She hadn't texted him either, she realised as the expression in his hazel eyes made her forget all the hurt. She stepped forward and placed her hands in his.

'I forgive you,' she mumbled. 'This time.' She lifted her face to his, but before anything could happen he pulled back, and she felt suddenly overwhelmed and a little awkward in her flimsy dressing gown. 'I'll just go and get dressed. Then we can put up that piece of wood over the fireplace. Can't wait to see it up,' she said in order to cool things down. 'I'll go and have a quick shower. Wait for me in the living room. I won't be long.'

Without waiting for a reply, Tricia went into the bathroom and had a shower in the old bathtub, then ran into the bedroom and dressed in a pair of jeans and a red T-shirt. She brushed her hair in front of the little mirror over the antique chest of drawers Sylvia had had brought over from the manor.

The bedroom wasn't quite finished and only had a bed and the chest of drawers on top of which Tricia had put a small lamp. Ted had rigged up a blind over the window, promising to put up a curtain rod later on. Still, even in this unfinished state, the room was fine to sleep in and she had fallen into bed every evening exhausted after all the work and slept all night until the dawn chorus woke her up. This morning, however, she had slept late and decided to drift into the day slowly.

But Cillian's arrival had interrupted her plan of a lazy morning. Seeing him standing there outside the front door had shaken her and she tried to calm her racing heart and think about how to handle the situation. She was afraid to be pulled into something that could be so sweet and romantic with someone who was connected to Fred and those happy days long ago. They were comfortable with each other the way old friends were, sharing memories that nobody else knew about. But they had both lived a long time after that, with other people in other places. The quote 'you can't go home again' kept playing in her mind as she got ready and she knew in her bones that it was true. She wasn't the same person he had known all those years ago – and neither was he. *We have to wipe the slate clean*, she thought, *and find out who we are now, in the present. The past is behind us and we can only be together if we look forward. I need to tell him everything.*

With that thought firmly in her mind, Tricia went into the living room and found Cillian holding the piece of driftwood over the fireplace.

'It'll look great once it's in place,' he said. 'But I have no idea how to fix it.'

'Ted will know,' Tricia said as she walked in and stood in the middle of the floor. 'I'll show it to him and he'll have it up in no time. It is actually perfect and will look amazing. It has a flat surface on the top so I can put a few things on it. I'll oil it with teak oil once it's up.'

'Good idea.' Cillian put the piece of driftwood on the floor. 'Who's Ted?'

'The builder who's doing all the renovations,' Tricia replied. 'I told you about him.'

'So you did,' Cillian said.

'Amazing guy,' Tricia continued. 'He's been a true hero, doing everything in super-quick time. Also so nice and kind.' She drew breath and laughed when she noticed Cillian's worried expression. 'He's a good friend, but that's all.'

'I'm glad to hear that. The Mr Fixit kind of man is usually very attractive to women.'

'I'm pretty good at fixing things myself,' Tricia said, attempting to reassure him. 'I'm not the helpless female who shouts for help you know.' She gestured at the sofa. 'But sit down. I'll get you a coffee or whatever you'd like.'

'That would be great. I didn't have breakfast, so...' He stopped and eyed Tricia's abandoned breakfast on the coffee table. 'Did I interrupt your Sunday morning feast?'

'Yes, in a delightful way,' Tricia said. 'So... Coffee? Tea? Toast? I have no idea what you usually have for breakfast.'

'Industrial strength coffee and toast with a slice of cheese and an apple,' Cillian replied. 'But whatever you have will be fine.'

'I think I can manage all that.' Tricia went to the kitchen and made coffee and toast with a thick slice of cheddar and an apple and then carried it all into the living room on a tray.

Cillian got up to take the tray, then they sat down on the

sofa, Tricia sitting with her hands in her lap watching Cillian consume his breakfast. There were so many things she wanted to say to him, but she didn't know where to start.

He swallowed the last bite of the slice of toast and looked at her. 'What?'

'Oh,' she said, startled out of her thoughts. 'I was just thinking...'

'About what?' he asked. 'You look like you're bursting with questions.'

'I am,' she confessed. She reached out and picked up her cinnamon bun. 'About you, about the past.'

'I have a feeling that the past is more like an obstacle than a help, to tell you the truth.' He drew breath and looked at her, his eyes troubled. 'That's my feeling, anyway. How about you?'

'I agree about that,' Tricia replied after a moment's silence. She wanted to tell him about the trouble she was in but something stopped her. Maybe he would judge her and think she was somehow guilty of what Sean's nephew accused her of. She wondered fleetingly if he was trying to tell her that he didn't want to know. The moment passed and the urge to reveal everything was suddenly gone. Maybe this wasn't the moment in any case. Better to leave things alone for the moment and just enjoy the feeling of peace between them.

'I can see that you have done a lot to this house since I was away,' he said, looking around.

Tricia nodded and nibbled at her bun, happy to change the subject. 'Yes, I've done a lot of the painting and polishing of all the floors.'

He seemed impressed. 'It looks so professional. I didn't know you were so good at stuff like that.'

'Well, I am and I love it. There you go, now you know more about me,' Tricia remarked. 'The present me, I mean.' She paused and put the bun back on the plate. 'So what do you do on a Sunday normally?'

'I usually go for a walk and then go to a pub for lunch. But today is different. I kind of invited myself to Sunday lunch at Sylvia's later today. There is something I want to talk to her about.'

'Really? What?' Tricia asked, intrigued.

He looked away. 'Oh, just something trivial,' he said airily. 'Your girls are coming too. Did she ask you as well?'

Tricia stared at him. 'Sunday lunch? Today? With the girls? No, she didn't. And they didn't tell me about it either. My phone is in the bedroom charging, so maybe they texted me or something...'

'Go and check it now,' he urged. 'I only talked to Sylvia this morning. She might have asked the girls on the spur of the moment.'

'Sylvia never does anything on the spur of the moment.' Tricia got up from the sofa. 'Why do you want to talk to Sylvia?' she asked again before she left.

When Cillian didn't answer, Tricia ran into the bedroom and found her phone on the windowsill. As she turned it on, she discovered several messages and two missed calls along with a voicemail. The text message included one from Lily, one from Rose and two from Vi, all telling her about the lunch. The voicemail was from Sylvia, as were the missed calls.

'I have tried to reach you several times,' Sylvia said in the voicemail, sounding annoyed. 'Just to invite you to Sunday lunch. There will be a surprise guest whom you will be delighted to meet and the girls, their husbands and children have all accepted. Let me know as soon as possible.' Then there was a click as she hung up. Tricia rolled her eyes, laughed and dialled Sylvia's number.

'Finally,' Sylvia said as she replied. 'Are you coming or not?'

'Coming, of course,' Tricia said on the brink of laughter. 'How can I refuse an invitation like that?'

'I should hope not,' Sylvia said, slightly mollified. 'It'll just be family and Arnaud is cooking.'

'Then I'll definitely come,' Tricia said. 'He's a five-star chef. Only family, you said, so who's the surprise guest?' she asked even though she knew.

'You'll find out when you get here,' Sylvia replied. 'One o'clock and don't be late,' she said and hung up.

'You were right,' Tricia said when she came back into the living room. 'Sylvia had invited me and now she's annoyed she couldn't get me straight away. So I will have to turn up and apologise for not being available when she wanted.' Tricia sat down beside Cillian. She wanted to ask why he had contacted Sylvia and what he wanted to talk to her about but she knew it was no use. It was obvious he wasn't going to tell her and she didn't want to start another argument.

Tricia wondered if Sylvia knew they had been seeing one another. Had Cillian told her? Sylvia couldn't have known about their relationship in the past, but if she knew, would she bring it up? How would she feel about Tricia's relationship with Fred's best friend? She felt so worried all of a sudden as all these questions whirled around in her mind. She wanted to share her fears with Cillian, but then she started thinking about Sylvia's plans for Violet and felt angry. 'I'm annoyed with her, too, to be honest. Nothing I want to bore you with, though, except...' She stopped, not quite knowing how to continue.

'Except what?' Cillian asked.

'Well, it has to do with your colleague, or whatever she is. Ilse, I mean,' Tricia continued, hoping Cillian might at least finally reveal why he and Isle were in town. 'It appears she's got very pally with Sylvia and now she seems to know everything about Vi's wedding plans, which were actually private. But Sylvia seems to have taken to Ilse big time and told her things that made me very angry.'

'Sylvia?' Cillian looked confused. 'And Ilse? I had no idea that they knew each other.'

'They met at the hairdresser's,' Tricia said. 'And started to talk. One thing seems to have led to another and now they're bosom pals.'

'What did Ilse tell you that made you so angry?' Cillian asked.

'Well, she said Vi is going to wear Sylvia's wedding dress, which is not true. Vi wants to wear my dress, actually. I'm afraid I'm going to have it out with Sylvia about this. She told a total stranger things we haven't had a chance to discuss yet. A private family matter too. I really don't like what this Ilse woman said to me. It is none of her business.'

'Ilse is like that,' Cillian said. 'I mean, she makes friends easily and gets people to talk. She's very charming when she wants to be.'

'When she wants to get close to important people, you mean?' Tricia asked, lifting an eyebrow. 'Sylvia being a very important person around here.'

'Yeah, well...'

Tricia sat up. 'Yeah well – what? You know I think it's time you told me about your work and how Ilse is connected to it. I can't stand you keeping secrets from me like this. You have to trust me or we will never be able to go forward.'

Cillian looked taken aback by her tone. He looked at her for a moment. 'I'm sorry. I really can't tell you until "they" give me the go-ahead. It's a very important project.'

'I thought you trusted me,' Tricia said, her heart beating faster.

Cillian frowned. 'Please, Trish, try to be patient. It won't be long till we tell the whole story.'

But Tricia had had enough. 'I need some space. And I need to think.' She got up to look out the window in an attempt to make him leave. It was all getting too much to cope with. All the stress and controversy was getting to her.

'Okay.' Cillian took his cue, and she could soon hear his chair move, and his soft footsteps as he left. The peace between them hadn't lasted long and she felt so confused about how to handle her feelings for him. He was constantly blowing hot and cold and Tricia was beginning to feel it might ruin everything between them.

21

Sylvia's Sunday lunch was not the quiet little family party it usually was. Tricia was happy to see Nora there too. She would be a great support if things went south. She had no idea what to expect. It started off very good-humoured and when Cillian arrived, the girls appeared delighted to meet him, with Sylvia introducing him as Fred's best friend. They listened intently all through lunch to him reminiscing about Fred as a young boy and then as a university student. They laughed at the scrapes the two of them had been through and all the pranks and jokes they had played on other people. Vi was especially entranced, hanging on every word about her late father who she had never known. And no one seemed to notice Tricia and Cillian's familiarity with one another – or the tension between them. Did Sylvia know they had been together earlier that day? And if she knew, was she upset? It was impossible to tell.

Tricia felt tears well up as she listened to Cillian's stories, Fred suddenly so alive just for a fleeting moment. It was like gazing through a looking glass at a time that had been so happy and carefree. She noticed that Sylvia was equally moved and that Arnaud held her hand in a tight grip all through to the end of the meal. Tricia wished she could hold Cillian's hand, but even though they were sitting together, she had to appear cool and detached, just as a friend. It was difficult but Tricia thought that they had managed it perfectly. In any case, the girls were all listening to Cillian with rapt attention and didn't notice anything at all going on between them. The children – Naomi, Liam and Sophie – were running around the table laughing and shouting but nobody paid much attention to them as they listened to Cillian's stories about Fred.

Tricia looked around the table at Lily, Rose and Vi, marvelling at how lucky they had been to marry such wonderful men. It was a lovely moment, full of happiness despite the feeling that two people were missing. But she felt that Fred was there and his father, Liam, too, as they all shared memories of them.

Was this all Sylvia had intended for the afternoon? An old friend visiting to share stories about Fred and the good times? It was a lovely thought and Tricia wished it would continue.

But then the spell was broken when someone arrived while Sylvia served dessert. Tricia stared in shock at Ilse standing in the door of the kitchen. 'Hello,' she said. 'Sorry to interrupt the family gathering. I just popped in to see Sylvia. But I don't want to disturb you, so I'll tiptoe out again.'

'What is she doing here?' Tricia mumbled to Nora.

'I have no idea,' Nora said. 'She seems to pop in to see Sylvia all the time.'

'Annoying woman,' Tricia muttered.

Sylvia got up and rushed over to kiss Ilse on the cheek. 'Please stay, dear Ilse. We're all so happy to see you. You're not disturbing us at all. Get a chair, Arnaud, and then you can have dessert and coffee with us.'

Arnaud found a chair and Ilse squeezed in between Cillian and Vi, beaming at them both. She shook hands with Vi. 'Hello, Violet. I'm Ilse, a friend of your grandmother. So lovely to meet you at last. You're even prettier in real life than your photos.'

'Thank you,' Vi said primly. 'You're very kind.' She smiled politely but Tricia could tell she was uncomfortable. *That woman seems to have a talent for getting up people's noses,* Tricia thought. *And what is she doing here, pushing into a family gathering like this?* Most people would have felt embarrassed at arriving to a Sunday family lunch uninvited, but Ilse seemed delighted to be there.

Ilse turned to Cillian. 'Hi, there. Nice to see you back. Did you have a good trip?'

'Yes,' he replied. 'Very good. I'll tell you about it later.'

Ilse winked at him. 'You can fill me in on your visit when we're on our own.'

Cillian squirmed. 'Okay,' he said stiffly. 'We'll meet up tomorrow as we planned and then I'll tell you about the meeting in Hamburg. I didn't expect to see you here, to be honest.'

Tricia felt that the comment from Cillian was an implied criticism of Ilse having turned up like this uninvited. But Ilse didn't look put out in the slightest; she only smiled and then started chatting to Sylvia across the table. Tricia looked at Ilse and wondered how she could appear so relaxed, gushing at everyone, pretending to be close friends with someone she had only met recently and trying to push into the family circle. But that could be because of loneliness. She didn't seem to have any family and was all alone in a foreign country. Not that her behaviour wasn't intensely irritating, but Tricia suddenly felt sad for this brash woman and decided to try to be nice to her. It would be hard but she had to grit her teeth and do her best.

'You look suddenly very serious,' Cillian mumbled in her ear. 'As if you're struggling with a problem.'

Tricia smiled. 'Struggling with myself, I think. I'll tell you later.'

'Okay.' He quickly squeezed her hand under the table for a second and let it go again.

It had been a fleeting gesture but comforting all the same

and Tricia suddenly felt much better. It was a sign that things weren't so bad between them. At least there was nothing going on between Cillian and Ilse; they were just working together.

But that was not what was bothering her – it was that Sylvia seemed to be so taken with Ilse. Tricia found that odd. Sylvia was usually hard to please and Tricia found it difficult to deal with her. There was tension between them despite Sylvia's many acts of kindness to Tricia: having the cottage cleaned from top to bottom and the gifts of items of furniture. But maybe that was because of Sylvia's fear of losing the girls' affections in favour of their mother.

'Tricia, you're not eating,' Sylvia said, her voice cutting into Tricia's thoughts.

'Oh.' Tricia looked at a plate with a slice of tarte Tatin that had been put in front of her. 'Sorry. I was thinking about something.'

'Something important?' Sylvia asked, looking intently at Tricia from her place across the table. Had Sylvia noticed Cillian's gesture towards Tricia?

'Do you know who the first tenants of the gardener's cottage were?' Cillian asked, changing the subject very suddenly. Tricia glanced at him, and their eyes locked for a moment. She could tell he wanted to save her by distracting Sylvia from Ilse, despite him making her promise to keep the drawings secret. 'The O'Gradys,' he went on and Sylvia nodded. 'What do you know about them?'

'Nothing much,' Sylvia said. 'They would be in the staff records. I think the house was built in eighteen sixty-nine, and they were the first family to live there.'

'That's right,' Rose cut in. 'I read through those records when I sorted everything out a few years ago. Mary and John O'Grady were the first tenants. He was head gardener then.'

'They had a son called Kieran,' Cillian said. 'At least that's what Tricia and I assumed from two drawings Tricia found in the cottage. Dated eighteen seventy-nine. Was he that famous painter?'

Sylvia shot a look at Cillian. 'Drawings?' she asked.

'Yes,' Tricia said, realising the cat was out of the bag. There was no point keeping it secret. 'Of a ship and another one of a family.'

'Kieran O'Grady?' Dominic cut in. 'You mean the one who became famous? But he was from Tralee, wasn't he?'

Lily picked up her phone. 'Just a sec. I'll google him. Yes,' she said after a moment. 'It says here he was from Tralee. So it can't be him but someone with the same name. Would have been great, though, if you found drawings by him.'

'Early work by Kieran O'Grady,' Rose said with a wistful look. 'How exciting.'

'They're just some scribbles by a child,' Cillian interjected. 'One of some stick figures and the other one a boat or something. Nothing that could point to a great artist.'

'You've seen them?' Sylvia asked, again fixing Cillian with a curious look.

'Eh, yes,' Cillian said with a quick glance at Tricia. 'I saw them when I called in to see the cottage. Before Tricia moved in,' he added.

'I found the drawings in a wardrobe in the attic,' Tricia cut in. 'One of them said it was drawn in eighteen seventy-nine,' she confirmed, hoping Sylvia wouldn't focus on the news that Cillian had been to the house.

'He was born in eighteen seventy,' Lily announced as she looked at her phone.

'That would fit as far as I remember,' Rose remarked. 'He would have been nine when he did those drawings. If he was the one, I mean.'

Lily put down her phone. 'I'm sure he's not the famous painter, but wouldn't it be fun if he was? I mean, as Rose said, an early work by Kieran O'Grady – wow.'

'Dream on,' Dominic said. 'That would be impossible to prove.'

'Of course it would,' Sylvia said and turned her attention to her tarte Tatin. 'But we're ignoring this wonderful dessert. Arnaud, you've surpassed yourself today. The whole meal was a masterpiece by a master chef.'

'You are too kind,' Arnaud said, looking pleased. 'I'm glad you like it.'

'Even the kids are quiet for once,' Dominic remarked, looking to the end of the table where the three children were tucking into the dessert. 'But it won't last long, of course.'

'They'll soon be bouncing off the walls,' Noel said. 'I think we'll let them out so they can run off the sugar fix in the garden.'

Rose joined Tricia in the living room while everyone else was having coffee on the terrace. 'Just for a little peace and quiet,' Tricia said. Her mind was reeling. Sylvia and Rose had confirmed a Kieran O'Grady did indeed live in the gardener's cottage. It sounded like she'd be hearing positive news from the National Gallery. She should have told everyone she had found a painting, too, and sent a photo off to be authenticated. But she was glad she hadn't. Sylvia's reaction to the news of the drawings had been odd.

Tricia tried not to worry further about Cillian and Sylvia whispering in the kitchen earlier. She sat down on the sofa, happy to have a moment with Rose. 'We haven't had any time on our own for a while. Come and sit here with me. You do look a little tired, Rose.'

'Well, yes, I am,' Rose said as she sat down. 'There was a wedding yesterday and I had to oversee everything because the wedding planner was off sick. It's nice to have a moment on our own. Mum,' she continued, 'I was thinking about what you said just now. About Kieran O'Grady, I mean. I know it says on the various websites that he was from Tralee. But it doesn't say he was *born* there, does it?'

'How do you mean?' Tricia asked.

'Well, he could have been born here and spent his early years in the cottage. Then he might have gone to Tralee for school or something and stayed with relatives. That often happened in those days.'

'I suppose,' Tricia said. 'But maybe your imagination is running away with you? I know how you love research but this might be an impossible task.'

'Oh, I don't think so,' Rose argued. 'There must be a way to find out. When you mentioned those drawings, I got really excited. I mean, Kieran O'Grady at Magnolia? How exciting is that?'

'Yes, but it's quite a common name,' Tricia said. 'And the biographies I've seen all say he was from Tralee.' She was tempted to tell Rose about the oil painting she had found but decided to keep quiet for now.

'Yes, but still...' Rose insisted, 'he could have said he was from Tralee when they asked about his education. He also went to study art in Dublin and then went on to Paris. He lived in an artists' community there and then went to somewhere in Normandy to paint those lovely landscapes he was famous for. He might have just told people he was from Tralee because he went to school there.'

Tricia looked thoughtfully at Rose. 'Yes, that's possible, of course.'

'I'd like to do some more research. I was wondering,' Rose continued, 'if you could mind Sophie for a day or two? Noel is going to Dublin for work next week and I thought I might go with him. I really need a break, Mum.'

Tricia patted Rose's cheek. 'Of course you do. I'd love to have Sophie for a few days. I could ask Lily to bring Naomi over so we'd have a little girly holiday.'

Rose brightened. 'That's a brilliant idea. Sophie idolises Naomi. She's always talking about her "big girl cousin".'

'That's settled, then,' Tricia said, feeling excited at the thought of having her two granddaughters to herself. 'When are you going?'

'Tuesday. We have to be back on Thursday evening. There's another wedding on Saturday, so I'll have to be there to supervise. Noel will be happy that we'll get a few days on our own. And I'll go to the National Gallery while Noel is at the conference. There has to be something about Kieran O'Grady in their records.'

'I'd be very interested to find out more,' Tricia said. 'I can't wait to have the girls.'

Rose kissed Tricia on the cheek. 'Thanks, Mum, you're the best grandmother.'

'Of course I am,' Tricia said. 'I love being with the kids. They make me feel young.' She smiled fondly at Rose, looking forward to the visit. She'd ask Ted if he could help her put together the bunk bed that had just been delivered. Then the girls could sleep in the little box room next door to her bedroom. She was sure he'd do it and then she'd be all set for a lovely few days with her little granddaughters. She'd have to put Cillian on hold for a while, but with everything that had happened tonight, and Sylvia's odd reactions, she thought that might be best.

22

Tricia had been right. When Ted heard that her granddaughters were coming to stay, he not only put the bunk bed together in double-quick time, but he also produced a doll's house he had made for his daughter who was now grown up. 'It's a little worn,' he said. 'And the furniture has seen better days but I think the girls will have fun with it. The dolls are also old and some of the clothes are threadbare but...'

'Oh, that doesn't matter,' Tricia assured him, touched by this lovely gift. 'They will adore it.'

'There is another thing I meant to ask you,' Ted said when he had made sure the bunk bed was secure and the ladder fastened.

Tricia put a mattress on the bottom bunk. 'What's that?'

'Well, maybe now is not the right time, but I was wondering if you'd like a kitten? My cat gave birth to four of them and I found a home for all except the last one. He's still with me and I have made sure he's house trained, so he won't cause any trouble.' Ted drew breath and looked at Tricia.

'A kitten?' Tricia asked. 'Oh, well, I hadn't planned to have a cat but now that you mention it, I think it would be nice. Great company and it will keep mice away.'

'But maybe we'll wait until after your granddaughters have gone back home,' he suggested.

'No, bring him over today,' Tricia said. 'Then we'll get to know each other and he can settle in. The girls will love playing with a kitten. It'll be fun for them.'

'Or it might cause mayhem,' Ted said, looking doubtful. 'It's a lively little thing.'

'Mayhem?' Tricia smirked. 'Bring it on. Couldn't be worse than two little girls running around the house. They're Fleury girls, you know.'

Ted laughed. 'I see. Well, in that case, the cat might be the least of your challenges.'

'Could be.' Tricia unfolded the other mattress. 'Please give me a hand with this one.'

'Of course.' Ted took the mattress and heaved it onto the top bunk. 'There. Anything else before I go to get the kitten?'

'No, I can manage. But it would be great if you could bring me the bed the kitten has been sleeping in to help him feel at home. And some food?'

'No problem,' Ted said. 'See you in about an hour, then.'

While she waited for Ted to come back, Tricia made up the beds and hung the curtains with a Barbie motif on the small window. Then she stepped back and looked at the room, happy with her labours. The room was tiny but the bunk bed fitted perfectly and the wall lights the electrician had put up would give the room a cosy glow and could be left on if either of the girls were afraid of the dark.

Tricia heard a car pull up outside and wondered who it could be. Was Ted here already? But he couldn't have come back from his house in Anascaul so quickly. When she opened the front door she found not Ted, but Cillian grinning at her from the driver's seat of a huge white campervan.

'Hi, Trish,' he called. 'Want to come for a spin? I have a few days off so I thought we could go for a little holiday together up the coast. I have a list of B&Bs that you can stay in if the campervan experience should be too much for you. What do you say?'

Tricia stared at him, unable to speak. She hadn't expected him to arrive like that unannounced, especially in his campervan. He had said he'd be in touch soon, but she had thought they'd have dinner together or maybe a walk on the beach and a picnic. But here he was, looking happy and hopeful, inviting her to go on some kind of holiday. She knew that in usual circumstances she'd jump at the chance to be alone with him, especially if they were to go away from here. It would be the most wonderful adventure that would kickstart a possible romance. *Oh, I wish I could*, she thought. *How perfect it would be to go away and get to know each other properly, and maybe take it a step further...* She knew by the way he looked at her that he was waiting for her to say yes, to pack a bag and hop into the campervan and take off.

'Oh, Cillian,' she said, walking closer. 'I'd love to but I can't. Not right now.'

His face fell. 'Why?' he asked. 'What's stopping you?'

'My granddaughters,' she said. 'I promised to have them for a few days and they're coming tomorrow.'

'Can't you cancel that?' he asked in a gruff voice. 'Maybe have them later on?'

'I can't disappoint them. They have been excited about it since Sunday.'

'Of course you can't,' he said, looking mollified. 'I understand that. I just felt we needed to talk. We finished on a bit of a bad note the last time I was here.'

'Yes we did,' Tricia agreed, feeling a slight chill as she thought about it. 'But if you're prepared to tell me about what you've been keeping secret, I think we could start off again and get to know each other properly. Trusting each other, for a start.' She studied him for a moment to see his reaction but was disappointed to see him frowning.

'I can't,' he said. 'And your lack of understanding is making me feel bad.'

'Your lack of trust is doing the same for me,' she countered. 'So it wouldn't be a good time to go off together anyway.'

'Yes, but I only have these few days,' Cillian said. 'Then I have to come back to finish up before the big reveal. When the news hits the media, we'll have to do interviews and explain what's going on before the press arrives here to take a look at what we've found. I had hoped we could be alone for a bit and talk before all that happens. The calm before the storm, so to speak.'

Tricia sighed. 'I understand all that, Cillian. But this situation between us is not improving things. Can we leave it at that for the moment?'

'I suppose,' he mumbled.

'Good.' She walked closer to the campervan. 'But hey, can I see inside? It looks like a hell of a van.' She wanted to cheer him up and make him understand that the impasse between them was temporary, even if it felt bad right now.

'It's not just a van, it's my home,' he said, looking slightly happier. He got out and opened the door at the side. 'I'll give you the grand tour. I bet you won't be able to resist coming with me when you see how comfortable it is.'

'Well, I...' Tricia started but stopped. 'Maybe I will, one day,' she said. Just to make him feel better, she climbed into the van and looked around, impressed with the interior that was like a mini-home with a sofa and table at one end and a little galley kitchen at the side and a tiny shower room at the far end. It was all very plush and well designed in blues and greens, with a few red cushions and a throw on the sofa that folded out into a bed, Cillian explained. The driver's and passenger seats were upholstered in what looked like dark blue velvet and the large windscreen was like a picture window. 'The interior is gorgeous,' Tricia said as she looked around. 'Very inviting, I have to say.'

'I knew you'd love it. Wait till you see the views as we drive along,' Cillian said. 'It's like being in a movie with special effects.'

'I'm sure it is,' Tricia said as she was about to get out. 'And I know I'll love it when we do that trip. But right now it's impossible.' She climbed back down just as her phone pinged and she fished it out of her pocket. Her breath caught in her throat as she looked at the text message. It was from Terence.

23

Tricia, you don't have a chance of winning this case. I have found evidence to prove that you acted illegally. I have contacted my solicitor about the matter and it will have serious repercussions if you don't agree to settle.

Cillian, who had got out after Tricia, stood looking at her for a moment. 'What's the matter? You're as white as a sheet all of a sudden.'

She pushed the phone into her pocket without replying. She had no idea what to do. None of her plans to raise funds in Kerry had come to anything; the house still needed work and the painting hadn't been authenticated. She was at a loss and felt as if she had come to an impasse. She had had such high hopes for her new life, but everything was crashing down before her.

'You look as if you've seen a ghost. What is it that scared you so much?' Cillian continued, stepping out of the van, and placing a hand on her arm.

'I can't tell you,' she said. She felt suddenly a wave of shame as she thought about the terrible mistake she had made that now looked like a crime.

'And you said I was keeping secrets from you.' He looked into her eyes. 'Trish, you've accused me of keeping the truth from you, but you're doing the same to me, can't you see that?' Tricia looked into his lovely hazel eyes and breathed in his special scent of salt and sea and a hint of sandalwood from the soap he used. She wished she could go with him on the adventure he had planned and she also wished with all her heart she could tell him about the trouble she was in. But there was no way she could reveal how foolish she had been, not until it was all over. Nor could she pull out of the arrangements she had made with Rose and disappoint the little girls who she knew were so excited to come for a sleepover at their granny's new house.

'Oh, Cillian,' she whispered. 'I wish I could tell you but I can't.'

'Why not?' he murmured against her hair as he pulled her close to him. 'It's important for us to be honest with each other and to spend some time together on our own, away from everyone here. Can't you see that?'

Tricia put her cheek against his chest and stayed there for a moment before she slowly pulled out of his arms. 'I know you're right, but I can't get out of having my little granddaughters. A promise to a child is sacred to me. I just can't break that. They'd never trust me again. And this message I just got... Well, yes it's a huge problem but it involves someone else and it's very complicated. Please try to understand,' she pleaded.

He nodded, still looking put out. 'I don't like being kept in the dark about something that's making you look so worried. And I...' He stopped as a small van pulled up behind the campervan.

'It's Ted with the kitten,' Tricia said and walked to where Ted had just parked, relieved to have a distraction. 'Hi, Ted.'

'Hi.' Ted looked curiously at Cillian as he got out of the driver's seat. 'Sorry, didn't know you were expecting visitors.'

'I wasn't really,' Tricia started. 'Anyway, Ted, this is my friend Cillian.'

'Hello.' Ted held out his hand. 'I'm Ted. The builder,' he added.

Cillian grabbed Ted's hand and shook it. 'Hi, Ted. I've heard so much about you. I gather you've been a huge help to Tricia.'

'Oh, I've just done a normal builder's job,' Ted said modestly.

'More than the normal builder,' Tricia protested. 'A lot more. Plumbing, carpeting, putting together a bunk bed from IKEA without swearing and now giving me a kitten for the girls to play with.' Her tone was jocular in an effort to hide her distress.

'That sounds like the work of several men,' Cillian said. 'But now I must be off,' he continued with a glance at Tricia.

'Don't go just yet,' Tricia pleaded.

'I think it's best,' Cillian said in a stiff voice. 'If you could move your van, Ted, I'll get out of the way of kittens and grandchildren and the like.' He shot Tricia a look of regret before he got into the campervan. 'I'll see you around, Tricia.' Then, as soon as Ted had moved his little van to the side of the cottage, he drove off without another word.

Tricia stood there, watching the taillights of the campervan disappear down the lane, wondering if she'd ever see him again. She knew he was disappointed that she hadn't been able to come with him and angry that she hadn't told him about the text message and everything connected with it. Ted's arrival hadn't helped matters much either.

Ted cleared his throat. 'Did I interrupt something there?'

Tricia squirmed. 'Eh, no, not really. Cillian wanted me to come with him for a drive up the coast. But I said I couldn't because the girls are coming tomorrow and I didn't want to disappoint them. He was a bit annoyed about that.' Tricia tried to sound unconcerned despite the lump in her throat and the tears that threatened to well up.

'You can't let kids down,' Ted said. 'Especially little girls. He must know that.'

'It's all my fault,' Tricia mumbled, fighting back tears. Then she couldn't hold it back any more. The tears ran down her cheeks as she felt despair overwhelm her. 'We were getting to know each other again after a long time apart, you see. I thought we might have something really good. Something that would last and might help us both heal. But I've ruined it.'

Ted moved closer and put an arm around her. 'I'm sure it's not that bad. He'll be back. I could see by the way he looked at you that he's mad about you. And who wouldn't be? A beautiful, intelligent woman like you with all those talents, what's not to love?'

'That's so kind of you to say. Right now, I feel like a foolish old woman who thought she could find love again.'

'You're neither foolish nor old,' Ted protested, taking his arm away. 'No one is ever too old for love.'

'I suppose you're right.' His words made Tricia feel a lot better. She sniffed and felt in her pocket for a tissue but found none. 'Of course I don't have a tissue so I have to blow my nose on my shirt.'

'No, you don't. Hold on.' Ted went to his van and came back with a roll of kitchen paper and handed it to her. 'Use as much as you need. And then maybe you can come and see the little guy I brought. He'll need a lot of loving now that he's been separated from his mother.'

Tricia used several sheets of kitchen paper to dry her tears. Then she blew her nose and pulled herself together. It was time to stop dreaming and count her blessings. She had a good friend in Ted, three lovely daughters, adorable grandchildren and she would just have to face Sean's nephew. Everyone might have to find out about the accusations against her. Sylvia would be disappointed and say that Tricia had finally ruined the Fleury name. But what more could she do? She knew she had to face it all soon.

Love and romance felt too complicated right now. She promised herself to try to forget Cillian, even if she knew he would haunt her dreams for a long time to come. She followed Ted to his van and watched as he took a kitten out of the back seat. He was black except for his white paws and a little white patch on his chest. 'Oh,' she said as she took the soft furry little bundle in her arms. 'He's gorgeous. What's his name?'

'He doesn't have one,' Ted replied. 'I thought your grand-daughters could find a name for him.'

'I'm sure they will. That'll be fun for them.' Tricia put her cheek against the kitten's soft head and heard him purr. 'I think he likes me.'

Ted smiled. 'He seems already at home with you. I'll get his bed and the food. Then I have to go and feed the mother cat and do a few jobs before dinner. Let me know how you get on with your new baby.'

'I will,' Tricia promised. She carried the kitten into the house and let him down on the floor, smiling as she watched him scamper away into the living room, then jumping up onto the sofa.

Ted came back with a round soft bed for the kitten and a bag of food. 'He'll eat some other things, too, but stick to this for a while. Hope you have fun with the little girls.' He put the things in the kitchen and was about to leave but stopped on the way to the front door. 'I was just thinking,' he said. 'About the painting we found...'

'I hid it well, don't worry,' Tricia said.

'And you haven't told anyone about it?' Ted asked.

'No, not even Cillian,' Tricia replied. 'I sent a photo of it to a curator at the National Gallery but I haven't heard back yet. That's the only person I've told.'

Ted nodded. 'Okay. It's just that if it should be by the real Kieran O'Grady, it could cause a few problems.'

'Like what?' Tricia asked.

'Like who actually owns it. The previous owner of the cottage might claim it belongs to them.'

'I hadn't thought about that. It would be Sylvia, of course.'

'Right.' Ted hesitated. 'Well, I'm sure you'd sort that out between you. But... there is a possibility that the family of the painter might also think they have a right to it.'

'Oh.' Tricia stared at him. 'I didn't think of that, either.'

'Well, maybe you should cross that bridge when you come to it,' Ted suggested. 'I just thought I'd mention it so you'll be prepared.'

'I'm glad you did,' Tricia said. 'But first things first: is that painting really by *that* Kieran O'Grady?'

'That would be good to know, of course,' Ted agreed. 'But now I really have to go. Have fun with the new member of the household. Let me know how you get on. And if there's any news from the gallery, of course.'

'I will,' Tricia promised.

'Good. Well, goodbye.' He waved and continued to the front door.

Tricia thanked him and said goodbye and then went to join her new charge on the sofa, feeling suddenly exhausted. She lay back and the kitten climbed onto her and went to sleep, purring loudly. It was oddly comforting to have that warm soft little cat on her chest, and Tricia let her thoughts drift.

Cillian's sour face and hasty departure played on her mind and she wondered if they would ever be able to sort out their differences. He had left both angry and hurt and that was probably the end of what could have been so lovely. That was sad but she would have to cope with it. Maybe she was too old for romance anyway. A bitter fruit to bite into, but she would have to face it.

Tired after the day full of controversies, with the kitten snoozing on her chest, Tricia felt herself nod off, only to be woken by her phone ringing. Startled, she picked it up from the coffee table, hoping it might be Cillian. But then saw that it was a Dublin number and wondered who it could be.

'Hello, this is Tricia Fleury,' she mumbled, still lying down with the kitten on her chest.

'Oh, hello, Mrs Fleury,' a woman's voice said. 'This is Barbara Delaney. I'm head curator at the National Gallery in Dublin. You sent me a photo of a painting a week or so ago.'

Tricia gasped and sat up, her heart racing, making the kitten jump away. 'Oh, yes, I did.'

'Sorry about not contacting you sooner but I've been on holiday until now.'

'That's okay. So you had a look at the photo?' Tricia asked.

'Yes.'

'And...?' Tricia held her breath while she waited for the woman to continue.

24

'Well,' Barbara Delaney continued, 'it's an interesting find and a very beautiful painting. But we'd have to see it in real life, of course, and do some tests before we can say who painted it and when.'

'I understand,' Tricia said. 'But maybe you could tell me if you think it *could* be a work by Kieran O'Grady. I mean, if you think it's in the same style.'

'I can't tell you much before I've seen it,' Barbara said. 'But...'

'But?' Tricia urged.

'Well, just between you and me, it looks very similar to some of his portraits. That was my take on it anyway. But then it could be a copy or someone trying to paint like him. We have to take a little sample of the paint and the canvas to establish when it was done. So, maybe I could come down to see it?'

'Of course you can,' Tricia almost shouted. 'That would be absolutely fine. And you can stay with me if you need to spend the night.'

'That's very generous, but I'll be fine in a nearby B&B or a small hotel somewhere in the area,' Barbara said.

'That's fine. Could you tell me,' Tricia continued, 'if you know anything about Kieran O'Grady? I mean, anything that's not on the very limited biographies online.'

'I will look up what we have here in the gallery,' Barbara promised. 'All I know so far is that he was from Tralee. Isn't that right?'

'Yes, but we think he might have been born here near Dingle, in the cottage where I live and then he might have moved when he...' Tricia stopped. 'Oh, it's a bit complicated. I can explain better when we meet.'

'Yes,' Barbara agreed. 'That seems like a good plan.'

'When can you come?' Tricia asked.

'Hold on. I'll check my diary,' Barbara said. 'How about... the end of next week? I'll bring my assistant who is also an expert of the Impressionists.'

'Brilliant,' Tricia said. 'Give me a call when you arrive and I'll tell you how to get here. We're only a few minutes' drive from Dingle town.'

'I know where you are,' Barbara said. 'It's easy to find on Google Maps. You're in a cottage in the grounds of Magnolia Manor, as far as I could gather.'

'Exactly.' Tricia thought for a moment. 'Actually, my daughter Rose will be in Dublin from tomorrow. She'll be doing some research into Kieran O'Grady and his life to find out more about him. Maybe you could tell me where she should look?'

'I'll have a look myself here at the gallery,' Barbara promised. 'But she might have better luck at Dublin Castle and maybe Trinity. They could possibly help her. And you could take a look at parish records in Tralee or even in Dingle town. That's all I can think of at the moment. But we'll know more when we've studied that painting, of course.'

'Thank you for the tips,' Tricia said. 'I didn't think of looking at this end.'

'We'll see what we come up with,' Barbara replied. 'I'm

looking forward to meeting you next week. Hopefully we'll know a bit more then.'

'I'll do my best,' Tricia said. 'Thanks for calling. See you next week. Bye, Barbara.'

Barbara said goodbye and hung up while Tricia looked around for the kitten. She found him on the floor cleaning his face. She smiled and scooped him up and then walked into the kitchen to feed him and make some supper for herself. The conversation with Barbara had been interesting. Next week might prove to be very exciting. But first, she had her new kitten and her little granddaughters to see to. The next few days would be eventful to say the least.

'Harry,' Naomi said. 'Like Harry Potter.'

'I don't like it,' Sophie argued, scowling at her cousin. 'I want to call him Wolfgang. That's my daddy's middle name.'

'No,' Naomi said. 'That doesn't suit a cat. We have to call him something better than a dad's name. Something like...' She paused, looking thoughtful. Then she shook her head and looked at Tricia. 'What do you think, Granny?'

'I think you should be the ones to choose.' Tricia topped up Naomi's glass. They were sitting at the kitchen table having milk and cookies while the kitten played with a felt mouse Tricia had bought for him. It was mid-morning and Lily and Rose had just dropped the girls off for their few days with their grandmother. The cousins had run around the house inspecting everything and Naomi declared that the house was 'delightful'. The sound of their feet on the floorboards, their happy voices and laughter made Tricia feel that the cottage was being inaugurated in the way she had hoped. And now, here in the cosy little kitchen, as they sat around the table together, it was like a dream come true. She had a fleeting image of Fred smiling at them and knew he would have been so happy to share this with her.

'I know Sophie hasn't read Harry Potter yet,' Tricia said. 'So maybe you could pick something from a story you both know. Or a TV programme or a cartoon. Or even someone you like a lot.'

'Paddington!' Sophie shouted. 'I love him.'

'Me too,' Naomi said. 'He's a teddy bear but I like the name. Would that be okay?' she asked, looking hopefully at Tricia.

Tricia nodded. 'Yes, but maybe we could shorten it to Paddy? What do you think, girls?'

'We'll ask him,' Naomi said and slid off her chair. She caught the kitten and held him in her arms. 'Dear little kitten, would you like to be called Paddy?'

The kitten let out a short 'miaow' and then wriggled out of Naomi's grip and resumed playing with the toy mouse on the floor.

'He said yes,' Naomi remarked and returned to her chair. 'So I officially name him Paddy,' she said solemnly and waved an imaginary wand over the cat.

'Paddy it is,' Tricia said. 'It suits him. Well done, girls.'

'Can I have another cookie?' Sophie asked.

'*May* I,' Naomi corrected. 'My mummy says it's may I, not can I.'

'Yeah, but I'm only four, so I can say what I want.' Sophie looked at Tricia. 'Please?' she added, batting her very long black eyelashes. With her blonde curls and bright blue eyes, she was the image of her mother. She looked like butter wouldn't melt in her mouth but Tricia knew she had a will of iron even at that tender age.

'How can I resist?' Tricia laughed and took another cookie out of the packet. 'I hope it won't ruin your appetite for lunch.'

'Lunch is a loooong way away,' Naomi said as she slurped her milk. 'What are we going to do today?'

'We could go to the beach,' Tricia suggested. 'Or to Ocean-world in Dingle if you like.'

'Beach!' Sophie shouted.

'And then Oceanworld tomorrow,' Naomi said. "Cause today is a sunny day and it might rain tomorrow. My mummy packed my swimming togs and armbands.'

'My mam did, too,' Sophie chimed in. 'Do you have any buckets and spades, Granny?'

'Yes, I do,' Tricia replied. 'I found the old ones your mothers used when they were small. They were in the shed behind Great-gran Sylvia's apartment. So we're all set.'

'Will Paddy the cat come with us?' Sophie wanted to know.

'No, we'll leave him at home.' Tricia smiled at Sophie. 'I don't think cats like the beach.'

'They don't,' Naomi said. 'They get sand in between their claws and they don't like getting wet.'

'But he'll be lonely.' Sophie stuffed the rest of her cookie in her mouth and looked at the kitten with sad eyes.

'He won't.' Tricia picked Paddy up from the floor. 'He'll sleep in his bed and then he'll forget we're gone. I'll leave his toys and some food and water and then he'll be fine. We'll just let him have a run in the garden for a bit before we go. We'll keep an eye on him so he won't get lost.'

'And he can do his business in the grass and not in the house,' Naomi agreed.

'What business?' Sophie asked, looking intrigued.

'You know,' Naomi started but stopped when a car horn tooted outside. 'Oh, there's someone here. Who is it?'

Sophie jumped down from her chair. 'I want to see who it is,' she said and ran to the front door. She pulled it open and peered out. 'It's a circus van,' she exclaimed.

Tricia went to the front door and looked out. 'Oh,' she said as she caught sight of the vehicle. 'What's he doing back?'

_____

25

Cillian stuck his head out through the window of the campervan. 'Hi.' He looked slightly awkward. Then he opened the door and got out, crouching in front of Sophie. 'Hello,' he said, smiling at the little girl. 'Remember me? We met the other day at your great-grandmother's house.'

Sophie nodded. 'I know. You're Mr Cillian, Granddad Fred's old friend. Why are you in a circus van?'

'It's not a circus van,' Naomi said behind them. 'It's a campervan. Can I go inside?'

'*May* I,' Sophie corrected. 'That's what you said we're opposed to say.'

'May I go inside?' Naomi asked. 'And it's *supposed*, not opposed.'

Cillian looked at Tricia and winked. 'Fleury girls, right?'

Tricia had to laugh. 'You got it.'

'Is it okay to show them the van?' he asked.

Tricia nodded. 'Yes. Let them have a look. And then you can tell me what you're doing back here after...' She stopped.

'I will. Just a sec.' Cillian opened the side door to the

campervan. 'Please step inside, girls, and take a look at my super-duper van. No circus, though.'

Naomi and Sophie climbed into the van while Tricia followed, making sure they were safe. Once they were inside, she got out and turned to Cillian. 'So...?'

'I came back to apologise because I know I behaved like an eejit,' Cillian said. 'Of course I get that you couldn't take off just like that. Your grandchildren have to come first. They will always come first to me, too. And then... whatever you're so worried about... It's hard for me to accept that you're keeping something important from me.'

'I know, but...' Tricia started. 'I just can't. One day, maybe, but not right now. Is that so hard to accept?'

He sighed. 'It's what's keeping us apart and I don't like it.'

'I'll tell you when I can.' Tricia smiled at him, feeling slightly more positive. 'I thought I'd never see you again. You were so angry.'

Cillian nodded. 'I was. Mostly about what you're keeping from me but it was also yer man standing there looking saintly that made me lose my head. For a moment, I thought... well, that you and he were more than friends, if you know what I mean. He seemed to be that kind of solid, dependable type that women go for. Especially women who have been through a lot.' He drew breath and looked at her.

Tricia shook her head. 'Cillian, you have no idea how silly that was. Ted is a true brick and he has been amazing, helping me with everything during the past few weeks. But he is just a friend, while you're more than that.'

'Am I?' he asked in a near whisper.

Tricia reached up and touched his face. 'Of course you are. A lot more. We go back such a long way, you and I. We share so many memories. You knew me so well when we were both young. But I want you to get to know the person I am now and what's important to me. And that includes my family. My daughters and grandchildren are my very first priorities. But that doesn't mean there is no room for you – or us – or that you aren't very dear to me. Do you see what I mean?'

'I'm very dear to you?' Cillian frowned. 'Is that all you can say?'

'Well, I...' Tricia stopped, lost for words. She wanted to say so much more to him but there was no time. The two little girls were in the campervan and would come out at any moment and wonder what was going on. Children, she knew, picked up vibes very quickly and the vibes that were in the air between her and Cillian would be obvious to them – or anyone that was watching them.

Cillian glanced at his van and then stepped closer. 'I'm going to say this very quickly,' he said, looking into Tricia's eyes. 'I'm sorry I flew off the handle and behaved like a six-year-old. I hope you can forgive me.'

'Of course I forgive you,' Tricia said. 'And I want to tell you—'

'I think I'm in love with you,' he cut in. 'That's how *I* feel. Think about that when you have the time. And you might also consider the problem of the lack of trust between us. If that can't be resolved, we have no hope of even being friends.'

Tricia put her hand to her heart, stunned by his words. 'Oh, Cillian. I'm sorry about everything. I know you're right. But I can't tell you anything until—'

They were interrupted by Naomi climbing down the steps from the campervan. 'This is an *amazing* van,' she squealed. 'There's a kitchen and a bathroom and a comfy sofa and curtains and even a TV!'

'It's the loveliest van in the whole world,' Sophie shouted from the open door. 'I want to sleep here tonight. Can I... I mean, may I?'

Cillian walked to the van and lifted Sophie down. 'You know what? It's not possible today because I have to go and see my sister. It's her birthday today and she would be very cross with me if I forgot. So I have to first buy her a present and then bring it to her and then have dinner and birthday cake.'

'Oh.' Sophie looked up at him. 'How old will she be?'

'Sixty-four,' Cillian said.

'Wow.' Sophie looked impressed. 'That's a lot of candles for her to blow out.'

'Oh, yes,' Cillian replied, bending down, his hands on his knees. 'So you see why I have to go?'

Sophie nodded. 'Yes. You may go. But come back another day and let me sleep in the campervan, okay?'

'Me too,' Naomi cut in.

'I will indeed,' Cillian promised. He rose and looked at Tricia. 'So I'll say goodbye now. Let me know how you feel about... that other thing. We have a long way to go before we can have anything to build on. Just think about that, okay?'

'I will.' Tricia nodded and shot him a shy smile, but he didn't return it. Then they all waved as he slowly drove off. She felt a surge of warmth towards Cillian and the way he handled Sophie. She was also touched by his declaration of love and his apology. She hadn't expected him to say that so soon, especially as she was still keeping secrets from him. But it had felt like it came straight from his heart. Maybe it would be all right in the end, even if it didn't seem so right now. Whatever way it was she hoped with all her heart that their differences could be resolved. But if not, she would have to accept it and move on. 'We have a long way to go,' he had said before he left. That was true. But this was not the time to dwell on such things.

'Bye, Mr Cillian,' the girls shouted after the van. 'See you soon.'

Tricia clapped her hands to attract their attention while she tried to shake off her thoughts of romance. 'Okay, girls, now we have to get ready for the beach. I'll make a little picnic while you find your stuff and then we'll get going. What kind of sandwiches would you like?'

The girls told Tricia they both wanted banana sandwiches and once the picnic was packed and their swimsuits and armbands had been found, they set off to the beach, the little girls skipping ahead while Tricia followed, carrying the bags. She thought fleetingly about Cillian and Ted and how different they were: Ted considerate, thoughtful and loyal, Cillian more of a free spirit and perhaps not as dependable. Ted made her feel cared for and cherished but what about Cillian? *He makes my heart sing,* she thought. *I feel so alive and young again when I'm with him. Ted is a friend but Cillian... He's someone I could spend the rest of my life with and never be bored. But it might just be a dream and we will never get together. Unless...*

She looked up at the blue sky and breathed in the fresh air that blew from the sea. She didn't know how she would tackle whatever happened next. The legal problem in Donegal seemed like an unsurmountable mess that would never be resolved. If she was found guilty of some kind of fraud, she couldn't explain her motives to Cillian. That would drive him away forever. She shivered as she thought about it and that threatening message and realised she needed help to tackle the lawyers who were after her. But where could she find it?

26

Later that evening, the girls fell asleep in Tricia's bed when she read them a bedtime story. She ended up nodding off herself as she lay between the two little girls with Paddy the kitten on her chest again. Then they were all jolted awake around ten o'clock by Tricia's phone ringing on the bedside table. Sophie started to cry and Naomi tried to comfort her while Paddy raced out of the room in a panic. The Tricia picked up the phone and discovered it was Cillian calling her. She had to tell him she'd call him back but it took over an hour to get everyone to settle.

She was finally able to pick up her phone an hour later and found a text message from him that made her heart skip a beat with joy.

I'm not giving up on us, he wrote. *I think we should spend some time together and see if we can find the solution to our problems. Let's take a walk on the wild side, throw all our fears and troubles into the wind and see what happens. What do you say? If you agree, I'll let you know what my plan is. Just give me a yes or a no.*

Tricia didn't hesitate. It made her spirits soar to learn that he didn't want to let go, either as a friend or something more.

She didn't care what he meant, she just didn't want to lose him. If they became simply friends, that would be better than having parted on bad terms with a strained silence between them. She quickly texted back with a *yes* and a smiling emoji.

His answer came back within seconds. *How about I pick you up on Friday evening for a magical mystery tour?*

Lovely, she replied. *Can I bring my new kitten? He is very well behaved.*

Yes, that would be nice. I like cats. We will explore new places and create new memories for only you and me. See you then. Cillian xx

Tricia smiled, knowing that they would go somewhere she had never been to with Fred or anyone else. This way they would have their own memories. That sounded good to her, even if his suggestion frightened her. It was like embarking on a journey without a destination or plan. It clashed with her love of order in everything. But he was that kind of man: a free spirit who would go where his latest whim took him. She wondered how that would work if they truly became a couple. He was right, though. They needed to be together away from curious glances and gossip. She knew she had to forget about the secret he was keeping from her and not press him about it. She thought about her legal tangle in Donegal, that she hadn't dared reveal to him. It had been on the tip of her tongue to tell Cillian but then she decided there was no point until she knew what would happen to her. It could change things between them when he found out. She wished she could tell him, but something had stopped her. But now, here he was, wanting to give them a chance.

Tricia sat back on the sofa and smiled into the darkness. This was what she needed. A mad adventure with a wild, unpredictable, sweet man who seemed to love her despite her age and wrinkles and slightly saggy body. How could she resist? She now felt a real need to tell him everything. If his feelings for her were as genuine as they seemed, then he wouldn't judge her too harshly.

The little girls went back home on the Thursday, happy with the 'Granny holiday', as they called it. It had been fun but exhausting, Tricia thought as she waved goodbye. She realised that minding small children at her age was quite a challenge. The girls had, on the whole, been well behaved but it had been quite difficult to stick to discipline about bedtimes and trying not to spoil them too much with treats and outings. They had tried it on several times, telling Tricia how Sylvia would give them sweets, buy them toys and let them stay up very late. But Tricia didn't fall for that, even though she did treat them to things they didn't get to do at home.

Rose had not managed to find out anything about Kieran O'Grady in Dublin, despite her efforts. There was nothing much about him at the National Gallery, apart from the biography they had gone through earlier. But she promised she'd take another look at the old papers in storage in the manor. 'You never know what might have been overlooked,' she said.

While she tidied up after the visit, Tricia thought of the weekend ahead. Spending a few days together in Cillian's campervan would be a good test of their relationship. It would answer many questions, not only about who they were now but also if they were truly compatible. It might end in tears – or be the beginning of something wonderful that would last for a long time.

When the phone rang later that night, Tricia was still thinking about Cillian and the weekend ahead. She answered with an absentminded 'Hello?' her mind on what she should pack.

'Tricia, it's Noel. I have something to tell you. Do you have a moment?'

Tricia sat down on the sofa. 'Yes? Did Naomi forget something? I thought I packed everything she brought.'

'It's not about Naomi,' Noel said, his voice serious. 'It's about something I heard from a lawyer at the conference I was at. Something about you and Sean's will.'

Tricia felt her blood run cold. Here it was. The sword that had been hanging over her since she left was finally coming down on her head. 'Oh,' she said. 'That.'

'Yes. Something about you pressuring Sean to sign something that gave his estate to you,' Noel said. 'Look, I haven't told Rose about this, nor anyone else. But it's very serious, as you must know.'

'Yes,' Tricia whispered. 'But, Noel, I didn't know what I was doing. I was so stressed and Sean was so ill and then... We needed to pay the medical bills so Sean gave me power of attorney.'

'You signed a document without having it witnessed,' Noel cut in. 'And then you tried to use it...'

'But nothing happened,' Tricia filled in. 'I didn't have to use it in the end.'

'I know, but the document is still there in the records. With your signature. That awful man Terence, the nephew, is trying to use it.'

'I know. It's been all over the local papers,' Tricia said, her voice breaking. 'I was so stupid. I knew it was wrong but...'

'It was both wrong and illegal,' Noel said. 'And then there is the issue of Sean changing his will in your favour.'

'Was that illegal too?' Tricia asked.

'No, it seemed to have been done according to the law,' Noel replied. 'But his nephew claims you manipulated your late husband when he wasn't quite himself.'

'That's not true,' Tricia snapped, feeling upset, mostly with herself. Was everyone going to find out what she'd done, before she had a chance to make amends? 'He's making it up. Sean changed his will just after we married a long time before he fell ill. The date is on the document and the witnesses...'

'Are all dead,' Noel said. 'But there is nothing illegal about that. It's the fiddling with the bank account that landed you in trouble. Do you have a solicitor?'

'No,' Tricia croaked, her throat dry with fear. 'Just the man dealing with the probate. I can't afford huge legal fees. So I thought I'd try and solve it myself somehow.'

'You can't,' Noel said. 'You need a solicitor, and you have one right here for free.'

'Who?'

'Me, of course,' Noel said. 'I'll see what I can do. Sean's nephew seems to want you to turn the farm over to him.'

'I know, and he's trying to scare me into it,' Tricia said. 'By threatening me.'

'Well, that's illegal, too, of course,' Noel said. 'Tricia, this is a huge mess but I'll do my best to find a way out. I won't tell anyone, not even Rose. I can't promise anything, but I will have a word with my colleagues up north and see if we can sort it out in some way. In the meantime, try not to worry.'

'That's easy for you to say.' Tricia heaved a huge sigh. What if everyone else found out this way too? 'But oh, Noel, you have no idea how relieved I am to have you on my side. I felt so alone with all this hanging over me.'

'Why didn't you ask me before? You must have known I'd be happy to help,' Noel said. 'I mean, I don't want to see my children's grandmother behind bars.'

Tricia tried to laugh. 'I know you're joking but that has seemed very real to me until now.'

'That was never a possibility,' Noel reassured her. 'Oh, my mobile is ringing and it's my colleague in Donegal. I'll call you back in a sec.' Noel hung up while Tricia sat there wringing her hands. She had been thinking about asking Noel for help, but then Rose might have heard about what trouble Tricia was in and that would have been hard to deal with. Of course Noel was not going to tell Rose, she realised now. He had to keep it confidential. How stupid she had been not to tell him. Then her phone rang again.

'Me again,' Noel said. 'It's going to take a little time to sort this out after all. So you have to be patient. It could mean you'll be found guilty of some kind of minor fraud. But I'll do my best to get you off the hook. That's all I can promise right now.'

'Thank you, Noel,' Tricia said.

They said goodbye and Tricia hung up with a feeling of dread. She had to tell Cillian before he found out from someone else. How would he react if he believed even for a moment that she had done something illegal just for money? Their little weekend trip was the only chance she had to tell him the truth. Her only chance to convince him she hadn't done anything wrong.

27

Cillian was outside in his campervan on Friday night just as darkness fell. Tricia was waiting in the front garden with her small bag and Paddy in a carrier for cats that she had bought that morning along with a bag of cat food. She was still stressed after her phone call with Noel, but she knew he was her only hope. What a relief it would be if it was finally over and she had Terence and his threats off her back. But she couldn't keep it from Cillian any longer, whatever happened.

Cillian climbed down from the van. 'All set?' he asked, peering into the cat carrier. 'Nice little cat. What's his name?'

'Paddy,' Tricia replied. 'Short for Paddington. The girls picked the name.'

'It suits him.' Cillian took Tricia's bag and the cat food. 'So off we go. If you're wondering why I'm so late, you'll soon find out the reason,' he said cryptically. They set off as soon as Tricia was in the passenger seat with Paddy on her lap.

'We seem to be going to Ventry,' Tricia said as they turned left and drove away from Dingle.

'We are,' Cillian said. 'But to the end of the bay just to look at the view.'

'What view?' Tricia asked, confused. 'There is no moon so we won't see much.'

'But the sky is clear and we have the stars,' Cillian replied. 'That's all I'm going to say until we're there. I would blindfold you but I don't think you'd agree to that. Just wait and then you'll see my surprise.'

Tricia studied his face in the dim light. He looked as if he was about to reveal something amazing and she decided to keep quiet until they had arrived to wherever they were going. And then, as they drove down the slope to the parking place that overlooked the little bay, she saw the surprise and it took her breath away.

'Oh,' was all she managed as she looked out the window at the still water that seemed to be illuminated from underneath with a bluish light that glimmered through the darkness. 'Plankton,' she said as they climbed out of the van and joined other people standing there silently gazing at this miraculous sight. She had never seen the plankton illumination – also called bioluminescence – but she had heard it was a beautiful sight. But it was more than beautiful, more than amazing, and she tried to find the words to describe it.

Cillian took Tricia's hand. 'It's like some kind of psychedelic experience. I've seen it before but it never gets tired.'

'Heavenly,' Tricia said as if to herself, forgetting all the tensions and misunderstandings between them as she looked at the ragged band of blue light and the reflection of the stars in the darker water beyond. 'Thank you for showing it to me,' she said and leaned against Cillian. 'I don't think I've ever seen anything so beautiful.'

He put his arm around her and drew her closer still. 'I thought it would be a nice start to our weekend.'

'The best start ever.' Tricia breathed in the soft salt-laden air and felt as if she was floating in the dark-blue night with the breeze caressing her cheeks. 'I could stay here all night.'

'We could if you want,' Cillian said. 'But I had other plans.'

She turned and tried to look at him in the dark. 'What plans were they?'

'That we'd drive to Dunquin and stay in a nice B&B. And then we'll continue on and climb Mount Brandon in the morning. It's a hike we never did even in the old days, I don't know why.'

'We thought it was too easy,' Tricia said. 'But now we're older and it might be a little too much for us.'

'It won't. That side of the mountain is not a hard climb. We can do it in a morning. What do you say?'

Tricia nodded. 'We should have a go. It will be our hike then and nothing to do with Fred.'

'That's what I was thinking but I didn't say it out loud,' Cillian said softly into the darkness. 'I thought you might be sad if we mentioned Fred.'

Tricia broke away from him. 'But we *should* talk about him,' she said. 'Because he's always with us. No longer standing between us but around us, smiling at us, happy that we're together at last. He's like a guardian angel to me, if that doesn't sound crazy.'

'Maybe he brought us together?' Cillian said with a smile in his voice. 'I see what you mean and it's a lovely thought. And maybe, just for this weekend, we could forget our arguments and secrets?'

Tricia nodded. 'Yes. Let's have a holiday from all that.'

'Good.' He shivered suddenly. 'It's getting a little chilly and I'm tired. Let's go on to the B&B in Dunquin and get a night's sleep. Separate rooms, of course, just so you know how gentlemanly I am these days.'

Tricia laughed. 'Well, you know what? I'm not as ladylike as I used to be. So if you had booked a room with a double bed I wouldn't have been upset. But...' She stifled a yawn. 'Tonight, I think I'd be too wrecked to do anything but sleep. So take me to the B&B so I can fall into bed. Do they allow cats? Paddy likes his carrier so he'll be happy to stay there for the night.'

'I'm sure that's not a problem,' Cillian said. 'Bridget, the woman who runs the B&B, is an old friend. Very relaxed about stuff like that.'

'Brilliant.' Tricia walked to the van and climbed in. Once settled in the passenger seat with Cillian beside her, she took a last look at the shimmery blue water. 'I had never seen this before. So it's the very first of the memories we have made together.'

'Many more to come.' Cillian started the van and they slowly made their way up the slope to the main road which would take them to Dunquin.

As they made their way to their destination, Tricia stared into the darkness. The image of the blue light under the water was still so vivid and she couldn't believe how lucky she had been to see it. *How well he knows me*, she thought. *Not just the old me but the new me as well. Maybe we weren't ready to be together all those years ago. We needed to grow and mature and deal with our pain. Will we discover that who we are now is what we have been waiting for? But when I tell him about the trouble I'm in will he think badly of me?*

She said a silent prayer that he would understand.

28

The Saturday morning proved to be as enchanting as the night before. Tricia found Cillian in the breakfast room in the B&B tucking into a full Irish breakfast of bacon, eggs, black pudding, sausages and grilled tomatoes. 'Just an occasional sin,' he said, looking slightly guilty. 'My diet is usually very healthy except for the odd slip-up now and then. I knew Bridget does a great fry-up, so I couldn't say no.'

'Of course not,' Tricia agreed while she helped herself to yoghurt, fruit, a slice of brown bread and a mug of tea. 'I'm afraid that's not my kind of treat and I'm no good at cooking it either. So if we're to spend a lot of time together, you'll have to say goodbye to the full Irish breakfast, except for when we stay in hotels.'

'You'll probably save me from an early grave,' Cillian said. 'I bet your choice of breakfast is the secret to your youthful looks.'

'You're not going to get around me with flattery,' Tricia remarked, trying her best to look serious.

'So how am I going to get around you, then?' Cillian asked.

'You don't have to.' Tricia opened the pot of yoghurt. 'Just be yourself and stop trying. I like you just the way you are, you know.'

Cillian smiled and put his hand on hers for a moment. 'Thank you for saying that. And also for coming with me this weekend when I knew you were in the middle of doing up your house and getting close to your grandchildren. Not to mention Vi's wedding and everything.'

'It was good to take a break,' Tricia said. 'I'm not that busy right now. Vi wants to do her own wedding with Jack so I don't have much to do about that except to help choose the flowers and get my old wedding dress altered to fit her. That is if she's going to wear that and not Sylvia's dress.'

'What does Vi want?' Cillian asked.

'She wants to wear my old thing that looks like a meringue with whipped cream.'

Cillian waggled his eyebrows. 'But you would love her to wear it.'

Tricia sighed. 'Yes, I would, to be honest. I thought I looked wonderful in it at the time.'

'You did. I was there, remember? Fred's eyes welled up when he saw you coming down the aisle on your father's arm. I was a little tearful myself too. You were a vision.'

'That's so sweet of you to say. Vi would look beautiful in anything so even the meringue dress is okay for her to wear. She has her heart set on it and I don't want to disappoint her.'

'Of course you don't.' Cillian finished his breakfast and drained his cup of coffee. 'If you're ready, we'll do that hike. And then we continue our voyage of discovery.'

'Fabulous.' Tricia swallowed the last piece of bread and got up. 'It's a nice day for a hike too. Not too warm and a nice cool breeze.'

'The views from the top of Mount Brandon are spectacular.'

The drive to the start of the hike didn't take long and they were soon walking up the steep slopes, both of them a little out of breath which forced them to stop and rest here and there. But then, finally, they were at the top and looking out over Brandon Bay and the islands beyond. They stood silently, hand in hand, and admired the view, smiling at each other. A man who had just arrived offered to take a photo of them and Tricia gave him her phone. Cillian put his arm around Tricia's waist and they both smiled as the stranger took several shots and then handed back the phone.

'You looked so cute standing there together,' he said. 'Are you on your honeymoon?'

'In a way,' Cillian said. 'We're on a kind of second-chance voyage, getting to know each other.'

'You look very much in tune already,' the man said.

They smiled at each other and then thanked the man before they walked back down the slopes to the car where Paddy the kitten greeted them with a loud 'miaow' as if he was wondering where they had been. Then they drove off, Paddy on Tricia's lap and Cillian humming a happy tune.

They continued back to Dingle and then took the road to Tralee and on to Listowel and Limerick, where they stopped for a quick lunch. Then off they went again, through the Burren and then through Galway to Clifden, where they could either stay in a hotel or in the campervan that they had parked in a designated spot at a camping site. They had also enjoyed a swim at the little beach near the camping site and then tried to decide where to stay.

'It's up to you,' Cillian said. 'I'm happy sleeping here but if you'd rather—'

'No, I wouldn't.' Tricia leaned over and kissed his cheek. 'But first I need to speak to you about something.'

Cillian looked intrigued. 'What is it?'

'Something I need to tell you. But maybe we could have dinner somewhere nice and talk?' She smiled reassuringly at him as she felt a surge of love for the man she had known nearly all her adult life. It felt like the right moment to tell him everything. She was sure he'd understand her once he knew what she was running from. He just had to.

'Sounds good,' Cillian replied just as Tricia's phone rang in the van. She rushed in and groped around in her large handbag and pulled it out and saw it was Vi calling.

'Vi? Has anything happened?'

'Yes,' Vi said and sobbed. 'It's Granny. She's in hospital in Tralee. Her heart...' Then there was more sobbing. 'She seemed to have had a heart attack or something. Can you come?'

'Oh, no,' Tricia said, horrified. 'How terrible. Is anyone with her?'

'Yes,' Vi replied. 'Lily went with her in the ambulance. Rose is on her way there now, so we should go too. Jack's on his way back so I'm waiting for him. But you could drive over and be there very soon, can't you?'

'But... but I'm not at home. I'm in Clifden.'

'What? In Clifden?' Vi exclaimed. 'What are you doing there?'

'I'm on a little bit of a break with Cillian. We're... Oh, never mind. I'll come as soon as I can.'

'Okay,' Vi said. 'See you there. I'll tell Lily to call you as soon as there's any news.'

'Thanks. I'll leave straight away.' Tricia hung up and then her knees wobbled and she had to sit down on the seat at the back of the van. She couldn't believe it. Sylvia having a heart attack. But she had seemed in such good form last Sunday. Tricia had always thought Sylvia was invincible, always in the middle of the action, always bright and present and on hand whenever she was needed.

Cillian walked back from the driver's seat. 'Trish? What's wrong? Who was that on the phone?'

'Vi,' Tricia said, still in shock. 'Sylvia has had a heart attack and she's in hospital in Tralee. We have to go back straight away. Oh, I can't believe it. Sylvia, the tower of strength, in hospital? It doesn't seem possible.'

'Well, you have to take her age into account.' Cillian sat down beside Tricia and took her hand. 'I know you're very fond of her despite your differences. She is – was – your mother-in-law, so you must be quite close really.'

'Of course we're close,' Tricia said irritably. 'You don't have to tell me that. Sylvia has always been important to me. Yes, we've had arguments and I always felt I wasn't really good enough for Fred in her eyes. But she was kind to me when we were first married and helped me through that tough time when I lost both my parents, one after the other. Liam was a darling, too, so they became like substitute parents when I was pregnant with the girls. I don't know how I would have managed without them.'

'And then Sylvia helped you with the girls after you lost Fred,' Cillian said quietly.

Tricia nodded as tears pricked her eyes. 'That's true. I think the girls were a huge comfort to her when she had lost her only child. Lily and Rose, anyway. I kept Vi close to me as she was so small then. Sylvia was there for me despite her own terrible grief.' She wrung her hands. 'I have to go and see her as soon as possible, if only to tell her how much she means to us all.'

Cillian got up. 'We'll go as soon as you're ready.'

'But it's late and you're tired,' Tricia argued. 'I can take a train or bus to Tralee.'

'Sylvia is important to me too,' Cillian said in a tone that didn't allow argument. 'We're going together and that's it. Now get dressed and we'll go.'

Tricia quickly changed out of her swimsuit and then, their romantic evening shattered, they began the journey back to Kerry and the hospital in Tralee.

Tricia hugged Paddy and stared ahead at the road illuminated by the headlights, thinking about poor Sylvia and what she might be going through. *Darling Sylvia*, she thought as if in a prayer, *please don't leave us, we wouldn't be able to cope without you. Hang in there and I'll be by your side very soon.*

Cillian glanced at Tricia. 'Sylvia is a tough old boot, you know. She'll get through this and then she'll be back home in no time annoying the pants off us as usual.'

'Do you think so?' Tricia asked. 'Or is it just wishful thinking?'

'I'm absolutely sure of it,' Cillian stated.

'I hope you're right. I wish we'd hear from Lily soon.'

They were approaching Limerick when Tricia's phone rang. Her heart raced as she picked it up. 'Lily?' she said.

'It's not Lily, it's Ilse,' the voice said. 'I know you're gone on a trip up the coast with Cillian but you must have heard the news by now. About Sylvia, I mean.'

'Yes,' Tricia said. 'Sorry, Ilse, I have to hang up. I'm expecting Lily to call any minute.'

'I know,' Ilse said, her voice trembling. 'I just wanted to say that it wasn't my fault. I just happened to mention the wedding dress and then everyone started to shout and then Sylvia... Oh, it was awful. That's all I wanted to say. I'll hang up now but we can talk later. Bye.'

'How weird,' Tricia said when Ilse had hung up.

'What did she say?' Cillian asked.

'Something about the wedding dress and a row and then Sylvia collapsing or something. What on earth was going on?'

They were interrupted by the phone ringing again. This time it was Lily.

'Mum? I just spoke to the doctor.'

'What did he say?' Tricia gripped the phone so hard her hand hurt while she waited for a reply.

29

'It's not a heart attack,' Lily replied. 'It was a panic attack. Quite frightening but not dangerous.'

'Ooooh.' Tricia felt weak with relief. 'Thank God in heaven.' She turned to Cillian, who had pulled up beside the road. 'It was just a panic attack. Sylvia's okay.'

'Phew,' Cillian said and relaxed some of the tension in his hands as they gripped the steering wheel.

Tricia turned on the speaker. 'How is Sylvia now? She must have been very frightened by that. I've heard panic attacks feel like a real heart attack, so it can be traumatising.'

'They gave her a sedative and she's asleep,' Lily said. 'They're keeping her in for a day or two to do some tests. Could be that her blood pressure is up and given her age, they want to make sure she's okay before they release her.'

'Very sensible,' Cillian said.

Lily let out a giggle. 'You should have seen Granny when she had recovered and the doctor started talking about her age. It appears she has been telling fibs for years. She's actually a whole two years older than she's let on and she was so annoyed when they told us. She said it was confidential and how dare they give such personal details to all and sundry like that. Then, when they said she had to stay in, she started getting out of bed and demanded they give her back her clothes and asked for a taxi to take her home.'

'Typical of Sylvia,' Tricia remarked, still wobbly after the scare.

'I know,' Lily said, still laughing. 'But they told her they wouldn't be responsible for what happened if she left. So she got back into bed and asked for a cup of tea. Earl Grey, of course, which they didn't have. Then they gave her a sedative and she fell asleep. So now we're going home but it would be great if you could go and see her tomorrow morning. We're all a little tired after all the drama, to be honest.'

'Of course you are.' Tricia thought for a moment. 'What brought on the panic attack? Ilse called and babbled something about a row to do with Vi's wedding dress. She hung up before I could ask her to explain.'

'Yeah, well...' Lily paused. 'I wasn't going to tell you right now but you should know what it was about. We were all in the kitchen having just finished dinner. Noel and Dominic left to take the kids home as it was getting late. Ilse was there, too, and she started talking about Vi's wedding and how lovely it was that she was going to wear Granny's wedding dress. But Vi said she wasn't and she was having your dress altered so she could wear that. And then Granny got upset and Ilse suggested Vi was being unkind to her grandmother. Rose agreed and said Vi should consider Granny's feelings. I said Rose should consider Vi's feelings and that it was her big day. Then I'm afraid we had a bit of a row and Vi burst into tears and Ilse kept going on and then...' Lily paused and emitted a sob.

'What happened then?' Tricia asked, feeling a dart of guilt. She had meant to take up the whole issue about the wedding dress with Sylvia but had been distracted by her outing with Cillian, and also the whole mess about the will. And now, because it hadn't been resolved, there had been this argument that landed Sylvia in hospital.

'Well, there was a bit of shouting,' Lily continued, 'and then Granny suddenly clutched her chest and said she couldn't breathe and she was in pain. She looked as if she was having a heart attack so we called an ambulance. It arrived very quickly, thank goodness. The ambulance men were amazing and put an oxygen mask on Granny and carried her out on a stretcher. Oh, Mum, I thought we were going to lose her. We all did.' Lily stopped and blew her nose.

'But you didn't,' Cillian cut in. 'It must have been very frightening but now all is well.' He glanced at Tricia. 'So we can continue our little outing and we'll see you soon.'

'I'll go and see Sylvia tomorrow,' Tricia promised her daughter. 'Bye for now and try to have good rest.'

Lily said goodbye and then Cillian started the van. But instead of driving towards Kerry, he turned the van around and began to drive back the way they had come.

'What are you doing?' Tricia asked. 'You have to drive me home so I can go and see Sylvia tomorrow. I promised Lily I would.'

'Sylvia is fine,' Cillian said. 'All is well and she's resting. Tomorrow is Sunday and she will have to stay in the hospital until at least Monday, I'd say. You can see her then.'

'But...' Tricia protested. 'She'll be so upset.'

Cillian pulled in at the roadside and stared at Tricia in the dim light. 'Tricia, this was supposed to be our special weekend. A day or two to get to know each other and to sort out where we're going. Then you got that phone call and we thought Sylvia was in real trouble. But now we've found out it was a false alarm and we can all relax. Sylvia is being taken care of by the excellent nursing staff in the hospital in Tralee. I'm sure she'd be happy to see you but she doesn't actually *need* you to be there. It's no longer a case of life or death.'

'I know, but I think she needs my support all the same,' Tricia argued. 'I feel it's partly my fault that they had that row that upset Sylvia so. I want to make sure she's okay. We can do this next weekend or any time after your press conference and I have heard from Noel about...' She stopped.

'From Noel about – what?' Cillian looked confused.

'Oh, nothing much. Just something to do with a legal problem. I can't discuss this right now.'

Cillian looked at her for a moment in the light of the dashboard without speaking. 'I have a feeling you're hiding something from me,' he said.

Tricia bristled. 'Oh, yeah, and you're not hiding anything? You told me some story about your job in Dingle that I now feel wasn't really true. You asked me to keep it quiet, which I did. But now I suspect it was all a ruse to lead me down a false trail. The real story is something different altogether, isn't it?'

Cillian gripped the steering wheel, staring straight ahead. 'We're both hiding secrets,' he mumbled. 'If we can't trust each other, then what are we doing here together?'

'I'm beginning to wonder that too,' Tricia countered with a horrible feeling deep down that their so-called romance was doomed to fail. She gritted her teeth and tried her best not to burst into tears. 'I think we should take a break from all this.'

'Yes, maybe we should,' Cillian said, looking as miserable as she felt. 'Do you want me to take you back to Magnolia? It's only about an hour and a half away.'

'If you're not too tired, yes,' Tricia said quietly. 'I want to go and see Sylvia as soon as I can tomorrow morning.'

'Well, I can see that I'm not at the top of your list of priorities, which tells me where we're heading.' Cillian started up the van and they rumbled down the road south.

Tricia felt the atmosphere become close to hostile. Gone was the resolve to tell him about her legal problem. He would probably think the worse of her if he knew. She stroked Paddy absent-mindedly, feeling the return journey was taking days instead of just a little over an hour. When the van finally pulled up outside the cottage, she gathered up her things and climbed down, relieved to be home at last.

Cillian stepped down from the driver's seat while Tricia fumbled with her keys at the front door. 'Will you be okay?' he asked.

'Of course I will. Don't worry.'

He took her hand when she had opened the door. 'I'm sorry it turned out like this. But it doesn't mean the end, does it?' He pushed his hand through his hair. 'We rushed things a bit maybe and I need time to think.'

'Yes, me too.' She hesitated. She wanted to tell him everything but it would be too rushed and he seemed in a bad mood. 'I was going to tell you something important, but it feels too much to talk about right now. I will tell you everything when I can.'

'It seems very serious,' he said, looking at her with concern.

'Yes it is,' Tricia admitted. 'But please believe me when I say that it has nothing to do with you and that I just can't talk about it right now.'

Cillian let out a resigned sigh. 'Okay. I understand where you're coming from. And I also see that there is, as you said, a lack of trust between us. You didn't trust me with your secret and I didn't trust you with mine. But in my case it was more to protect you. I didn't want to burden you with a secret that might result in a lot of problems and accusations.'

'I see.' Tricia suddenly felt a wave of fatigue wash over her. 'I know what you're saying about trust. But right now, I'm so tired I think I'm going to go to collapse right here on my own doorstep. I need to sleep and so do you. Park the van here and stay the night. You're just as tired as I am.'

Cillian shot Tricia a pale smile. 'Thanks, but I'll trundle

over to Orla's. She'll be over the moon to see the van outside her house again.'

Tricia returned his smile and briefly touched his cheek. 'Okay. Sleep well. We both have stuff to deal with. But I did have a lovely time before that phone call about Sylvia. I'm sorry we couldn't work it out. Goodnight, Cillian.' Then she opened the door and went inside, closing it gently behind her while her heart broke into a thousand pieces.

She had failed to tell Cillian the truth, but she didn't want to keep anything else from Sylvia. She'd been too scared to confront her about Vi's wedding dress, and it had resulted in a horrible altercation that had landed Sylvia in hospital. Tricia knew she should tell Sylvia about her legal problem and all the horrible rumours that had been spread. But was this the right time to reveal all? And when she did, would Sylvia be so shocked she would ask Tricia to leave Magnolia and her lovely cottage?

30

Sylvia was sitting up in bed reading the Sunday papers when Tricia arrived at the hospital the following morning. Her grey hair was immaculate and she was dressed in a frilly white night-gown under a pink cashmere cardigan. She had, somehow, managed to get a private room and it had taken Tricia half an hour and a lot of searching before she found the right door.

Sylvia looked up and smiled as Tricia approached her bed. 'Tricia! How kind of you to come and see me. I thought you had gone for a bit of a drive with Cillian.'

Tricia pulled up a chair and sat down. 'I had but then I got a call to say that you had been taken ill. So we turned around and came straight back. Thank goodness it wasn't anything serious. You look as fit as a fiddle, I'm happy to say.'

'And so I am,' Sylvia said, putting down the newspaper. 'A lot of fuss about nothing. I shouldn't be here taking up a bed that's needed for someone who is really ill. But they insisted I stay in so they can stick needles in me and tell me I'm old and frail.'

'And you got your own room,' Tricia remarked. 'How on earth did you manage that?'

'It must have been some kind of storage room at some stage,' Sylvia replied. 'It's the smallest room I've ever slept in. But they wheeled me in here last night saying I was talking too much and asking too many questions.' She shrugged. 'That's their story. I was just chatting to the other patients in my ward, asking them about their families and where they were from. I didn't want to share a room with total strangers. If I knew a bit about their background, I'd feel I knew them better.'

'And did you also give them advice on health matters?' Tricia asked, trying her best not to giggle.

'Weeell,' Sylvia said, looking only slightly guilty. 'I might have said that if they had had a healthier lifestyle they might not be in hospital. Especially the woman in the bed next to me who was larger than she should be, if you see what I mean.'

'I do,' Tricia said. 'But what about you? How are you feeling? You gave us all a fright yesterday evening. The girls were so upset. It must have even worse for you.'

'It wasn't a pleasant experience, I have to admit. It felt like a real heart attack, so thank the Lord above that it wasn't. I'm fine now and we should forget all about it.' Sylvia sipped tea from a cup on the bedside table. 'I'll be out of here as soon as I can see the doctor tomorrow morning. She's going to give me a prescription for my blood pressure as that's a little high. Nice woman, if a little overbearing. But those career women often are.'

'I know what you mean, as I used to be one,' Tricia quipped.

'You were never overbearing, just very driven,' Sylvia said. 'But you're calmer now.' She paused and sat up straighter, studying Tricia. 'Why didn't you carry on with your weekend trip once you knew I was all right?'

'We turned around when we heard the news.'

'But then you must have heard it was a false alarm,' Sylvia said, looking confused. 'Why didn't you turn back to continue your nice weekend?'

'Because...' Tricia started. 'Sylvia, have you known all this time that Cillian and I have been seeing each other? And that we were getting to be more than friends?'

'Yes.' Sylvia replied. 'But please don't worry about my feelings about the two of you. I was pleased when I realised what was going on between you and Cillian. And I think Fred would want you to be happy. I see the way you look at each other and it makes me happy too in a strange way. It seems right for you to be together. I've always been very fond of Cillian.'

'Oh, that's lovely to hear,' Tricia said. 'I thought you might think I didn't have time for my grandchildren if I started dating. And then I was worried you would be upset about Cillian and me.'

'Tricia,' Sylvia said in a stern voice, 'I think you have taken your role as mother and grandmother and daughter-in-law far too seriously. You don't have to be at the beck and call of every single member of the family all the time. You have to have your own life too. And when true love comes your way, you have to grab it and hold on to it for dear life.'

'I thought I was too old,' Tricia mumbled. 'I have been so lucky to have been with two wonderful men. Shouldn't that be enough for any woman?'

'Says who?' Sylvia asked.

'I don't know. Someone up there in heaven or something.'

'Rubbish,' Sylvia snorted.

Tricia looked up again and met Sylvia's critical gaze. 'I do care about you, despite our differences. And I just didn't want to upset you.'

'It was guilt that made you push Cillian away?' Sylvia asked.

'Not quite.' Tricia tried to explain how she felt even though it was complicated. 'There's just been so much going on...'

'Like what?' Sylvia asked, sitting up in bed. 'I feel you have something on your mind that you need to get off your chest.' She laughed. 'Well, that sounded a little complicated. But go on, tell me what's troubling you. I can tell it's something serious by the haunted look in your eyes.'

'It is,' Tricia said. Then she took a deep breath and started to tell Sylvia the whole story, not leaving out a single detail, even her own actions. 'So there you are,' she ended. 'That's the dark secret I've been keeping from you. I did something stupid and borderline illegal so I could get Sean the best care there was.'

Sylvia's eyes softened and she reached out and patted Tricia's hand. 'I'm glad you told me. How terrible it must have been for you. I can understand that you would have tried everything to make sure your Sean had the best care during his last days, even something slightly illegal.'

'Oh, that's wonderful to hear,' Tricia said, feeling a huge sense of relief. 'I thought you might be shocked by what I did.'

'It would take a lot more to shock me,' Sylvia said. 'And now that Noel is dealing with all this, I'm sure he'll have a solution. Don't worry about gossips; I'll make sure it won't get around. You're family and nobody would dare talk about you behind your back.'

'Thank you,' Tricia said, wondering how Sylvia would be able to stop the tongues wagging. But she was such a formidable woman who could do anything.

'I don't think anything can be worse than watching someone you love suffer,' Sylvia said.

'No, that's true,' Tricia said.

'All will be well,' Sylvia soothed.

'I hope so,' Tricia said. 'But there is another thing that's puzzling me. That woman, Ilse, seems to have crept into your heart. She seems to want to be in on every family occasion, including Vi's wedding.'

'Yes, she is a little overwhelming, all right,' Sylvia agreed. 'And I'm very cross with her for starting that row. I have no idea why she tried to get involved. In any case, Vi can get married in a swimsuit for all I care. The only thing that matters is her happiness. Ilse didn't realise that and tried to earn Brownie points with me by butting in. *Nul points* to her, is all I can say,' Sylvia added with a cheeky smile.

'She might be trying to get around you for some reason,' Tricia suggested. 'I don't exactly trust her.'

'She can't get around me, don't worry,' Sylvia reassured Tricia. 'But about what you just told me...'

'Yes?'

'You've been keeping all of it from Cillian, too, I imagine?' Sylvia asked. 'All this stuff about Terence?'

Tricia nodded. 'I was going to tell him but then I got the phone call about you and...'

'I'm sure he'll understand,' Sylvia said.

Sylvia was right, Tricia thought. 'He's been hiding things from me too,' she said. 'I have found it hard that he hasn't been honest with me about his work.'

'Perhaps you need to give him a bit of grace?' Sylvia replied. 'You've been trying to protect us; maybe he had a good reason for not telling you his story.'

Tricia nodded, and looked out of the window, deep in thought. Everything Sylvia was saying made complete sense. Had she been too harsh on Cillian? 'Maybe you're right.'

'Of course I am,' Sylvia stated, picking up her newspaper. 'Now, I just want to read the papers and have good rest before I face the doctor tomorrow. And you, young lady, will go and find Cillian and try to get him to cool down. I'm sure he'll be very happy to hear what you have to tell him.'

'What's that?' Tricia asked.

Sylvia looked at Tricia over the news section of *The Sunday Times*. 'I think you know. You will have to eat humble pie and tell him you have been really silly and then tell him you love him. Now off you go and try to be just a little bit selfish. Arnaud is coming to see me in a little while.'

'Where was he last night?' Tricia asked.

Sylvia lowered the newspaper. 'He was in Dublin when all this happened, thank goodness. I wouldn't have liked him to see me the way I was.'

'I'm sure you weren't that bad,' Tricia protested.

'Yes, I was. Now, you must get Cillian back, but don't rush to him right this minute. Let him miss you and wonder where you are and what you're thinking.'

'I suppose so,' Tricia said, knowing that she couldn't talk to him until that other matter had been resolved, the one Noel was helping her with. Now that Sylvia knew, it might be better to wait a little.

'Take it easy and don't rush things. Now off you go and I'll see you soon.' Sylvia picked up the paper and started to read it.

Tricia, knowing she had been dismissed, said goodbye and left the room, going over the conversation. She knew Sylvia was right; she had been overthinking everything. She had pushed Cillian away. She wouldn't go and see him straight away even though she was burning to tell him everything about her problems with the will. After that, she would be ready to commit to him if he still wanted her. But she would wait until after the press conference. Then his project would be over and he would have time and peace to think about their relationship. If they were to have one.

31

The following week was eventful to say the least. The press conference on Tuesday was broadcast on the evening news and everyone was amazed at what was revealed, most of all Tricia. She listened with bated breath to the story Cillian and Ilse told the press and realised that it was far from what Cillian had hinted at. She had thought he was digging out a Viking grave full of treasure and that nobody must know or the grave would be plundered. The real story was much more amazing and as she listened, all the dots connected and she saw the whole picture. The diving in the bay, Ilse and her team, the rib and the boat and everything else suddenly made sense. And after her chat with Sylvia, Tricia finally felt at peace with Cillian's need to keep it secret.

The find of an ancient ship from the Spanish Armada was big news indeed. The ship had been loaded with gold and silver and some jewellery worn by the officers of the day. The fact that around twenty-five ships of the Armada had sunk all the way up the Wild Atlantic Way was something she had heard about from time to time but thought of as fantasies and myths. The ship in question was the best preserved of the ones that had been found around the west coast of Ireland. Cillian and Ilse replied to all the questions from the reporters in detail and it was featured in all the newspapers the following day. But Tricia still hadn't heard from him. She assumed he was overwhelmed with all the attention he was getting.

The most exciting event of the week, however, was when Rose arrived at the cottage the morning after the press conference with a letter she had found in the storeroom at the manor. It was a letter to Mary O'Grady from her cousin in Tralee dated September 1880, telling her that Kieran had arrived safely and would start school the following week. He would visit his family at Magnolia Manor at Christmas time and Mary was not to worry about him as he would be well looked after.

'Oh,' Tricia exclaimed when she had read the letter sitting on the sofa in the living room. 'This proves without a doubt he was the lad who grew up to become the famous painter.'

'It certainly does.' Rose hugged her mother. 'Isn't this exciting?'

'It's about to become even more exciting.' Tricia told Rose about the painting she had found and that the expert from the National Gallery would come and take a look at it. 'I have to tell Sylvia,' she said.

'Oh, yes,' Rose agreed. 'She'll be so excited.'

'It's up to her to decide what to do with the painting,' Tricia stated. 'It belongs to Magnolia, after all.'

'It does,' Rose agreed. 'I'm sure Granny will want it to hang in her sitting room.'

'We'll have to wait until Friday and then we'll see,' Tricia said. 'If it's the real thing, there will be complications with insurance and so on.'

'I didn't think of that,' Rose said. 'But we'll find a way. Granny always does.'

'She does indeed.' Tricia nodded, knowing that it was true. Sylvia always found a solution to most problems and managed to have a life as well as looking after everyone at the same time. *I used to resent that*, she thought. *But now I admire it and want to be like her. How strange...*

'She said you and Cillian are together,' Rose said, looking at Tricia with an odd expression. 'Is that true?'

'I hope so.' Tricia felt her face turn pink. 'We were but then there was a misunderstanding between us and he left looking very annoyed. I'm hoping to patch things up between us and then... well, I hope we'll start dating. You don't mind?'

'Of course not,' Rose exclaimed. 'I'll be happy for you. We all like Cillian very much, you know. We were worried you'd be lonely here in the cottage all by yourself. Now you have that little cat and then hopefully Cillian to keep you company.'

'In that order?' Tricia laughed. 'I suppose Paddy will be here all the time, but Cillian might not. He's a free spirit and I'd hate to tie him down. He'll be off on jobs all over the country. I'll join him sometimes and he'll be here when he can. I think that's the best way for us, to be honest. We'll never get tired of each other.'

'Great idea,' Rose agreed. 'Everyone needs a little "me" time occasionally. Just look at Granny and Arnaud. They have this agreement never to put in on each other. Seems to work beautifully.'

'She's a very clever woman,' Tricia said warmly. 'I admire her enormously. She's a real powerhouse.'

'You admire her?' Rose stared at her mother. 'Really? The two of you used to be on opposite sides of every argument. What changed your mind?'

'A bit of a wake-up call and a few honest words from Sylvia.' Tricia smiled. 'I'm not saying we'll always be bosom pals, but there is a new respect between us. We know where we stand, so to speak.'

'That sounds good,' Rose said. 'So when are you going to talk to Cillian?'

'Tomorrow morning, I hope,' Tricia replied, feeling nervous just thinking about it. She had left him a voicemail message. 'Keep your fingers crossed that he'll forgive me.'

'I'm sure he will,' Rose declared. 'Sure he's mad about you. Everyone knows it.'

Tricia sighed. 'I hope you're right.' *And I hope he'll understand about the trouble I got myself into,* she thought.

Later that day, when Tricia was tidying up after lunch, Noel knocked on the door to the cottage. 'I thought I'd come and tell you in person,' he said, his pale blue eyes sparkling.

'Tell me what?' Tricia sked, her stomach in knots. 'Good news or bad?'

'Good news,' he said, hovering on the doorstep. 'Are you going to let me in?'

'Of course.' Tricia laughed and opened the door wider. 'Come in. How about a cup of coffee? I was just about to make some.'

'Yes, that would be nice.' Noel followed Tricia inside.

'In here.' She led the way into the kitchen and Noel sat down while she busied herself with the coffee machine. When she had filled two mugs, she put them on the table and sat down, looking expectantly at him. 'So,' she said. 'Tell me the good news, then.'

'Well,' Noel said when he had taken a sip, 'I have had a long conversation with both solicitors – the one handling Sean's estate, as he also happened to be one of the executors of the will.'

'I know. I've been working with him on the probate,' Tricia said.

'Of course. But I also spoke to the other one representing Terence.'

Tricia nodded. 'I see. Go on.'

'Well, it appears you did nothing wrong at all. Except maybe being a bit hasty when you cobbled together that document. It wasn't valid as proof of power of attorney.'

Tricia sighed. 'I had all those horrendous medical bills to pay. I just wanted Sean to have the best care during his final days.'

'Of course you did. But the speed of it is what made Terence so upset, and suspicious.'

'Yes,' Tricia admitted. 'I have been kicking myself for that ever since. But I was so stressed and he was so ill and needed all the help he could get.' Tears welled up in her eyes as she remembered those heartbreaking months when she had fought so hard to try to save him. But nothing could and he had died despite her efforts. 'It was all for nothing, anyway,' she mumbled and reached for a piece of kitchen paper to dry her eyes.

'It must have been such a tragic time for you,' Noel said quietly.

Tricia nodded and tried to compose herself. 'Yes it was. Horrendous. But it's over now and here you are trying to help me. I've been worried sick for months. Please give me that piece of good news you said you had.'

Noel nodded. 'Okay. Well, the other executor looked into Sean's bank account and then discovered that you hadn't touched any of Sean's money, only used everything in your joint account. The one you and he shared.'

'That's right. There was enough there in the end. I had forgotten the code anyway so I couldn't log in to his own account and he was too weak to remember it himself.'

'So that was quite okay, actually,' Noel said. 'Your joint account was yours when Sean passed away. So...'

'So I didn't do anything wrong, then?' Tricia asked, feeling a dart of hope. 'Terence has nothing on me at all?'

'Not a thing. In fact, you could report him for blackmail and slander after what he's been telling the local newspapers.'

'I could?' Tricia brightened, but she knew Terence had only done this out of sadness. Grief did terrible things to people, she knew that, of course. Tricia met Noel's earnest blue eyes and felt a surge of affection for this sweet man who had made Rose so happy. He was doing his best to help her. When she thought of Terence, she realised that revenge wasn't in her nature. 'I don't think I will. But thank you,' she whispered, taking his hand.

'No need,' Noel said. 'I didn't do much. Just a few phone calls and emails here and there. You can relax now and go forward.'

'Oh, I will,' Tricia said. 'But first I have to talk to someone who might not feel I was that innocent in all of this.'

'Oh, I'm sure whoever you mean will understand that you were all alone and trying to cope during a terrible time in your life.'

'I hope he will,' Tricia said, feeling less than confident. Cillian might not understand why she had tried to fake a power of attorney to get access to her late husband's money. There were so many secrets and misunderstandings to sort out before they could regain the trust between them. It would all be decided when they met tomorrow and she told him everything.

32

All was quiet outside Orla O'Malley's house when Tricia arrived in her car just before lunchtime the following day. The campervan was parked just outside the front garden, looking equally deserted, except for a bike leaning against the side. Tricia saw a curtain move in the little side window. He had to be there. Her heart beating, she got out of the car and went to the side door and knocked. There was a moment's silence before the door slowly opened and Cillian peered out. 'It's you,' he said.

'Yes.' Tricia looked at him for a moment, trying to gauge his mood. But the hooded hazel eyes were bland and his mouth unsmiling, which unnerved her. She knew she would have a hard job convincing him that she meant what she said and that from now on, she would take a step back from her family in his favour. 'I went to see Sylvia last Sunday,' she started. 'And she gave me a roasting.'

'About what?'

'Can I come in?' Tricia said. 'I can't tell you standing here outside your campervan.'

He opened the door wider and stepped aside. 'Yes, of

course. Please come in. I was making a cup of coffee. Would you like some?'

'Yes, please.' Tricia shivered slightly as she brushed past him into the van. Inside, there was a lovely smell of coffee and newly baked cinnamon buns that sat on a plate on the table by the window. There were also bits of paper and what looked like a chart on the table.

'Please sit down and I'll make more coffee,' Cillian said. 'I have this fancy espresso maker I bought just last week. I love a good cup of coffee as you know.'

'I do.' Tricia shot him a nervous smile, feeling somehow she was on trial. What she said next would decide their future – if they had one.

There was suddenly a noise from the back of the camper-van. Tricia gave a start as Ilse appeared through the bathroom door. 'Hi, Tricia,' Ilse said, looking as if she was just as surprised as Tricia but not in a pleasant way. 'What are you doing here? We're working, as you can see by what's on the table. Winding up the project.'

'Oh,' Tricia said, still hovering by the door. 'I didn't know you were still working on it. I thought Cillian was here on his own. Do you want me to leave? I wouldn't want to disturb you.'

Cillian shot Ilse a glance. 'We had nearly finished. And Ilse was just about to leave, weren't you?'

'Not really, but...' Ilse stopped. 'I have feeling something is going on, so I'll leave now.'

'Tricia and I have to talk about something important,' Cillian said. 'But first we should ask how Sylvia is.'

'Yes, of course,' Ilse said, looking only slightly guilty. 'How is she?'

'She's fully recovered and back home safe and sound,' Tricia replied. 'And you know what? She doesn't give a hoot about Violet's wedding dress. She said she never really did. Don't know why you brought it up.'

'I didn't really,' Ilse protested. 'It just came up in conversation.'

'Well, it wasn't really the best thing to bring up, was it?' Cillian remarked with a touch of irony.

'I suppose not.' Ilse looked a little sheepish. 'Silly of me to mention it.'

'I'm sure you didn't mean any harm,' Tricia soothed, feeling sorry for Ilse. 'Sometimes we say things without thinking.'

'Yes, that's true,' Ilse said. 'It was an accident.'

'Could happen to a bishop, as my mother used to say,' Cillian quipped.

Ilse laughed, looking relieved. She picked up a bicycle helmet from one of the seats. 'I'll be off now. Give me a call if you need to discuss anything further, Cillian.'

Cillian nodded. 'Grand. See you, Ilse. I'll be in touch before you go back to Germany.'

'Okay. Bye,' Ilse said and left closing the door behind her.

'She was annoyed,' Tricia said. 'I'm sorry if I interrupted your work.'

'You didn't. We had finished. After the trouble she caused with Sylvia, I don't feel I want to spend much time with her.'

'She didn't mean any harm,' Tricia said.

'I know. In any case, our job is finished now and then the other team will take over.'

'The other team?' Tricia asked.

'I'll tell you the whole story. You deserve to know. Sit down.' Cillian cleared a space on the seat by the table. 'Wait, I'll get the coffee. Do you want a bun?'

'Weren't they for you and Ilse?' Tricia sat down.

'Well, she isn't here now, so go ahead. They're from that amazing bakery in Dingle.'

'I don't mind having one, then.' Tricia picked up a bun and nibbled at it while Cillian busied himself with the coffee machine.

'So,' he said as he placed a steaming cup in front of Tricia. 'First about the project, then whatever you have come to say. Okay?'

Tricia nodded. 'That's fine.'

He sat down on the seat opposite her. 'I'm sure you know all about it by now,' Cillian began.

'Of course,' Tricia said. 'I saw the whole thing on TV. But when was the shipwreck discovered?'

'It was found by divers way back in April. They have been diving in the bay just outside the Magnolia beach since then. First trying to establish what kind of ship it was and then when we did, trying to salvage as much as we could from it. At first we thought it was a ship that had sunk about a hundred and fifty years ago. That's why that little drawing you found shocked me so. I thought we were barking up the wrong tree and the find would turn out to be something a lot less exciting. But then once we had examined the samples, we realised it's much older than that.'

'Amazing,' Tricia cut in. 'I can't imagine how it would have felt to find a ship from the Spanish Armada.'

'We were over the moon,' Cillian said. 'Sorry I had to tell you that lie.'

'I thought you might have found a Viking grave or something. Full of treasures.'

'We found treasure all right,' Cillian said. 'But under the sea, not in any grave. There were a lot of gold coins and other things there that have now been salvaged and sent to Spain where it all belongs. The canons and other things will be taken up slowly by the next crew. It's a very important find.' Cillian drew breath and drank some coffee.

Tricia stared at him, forgetting her anger. 'So that was what the diving was all about? Did you dive yourself?'

'No, I don't have those kinds of skills. Ilse and a guy who

works for her company are both marine archaeologists. I just examine whatever they bring up and catalogue it.'

'Amazing. But why all the secrecy? Was it because you thought other divers would go down and steal the treasures?'

'Exactly. That happens a lot. There are people who plunder shipwrecks for profit. It's dangerous and illegal but there is no way to stop them, other than to keep quiet about finds like this as much as possible. It wasn't that I didn't trust you, Trish. I just didn't want you to be blamed if you told anyone by accident.'

'I see.' Tricia broke off a piece of bun and ate it without really tasting it. She knew the time had come for her to tell Cillian how she felt. She didn't know how he would react or if he would believe that she wanted them to resolve their differences and maybe get close again. 'That's some story,' she said, looking at him.

'I had to tell you a fib to get you off the scent.'

Tricia nodded as she tried to swallow the piece of bun. 'I do understand, though,' she said when she had managed to get it down. She drank a little coffee to help ease her dry throat.

'I'm glad you do,' Cillian said. 'But enough about that. You had something to say, didn't you?'

'Yes,' Tricia said. 'I came here to tell you something. But I'm not sure you'll want to listen after what happened between us. I'm not sure where to begin.'

'Ah go on, Tricia.' He took her hand and held it in a tight grip. 'I do want to hear it.'

The touch of his hand gave her the courage to go on. 'First of all, I need to tell you what happened in Donegal when my late husband was so ill. I did something that wasn't quite right.' She stopped for a moment and then started again, a strange force driving her to reveal the whole story. 'I needed to pay his medical bills, and he and I sorted some paperwork out just before he died. It allowed me to help him, but it also created some legal issues. I was accused of trying to act illegally, to take his money. Which I've never really been interested in. Though, I am entitled to most of his estate, as his widow.' She went on to tell Cillian the whole story, not leaving out a single detail. 'That's what that text message was all about,' she ended. 'Terence, Sean's nephew, had found out about that document and he thought he could blackmail me into signing over the farm to him.'

'But I thought you had sold it,' Cillian said.

'It's on the market but it hasn't been sold yet,' Tricia replied. 'But that's not the issue here.'

'No. It's about you doing something dishonest,' Cillian said, looking serious.

'Yes.' Tricia sat there waiting for him to say something, but he stared out the window and seemed deep in thought, still holding her hand. 'I came here wanting a solution to my problem. To find the funds to just become independent and tell Terence he could keep the farm. I thought I could sell the cottage once I'd renovated it. But I didn't realise it was in such bad condition. Then I thought I could sell Kieran O'Grady's works...'

He turned and looked at her. 'It must have been tough, with Sean.'

She nodded. 'Yes. Sean was so ill and he needed the best care, even if he wasn't going to make it. So I had him admitted to a private nursing home where he could have a room to himself and be properly looked after. I wanted him to have peace and calm and not be in a crowded public hospital.' She held back her tears that were threatening to spill. Cillian didn't need to be part of her sadness; it wouldn't be fair to expect it. 'That's why I needed the money,' she explained.

'But you didn't do anything wrong,' Cillian said. 'And even if you had, it would be completely understandable and forgivable, I have to say.'

Tricia felt suddenly flooded with relief, touched by his empathy. 'Thank you. That's what I needed to hear.'

'I hope you can put it all behind you,' Cillian said, squeezing her hand. 'I don't want you to dwell on that or feel guilty. Sean was a lucky man to have you there until the end.'

'That's lovely of you to say.' Tricia leaned over and kissed him on the cheek. 'I just wanted to say that I know I was wrong the other night. We should have continued our weekend. I rushed off to see Sylvia the next morning because I was scared. Scared of telling you the truth. Scared of what this could be. But Sylvia put me straight.'

Cillian's mouth quivered.

'She's right,' Tricia said. 'I've been trying to protect my family, and to be there for everyone. But I need a life too. I need *you*.' She stopped, not knowing what to say next.

'But what do you want?' Cillian asked as a smile played on his lips.

'I want you in my life whatever way suits you,' Tricia replied. 'Our time together is important to me. I know it might be hard for you to cope with my daughters and my grandchildren as they aren't yours, but—'

'They're Fred's children and grandchildren,' Cillian cut in. 'So maybe, in some little way I could be a link to him through you and the childhood I shared with him. Does that sound cracked to you?'

'It sounds wonderful,' Tricia said.

She smiled at him as he got up and then, before she knew how, they were in each other's arms. The kiss was long and tender and full of love and the pent-up feelings that had been waiting to come to the surface. Tricia closed her eyes and let herself be carried away by the feel of his soft lips and his clean, fresh smell, kissing him back with fervour.

'That's what I call making up,' Cillian said when they broke apart. 'Now there will be no more misunderstandings or resentments, will there?'

'And no more secrets,' Tricia said, feeling as if her heart would burst with joy. 'I'm sure we'll argue like mad, but in the end we know that we belong together for as long as...'

'As we both shall live,' Cillian filled in as he gazed into her eyes. 'That's how I feel anyway.'

'Oh, me too, my darling.'

He stepped back and smiled at her. 'You know what? I think we should start from the beginning and go on a date. A proper one where I bring you flowers and then we go to a restaurant and then I drive you home and kiss you goodnight on the doorstep even though I want to do a lot more. What do you think?'

Tricia laughed. 'That would be perfect.'

'I'm glad you agree. So when will we have the first date?'

'Saturday night?' Tricia suggested.

'Good idea. I just want to say one thing before we go on,' Cillian said. 'It might annoy you, but I have to say it.'

'Go on,' Tricia said.

'God bless Sylvia.'

Tricia squeezed him tight. 'Amen to that.'

Then everything fell into place. At the end of the week the curator from the National Gallery arrived and examined the painting Tricia had found. It didn't take her long to decide that it was indeed a work by Kieran O'Grady. A few days later the story broke and there were features in all the newspapers. By then the painting was already hanging in the National Gallery with a label that said: *On loan from the Fleury family*. Sylvia had immediately decided that it was too valuable to have on the premises but she wanted it to stay in the family should they need to sell it. As no relations of Kieran O'Grady were still alive, the painting was assumed to belong to Magnolia Manor as it had been found there.

The most important day of the whole summer, however, was Vi and Jack's wedding on a beautiful summer's day in late August. Tricia's eyes were full of tears as she watched Vi walk up the aisle of St Mary's Church on Arnaud's arm. He had formed a strong bond with all the girls ever since he and Sylvia had become a couple. He had been there in the background, a support and a shoulder to cry on, a kind of grandfather to them all, who asked for no favours but gave enormous love and attention to anyone who needed it. Vi was especially fond of Arnaud as she had no memory of her real grandfather. Tricia heard Sylvia sob quietly into her lace handkerchief and noticed many people in the congregation dab their eyes as the handsome Frenchman walked his step-granddaughter down the aisle looking proud of this beautiful young woman about to enter into marriage with the man she loved.

Vi wore Tricia's dress and Sylvia's veil with a wreath of flowers from the garden at Magnolia Manor on her head. Jack turned around as Vi and Cillian approached and looked at his bride with love and pride. Then they said their vows in front of the priest and walked out into the sunshine in a storm of confetti as everyone clapped and cheered. There were no photographers outside the church as they had managed to keep their wedding plans away from any publicity. A friend of Dominic took the official photos and then the guests boarded a bus that would take them to the orangery where there would be a barbecue and dancing late into the night.

It was a wonderful party that even Sylvia enjoyed. She and Arnaud did a much-applauded cha-cha number on the terrace in the walled garden to the tunes of the salsa band Vi and Jack had hired. Then they declared they would leave the dancing to the young and walked slowly up the path back to Magnolia waving at everyone.

'The king and queen have retired,' Cillian muttered in Tricia's ear as they danced cheek to cheek to the now slower music. 'Do you think we could slip away as well?'

'Not until the bride and groom have driven away in Jack's Morris Minor,' Tricia protested. 'We have to give them a proper send-off.'

'You're right,' he said and twirled her around, bending her over in a deep dip. 'In the meantime I'm not going to let go of you.'

'I'll hold you to that,' Tricia whispered into his ear. She felt a huge sense of relief and happiness that things were finally settled between them. They had been on some wonderful dates, having dinner, going to the cinema or a cosy pub to listen to Irish music, or do line dancing that was great fun. Sometimes they went on hikes up the mountains that felt nearly like the old days, even if Fred was missing and they couldn't manage the steep slopes like they used to.

'We didn't get to the top, but hey, we're enjoying the best views in Ireland,' Cillian had said as they sat on a ledge in the MacGillicuddy's Reeks on a sunny day looking out over the deep blue waters of the Atlantic. And now, as they danced under the stars, Tricia felt she couldn't ask for anything more than this: Cillian's arms around her, Vi and Jack married at last, Lily and Rose content and Sylvia and Arnaud happy in each other's company. She was no longer afraid of the future or of growing old. Whatever fate had in store, they would face it together in their own way.

EPILOGUE

Exactly a year later, Tricia held her fourth grandchild in her arms. Rose had given birth to a son who they would call Fred. Tricia had rushed to Tralee hospital as soon as she heard the news.

'He's beautiful,' Tricia said and touched the baby's head covered in soft reddish down. 'So like his grandfather already.'

'He'll have red hair like Vi and Dad,' Rose said from the bed. 'Isn't that wonderful?'

'Yes.' Tricia looked into the baby's blue eyes. 'Hello, little Fred,' she said softly.

'Fred Wolfgang Quinn,' Rose said with a giggle. 'Such a mouthful, but there was no getting away from it. Noel's real first name is Wolfgang and he insisted.'

'A noble name,' Tricia said, not taking her eyes away from the baby. She breathed in the lovely scent of baby powder, milk and soap. 'He'll be tall and handsome like his father. And good at maths like his mother. Such a lucky little chap.'

The baby whimpered and squirmed in Tricia's arms.

Rose held out her arms. 'Here. Give him back to me. He's hungry again.'

Tricia carried the baby carefully over to the bed. 'Here you go, little Fred. Back to Mummy for a good feed.'

Rose put the baby to her breast. 'Where is Cillian? Gone off again to some far-flung place to dig up the past?'

'Not so far-flung at all,' Tricia replied. 'Just to Roscommon where there is a Viking grave. He'll be back at the weekend.'

'How is it working out?' Rose asked over her baby's head. 'The on-again-off-again arrangement you have, I mean.'

'It's perfect for us,' Tricia replied. 'Believe it or not, I'm really happy. I get to have my own space, my own life and then these lovely times with a man who makes my heart sing every time he comes back. It suits us both, you see. He has the freedom he needs and I get to spend time with my family when I want.'

'As long as you're happy.' Rose put her cheek against her son's head. 'We love being with you, too, you know. And we do like Cillian so much.'

'I know. And he loves you all. It's just that he isn't cut out to be a dad and we have to accept that.'

'He's a very good friend, though,' Rose said. 'You always feel he'll be there if he's needed, wherever he is.'

'He's my rock,' Tricia said. 'Even if he's absent from time to time.'

'Maybe that's the secret to keeping a man like him,' Rose pondered. 'Letting him go so he'll want to come back. Weird, but wonderful at the same time.'

'Ask Sylvia. It works for her and Arnaud,' Tricia said. 'Could be that when you're older, this kind of relationship works best. Not leaning on each other but enjoying being together when we want.'

'You're getting more and more like Granny,' Rose said. 'Even though you're not related.'

'But we're alike in our personalities,' Tricia remarked. 'That's why we clash from time to time.'

'Fleury girls to the core,' Rose said. 'If not by blood, by spirit.'

'You said it.' Tricia went over and kissed Rose on the cheek. 'I'll be off. I'm sure you both want to sleep.'

Rose smiled. 'Yes, we do. I'm trying to get all the sleep I can before I have to go home and tackle being a mum of two. Sophie is looking forward to being the big sister, so she'll be a big help.'

'She will. It's surprising how helpful a five-year-old can be. Especially a girl.' Tricia gathered up her bag and her phone. 'I'm only a phone call away if you need me.'

'I know, Mum. It's great to know I can count on you.'

'Of course you can. Bye for now.' Tricia smiled at her daughter and brand-new grandson as she slipped out of the room.

The campervan was parked outside the cottage when Tricia got home. Cillian was home earlier than she had expected. She pulled up, jumped out of the car, ran to the front door and flung it open as soon as she got there. 'Cillian,' she called. 'I'm home. Where are you?'

'In the kitchen,' Cillian's voice replied. 'I'm cooking up a storm here. How's the new member of the family?'

'The most beautiful baby in the world,' Tricia replied as she walked into the kitchen, where she found the table set for two with candles, a red rose in a vase and a little box with a red ribbon by her place. There was a delicious smell of something cooking in red wine and herbs.

'Sit down,' he urged and pulled out a chair.

Tricia sat down. 'What's this?' she asked, touching the little box.

'Open it and find out,' Cillian said.

Tricia undid the red ribbon and opened the box. She gasped

as she saw the Claddagh ring set with tiny diamonds. 'Oh, Cillian, how beautiful. But it's not my birthday or anything.'

'It's my way of saying I love you,' he said, standing beside her. 'And it's not exactly an engagement ring either as you said you didn't want that. It's just a ring that means you're mine and I'm yours, that's all.'

'What a lovely thought.' Tricia put the ring on the ring finger of her right hand, the bottom tip of the heart pointing inward. 'I think this is the way to wear it if you're in a relationship.'

'That's right. In love but not married.' Cillian pulled Tricia to her feet. 'I thought that was the right thing for us to be. Together but apart from time to time. But always with each other in our minds and hearts wherever we are. Does that sound good to you?'

Tricia looked into his kind and earnest hazel eyes. 'Perfect,' she whispered.

A LETTER FROM SUSANNE

I want to say a huge thank you for choosing to read *The Widow's Irish Secret*. If you did enjoy it, and want to keep up to date with all my latest releases, just sign up at the following link. Your email address will never be shared and you can unsubscribe at any time.

www.bookouture.com/susanne-oleary

I have hugely enjoyed writing this story and I hope you have felt swept away to the beautiful shores of Kerry in the southwest of Ireland. I am currently working on the next book in the Magnolia Manor series, with even more adventures and mysteries to solve for the Fleury family. I hope you will enjoy it.

I hope you loved *The Widow's Irish Secret* and if you did I would be very grateful if you could write a review. I'd love to hear what you think, and it makes such a difference helping new readers to discover one of my books for the first time.

I love hearing from my readers – you can get in touch on my social media or my website.

Thanks,

Susanne

KEEP IN TOUCH WITH SUSANNE

www.susanne-oleary.co.uk

 facebook.com/authoroleary

 bsky.app/profile/susanneol.bsky.social

 instagram.com/susanne.olearyauthor

goodreads.com/susanneol

ACKNOWLEDGEMENTS

Huge thanks, as always, to my wonderful editor, Jennifer Hunt, copyeditor Jon Appleton, Proof editor extraordinaire, Becca Allen and all at Bookouture. I couldn't thank them all enough! Thank you also to my friends and family who cheer me on and listen to my weird ideas for more stories. Most of all I want to thank my readers for the lovely messages and the support, enthusiasm and kind messages on my social media pages. You make all the hard work worth my while!

PUBLISHING TEAM

Turning a manuscript into a book requires the efforts of many people. The publishing team at Bookouture would like to acknowledge everyone who contributed to this publication.

Commercial
Lauren Morrissette
Hannah Richmond
Imogen Allport

Cover design
Debbie Clement

Data and analysis
Mark Alder
Mohamed Bussuri

Editorial
Jennifer Hunt
Charlotte Hegley

Copyeditor
Jon Appleton

Proofreader
Becca Allen